Dear Anem

Enjoy

Daljit Ranajee

# ECHOES FROM PUNJAB

*Metamorphosis of a Woman*

Daljit Ranajee

First Edition: February 2015

Printed in the United States of America

ISBN: 978-1-939237-35-4

Published by Suncoast Digital Press, Inc.

Sarasota, Florida, USA

Cover art: "Jasmine," an original painting by Daljit Ranajee.

# Dedication

*In memory of my mother, and my friend, Sherry*

# Table of Contents

# Acknowledgments

First of all I must mention my husband, **Jagjitnar Singh**, who passionately kindled my imagination to follow my heart in writing and painting. Without his encouragement and appreciation, I would not be what I am today.

I am deeply indebted to my wonderful editor and friend, **Barbara Dee**, president of Suncoast Digital Press. She not only edited the manuscript, she uplifted my spirits by understanding my culture so well that her ideas resonated with mine. Without her input and admiration, I would not have felt so confident to share my story with readers.

Another great lady I have much gratitude for, is my mentor, **Dorothy Conlon**, author of many books, who made intuitive suggestions and encouraged me to continue writing. I was about to complete my manuscript when she, in her late eighties, passed away. God bless her soul!

I am especially grateful to **Professor Stuart Richman**, for his insightful comments and praise for my writing that encouraged me to complete the novel. He traveled, along with Jasmine, through her winding path, flecked with humor and pathos.

In addition, I am indebted and thankful to my many relatives and friends who encouraged me along the way to finish the novel sooner than later, and their many kind words encouraged me to continue this journey.

My grateful admiration extends to bestselling author, **Bob Delaney**, who recognized my writing talent and quickly put me in touch with his agents.

Last, but not the least, I greatly appreciate **Professor Patricia White** and **Aroon Chaddha** for their input and final touches on my manuscript.

"Your living is determined not so much by what life brings to you as by the attitude you bring to life; not so much by what happens to you as by the way your mind looks at what happens"

— Kahlil Gibran

# 1

# Yogi's Prediction

"When will the monsoon ever start? July is almost over and this agonizing heat is so unbearable," says Jasmine, sitting under the *pipal* tree, fanning herself with her scarf. She is playing a mango game with her siblings and friends in the courtyard of her house in the northwestern Indian state of Punjab. A bucket of small, juicy mangoes is placed in the center. They are to be squeezed thoroughly into one's mouth within a set time limit. At the end, the leftover pits are counted and the person with the highest number wins. Little does she know that this is to be the last time she will play this game for a long time to come.

Jasmine, a beautiful, slim girl with intoxicating eyes, is a student in the nearby college. Little does she know that she, a simple, carefree girl of seventeen years, would soon become a bride, destined to live a life of responsibility and sophistication far, far away.

With no electricity in the village, meaning no fans or air-conditioners, sitting in the shade and breeze of the tree is a real treat. Their front door stays open all day long, and beggars, bangle-sellers, and the *kulfi-wallah* (ice-cream man) routinely walk in and out of their courtyard. After finishing their morning chores, the neighborhood women often drop by to gossip and to rest for a while under the tree.

"Ah, I heard that last night the butcher beat his poor wife again," Lajo whispers in Bibijee's ear.

"Oh, *merya Rubba*, women are so weak and helpless," Bibijee, Jasmine's mother, laments loudly, holding her head.

"Women aren't weak," Jasmine's *daadijee* (grandmother) says. "Some of them are really bad and deserve to be beaten. Do you know how badly that woman treats her mother-in-law? One day her husband caught her red-handed when she was pushing his mother out of the house with a broom."

"*Ahaho* [oh, yes], the times have changed," Lajo replies. "It's no longer our era, the *Satyug [good era]*, when women understood that their place in the household was to serve their in-laws tirelessly. Now, it is a new age and women, especially the educated ones, have become more daring."

"Only a few classes of education transform them into birds with wings," Preeto says.

"A woman is like a brass vessel: the more you rub, the more it shines," says Jasmine's *bhuajee (paternal aunt),* joining the conversation.

Lajo starts to sing a folk song referring to a woman's life:

> *I'm a piece of driftwood*
> *Kicked, pushed for centuries*
> *Broken from my family tree*
> *Rattled in the stormy river...*

Jasmine exchanges disapproving glances with Bibijee, but keeps quiet. There is never a winning situation with these illiterate women.

One day as soon as they finish afternoon tea, a *yogi*, dressed in a deep orange ankle-length *chola* (garb), with long sticky hair, walks into their courtyard, chanting, *"Hari Rama Hari Krishna."*

He keeps staring at Jasmine. "Your *bitiya* [daughter] is born with lucky stars," he tells her mother. "Her unique beauty tells me God has devoted many years to create such a face with those enchanting eyes."

Immediately Bibijee reacts with outrage. She scolds, "Go, go away, yogi! I have seen many charlatans like you. What a shameless person, flirting with my daughter."

"Believe me or not, I am telling you, this girl is born with lucky stars," he repeats. And without hesitation, he asks Jasmine to show him her palm. Curious, she obliges him.

"You are getting married very soon, believe me or not," he says.

"Tell us, yogi, is he handsome?" Jasmine's friend, Simran, jumps in.

"Yes, I see a tall, fair, handsome life partner," the yogi continues. "I see you will cross the seven seas. You will have so much money that you will bathe in milk and honey."

Bibijee, always skeptical of palm readers, gives the yogi alms and tells him to leave. Jasmine, however, is quite concerned, and asks Bibijee several questions.

"You are only seventeen and still have a year to complete your college degree," Bibijee assures her firmly, putting an end to the talk of inevitable arranged marriage.

Bibijee's words put Jasmine's mind at ease. But fate intervenes. Within a week, Jasmine's economics professor, Ajit Singh, approaches her father with a marriage proposal. He had fallen in love with Jasmine at first sight, but, fearing scandal, had kept it to himself. He intended to wait until Jasmine had finished college, however, he was motivated to act after he was granted admission to a Ph.D. program in America earlier than expected. Ajit hoped to marry her and leave for the USA by the third week of August.

Ajit presents his plan to Jasmine's father, who, eager to join his daughter with a respectable and ambitious intellectual, agrees that the marriage can take place as soon as possible. Since Ajit had already obtained his student visa and passport that he had applied for months ago, Jasmine's visa and passport are ready within two weeks.

At Jasmine's wedding, Bibijee blesses her daughter, "Break the old wives' ignorant belief that a woman is a piece of driftwood or a brass vessel," she says. "Live your life with dignity, self-respect, and traditional values."

Jasmine is silent. The sudden change in her destiny has numbed her senses. Her friends, realizing her inner turmoil, console her, "Ah, you are so lucky to marry a handsome man and to go abroad."

After the ceremony, as Jasmine's friends and sister get her ready for the *Doli*, the departure from her parental home, they sing a folk song customary for this ritual.

> *We, the daughters, are a flock of sparrows, oh babul (dear father). One day we will fly, leaving our childhood nests. Our journey is unknown and some of us will fly far, far away.*

Normally the departing daughter cries inconsolably, but Jasmine could not shed a single tear.

# 2

# The Land of Milk and Honey

"You have made me the happiest man in the world, Jasmine,"
Ajit says, squeezing his new wife's hand as they sit together
on the plane. She is looking at the clouds, totally mesmerized
by the magical sky. Her husband's romantic gesture does
not penetrate her enchanted world. She feels no distinction
between dream and reality. She is in a trance just as the
Sufi poets who dance and dance in circles in anticipation of
meeting their beloved God.

After only two weeks of marriage, they have embarked on
this journey to the West from Punjab, India. Ajit had studied
in a convent school in New Delhi and was well-versed in
English and western culture; Jasmine, however, had studied
English as a second language and had never spoken a word of
it. Their plane lands at Philadelphia International Airport late
at night. The cab drops them at the YMCA where they are to
stay until they can rent an apartment near the University of
Pennsylvania, where Ajit will start his Ph.D. program after
Labor Day, 1957.

Early the next morning, Ajit goes downstairs to the
YMCA coffee shop and brings back two cups of coffee.
Gingerly, Jasmine takes a sip.

"Ooo… this tea tastes like a bitter gourd," she says,
wincing. "It looks and smells strange too."

"It is coffee, not tea," Ajit tells her. "They don't sell tea in
the shop downstairs."

"I must have my tea in the morning," Jasmine says.
"What if we never find any shop selling tea in America?"

"I don't know when we will find such a shop," Ajit says.
"I think Americans mostly drink coffee; tea-drinking is
British. Just close your eyes and imagine a delicious cup of
tea and drink it. I don't like the taste either, but something is
better than nothing."

Jasmine closes her eyes and imagines sipping the spiced
tea her mother gave her every morning along with buttered
toast. Thinking of the aroma of cardamom, cinnamon,
cloves, and fennel, she takes another sip of coffee. The acrid
coffee jolts her back to reality and she runs to the bathroom,
cupping her mouth with her hand. "I can't, I just can't," she
cries. Tears irrigate her cheeks.

They go out to look for a restaurant where they can find
tea. Jasmine, coming from a small village, is overwhelmed
with the novelty of everything: people with blue eyes,
skyscrapers, elevators, and the unfamiliar smells.

Standing on an escalator, holding Ajit's arm to steady
herself, she takes off her pencil heel sandals for fear of
getting them stuck in the grooves. She is glad when the ride
is finished and Ajit helps her step off. Dressed in a Punjabi
outfit, a *salwar kameez*, with her long braid swinging left

and right, lightly hitting her hips, she strolls with a style she learned at college.

First they go to the Philadelphia National Bank to withdraw money.

"Money is not yet transferred from your overseas bank," the teller informs Ajit. "There is no money in your account."

"Madam, can you expedite it please?" Ajit asks. Twitching his eyes, he holds up his wallet with only eight dollars inside.

"No sir, there is nothing I can do on our end," the teller says. "You have to contact your bank."

The couple's disappointment is lightened at a corner grocery store where Jasmine is happy to find tea. For six dollars, they purchase a small box of tea bags, a loaf of white bread, grape jelly, a small carton of milk, a box of corn flakes, and sugar.

They bring it all home and Ajit puts out the paper cups, plates, and spoons he had taken earlier from the coffee shop. They make tea with hot tap water and eat cornflakes with milk. This is all they have to satisfy their hunger for a few days. Jasmine refuses to eat the bread because it smells very different from what she had back home.

Fortunately, their money becomes available on the third day. They rent a one-bedroom apartment on Market Street quite a few blocks away from the university. The apartment is unbelievably filthy. It appears to them that the previous student tenant never cleaned the refrigerator, bathtub, or kitchen sink. Jasmine, coming from a family where the servants did such chores, is horrified at the squalor. She remarks innocently to Ajit, "I think their servant is *nickamma* [useless]. We should tell the landlord to send a new one."

"Which servant are you talking about?" he replies. "There are no such luxuries in America. Even the rich do everything themselves." He surveys the kitchen, peering at the sink from a safe distance. "I can ask the landlord to have the place cleaned, at least one time."

The landlord tells Ajit that the cleaning lady is not available until next week. Frustrated and unable to wait that long, Jasmine cleans the apartment herself with whatever cleaning supplies she finds. The next day, writing to Bibijee back home, she jokes that the yogi forgot to tell her that before sitting in the bathtub filled with milk and honey, she would have to clean it herself!

Ajit's workload is strenuous and he comes back home from the library quite late every night. Jasmine, meanwhile, spends her days writing letters and exploring the nearby stores. She is fascinated by the variety of things offered for sale and by the colorful crisp autumn season. At the same time, though, she is terribly lonely. Almost two months have passed and she has not come across a single Indian. On top of that, Ajit has put a condition on her not to speak Punjabi so she can practice and perfect her English. Due to Jasmine's reluctance or diffidence, her input in their conversations is typically limited to *yes* and *no*.

She walks every day on the university lawns hoping to find someone from her country, especially a Punjabi with whom she can talk to her heart's content. Her seventeen years of life had been spent in a house full of relatives and neighbors. All day long their entrance door stayed open and there was always something cooking in the kitchen. Compared to such an environment of hustle and bustle, the stillness of the apartment stifles her.

One lucky day, while shopping in the grocery store, Jasmine is thrilled to overhear a Punjabi conversation in the next aisle. She leaves her shopping cart and runs over to see who it is. She finds a couple, a man and a woman in their thirties.

"*Tussi Punjabi ho* [you are Punjabi]!" she exclaims, and continues speaking in Punjabi, nonstop. "My name is Jasmine, my husband's name is Ajit, we came to America in August. You are the first Punjabi I have met. I am so happy to meet you. I have been looking for some familiar faces in this sea of strangers."

"*Array wah* [How great]!" the woman replies. "My name is — well, people just call me Mrs. Khan. My name is too complicated for this country. No one can spell or pronounce it correctly. Sometimes they call me *Kushu* and then I think, oh my God! How can I tell them '*Kushu*' means 'turtle'?" The two women laugh so loud that they put their hands over their mouths, not wanting to make too much noise in the store.

"I do know what you mean. My name is actually 'Jusmeen' but 'Jasmine' is what everyone hears, so I just go with that."

"And I am Arshid, her poor husband," the man says. "Her name is Kushuliya, by the way."

"In my school there was a girl named Kushuliya – we used to call her *Shaloo*," Jasmine says.

"*Array wah*!" Mrs. Khan exclaims, hugging her. "You solved my problem, Jasmine! That is easy to pronounce and spell. From now on I will tell everyone to call me 'Shaloo'."

"Can I call you Shaloo *didi* [sister]?"

"Oh, absolutely. I would love to have a beautiful little sister," Mrs. Khan says. The happy exchange ends with Mrs. Khan inviting Jasmine and her husband for dinner that evening.

Jasmine can hardly wait to tell her husband that she has met a beautiful and very nice Punjabi lady. She wants to tell him that Mr. Khan also appears to be very nice and humorous. She wants to tell him that Mrs. Khan does not look Indian at all. She wears western clothes, and if she had not heard their speaking in Punjabi, she would not have met them. But she must speak English with Ajit and she is afraid she might make an error, and then she would have to listen to his lecture. Therefore, she decides to tell him briefly about the invitation and that Mr. and Mrs. Khan are from Punjab.

"How can we go tonight?" Ajit protests. "You know I have a term paper due tomorrow. Tell them we will come another time."

"You tell them," Jasmine says, handing him the phone and their number.

Seeing Jasmine's teary eyes, Ajit says, "We can go for a short while."

Jasmine feels as if she has found a lost gem. For the first time since coming to America, she feels like wearing makeup and a beautiful Punjabi outfit complemented with matching jewelry. When she comes into the living room after getting ready, Ajit is transfixed.

"Wow!" he says. "You look stunning! I am afraid Mr. Khan might fall in love with you."

"Why would he?" Jasmine asks, teasingly. "His own wife is very beautiful."

"Nay, no Indian woman has your light eyes, nor your silky hair and fair complexion," Ajit says, embracing her. "You know what the students used to call you in college? *Kashmir ke kali* [Lilly of Kashmir]. I think you resemble a Russian movie star, I forget her name."

They live within walking distance of Mr. and Mrs. Khan. The October air is a bit chilly with a soft drizzle, but this evening Jasmine does not mind walking. With her spirits lifted and her overpowering desire to eat Punjabi food, she does not feel the chill at all.

As soon as they enter the Khans' apartment building, the aroma of Indian spices fills their nostrils. They head to the third floor, Jasmine following behind Ajit as they walk up the steep spiral staircase. Mrs. Khan opens the door and the couple steps in, breathing in the wonderful and familiar aromas. The apartment is artistically decorated with Indian ambiance and special Punjabi touches. A *sitar*, a *harmonium* and a *dholak*, all Indian musical instruments, adorn one corner. On the living room wall, above the sofa, hangs a hand-embroidered Indian tapestry. In the armoire there are several decorative pieces collected from different places. Standing out among the familiar décor is a French provincial sofa which Mrs. Khan says they have just purchased from the landlady downstairs. Mrs. Khan informs them that the old lady still has several items worth buying.

When Mr. Khan comes out from a back room, introductions are made. Arshid is a medical doctor, doing his residency at the Pennsylvania University Hospital, and Mrs. Khan is a marriage counselor, working part-time.

"You have exquisite taste," Ajit says, admiring their beautiful art collection.

"My wife is a scavenger," Arshid says. "We came to the States with only two suitcases and musical instruments, and now this little apartment is overflowing with artifacts."

"*Janaab*, what are you talking about?" Mrs. Khan interjects in Punjabi, "Had I left it to you, we still would be sleeping on the floor."

"Okay, madam, I agree with you wholeheartedly," Arshid answers in Urdu.

At the dinner table, Dr. and Mrs. Khan talk simultaneously, their colorful personalities keeping the evening lively. From Mrs. Khan's English conversation, it is clear that she had studied in a convent school, but when she speaks Punjabi, she gives the impression of a country girl just like Jasmine. Dr. Khan speaks Urdu, English, and some Punjabi. They make a very handsome and interesting couple.

While they are talking, Jasmine is quietly enjoying every bite of the dinner. The chicken curry tastes almost like her father's, and the *gobhi-aloo sabzi* (cauliflower-potato dish) is prepared exactly like her mother's.

Jasmine learns that Mrs. Khan's grandparents live in a town quite close to her own parental village. They have so much in common; this is the first time Jasmine has begun to feel at home in this foreign land.

The lively conversation goes on for hours. Since the Khans have been living in America for almost a year, they know much more than them about this country. They tell Ajit and Jasmine about the safe and unsafe university areas. The news about dangerous places is shocking to Jasmine; she was under the impression that all Americans were rich, and there were no beggars or burglars.

"You live on an unsafe side of the university and you must move from there," Mrs. Khan warns. "Ajit, you walk home from the library at two o'clock in the morning? And Jasmine stays home alone without bolting the door so you can open the lock without disturbing her sleep? Oh, my goodness!"

"This building is relatively safe and a second floor apartment will become vacant next month," Arshid says. "You must move here."

"We can secure you this much better, and of course safer, apartment for about seventy-five dollars," Mrs. Khan says.

Jasmine is excited to hear of the possibility of becoming neighbors with the Khans. She clears the table and starts to wash the dinner dishes while Mrs. Khan packs all the leftovers for her to take. On the way home, Jasmine wants to discuss the evening and their new friends with Ajit, but she remains quiet so she doesn't spoil her happy mood by risking a language lecture.

The next day, Mrs. Khan talks to her landlady downstairs, bargains with her, and gets the apartment for them. With Mrs. Khan's help, they are able to purchase a second-hand sofa, a chair, a desk, and a television. They move into the apartment on the second floor of the building.

From then on, Mrs. Khan and Jasmine spend most afternoons together. To Jasmine, Mrs. Khan is now Shaloo *didi*, but Ajit always addresses her as "Mrs. Khan." He does not like names that have no meaning, and moreover, he advises Jasmine not to refer to her as Shaloo *didi* in front of other people, especially Americans, who will be confused.

The month of March here is quite cold compared to Punjab. In Jasmine's village, spring season is quite thrilling with all its festivals. The farmers get ready for harvest, and anticipate the *Baisakhi* celebration on the horizon. The *Holi* festival, involving sprinkling colors on people you love, is silly, but enjoyable. Jasmine and Mrs. Khan receive letters from their relatives describing the festivities, which make them homesick.

One day, after several days of complete silence, Jasmine dares to converse in broken English with her husband as soon as he comes home.

"Mrs. Khan's father dead," she says. "Telegram came in the morning. She's crying and crying in telephone…I make some food to take them."

"Oh wonderful, Jasmine!" Ajit says excitedly. "You're speaking English! With time you'll overcome your hesitation. You see, any language, not just English, must be spoken fluently and correctly. A person can appear educated and intelligent just by the way he or she talks. Listen to Dr. Khan's Urdu language. Every sentence he utters comes out as a string of pearls."

Jasmine looks strangely at her husband in the midst of his cheerful lecture. She wonders to herself, *does he not have any sympathy for poor Mrs. Khan who has lost her father, oceans away?*

After dinner, they go upstairs to the Khans' apartment. Ajit knocks on the door and, hearing Arshid's loud voice, shakes his head. "Oh no, they are bickering again," he says. "I am going back." He motions for Jasmine to go in alone. Ajit is just about to turn towards the stairs when Arshid opens the door, muttering, "*Bavekoof auarat* [silly woman]." He shakes hands with Ajit and says, "*Yaar* [my friend], why do women need so many things?"

He turns his head back towards the apartment, addressing his flustered wife. "Oh madam, you have only ten minutes to leave for the airport," he tells her. "Otherwise you will miss your plane."

Arshid explains the situation to Ajit and Jasmine. Apparently, Mrs. Khan has managed to get a seat on an Air India flight that leaves that night from JFK International Airport. She is now sitting in front of two suitcases. One suitcase is ten pounds over the allowable weight. Arshid is helping her remove some items. He pulls out a pressure cooker. "This is where your ten pounds are," he scolds. "Take this damn thing out. Don't they have pressure cookers in India? Why is it so heavy?" Opening it, he finds a five-pound bag of almonds inside.

"No, no, no," Mrs. Khan insists. "My mother has written to me so many times to bring this exact cooker because the Indian brand is not of good quality. She says her neighbor's daughter had brought one …and almonds are very expensive in India. I'm taking them to my brother who is very weak after being ill with jaundice."

Arshid pulls out a blender, in which there are a few small bottles of perfume. Before Arshid can open his mouth, Mrs. Khan grabs the blender. "I must take something for my *Bhabi* [sister-in-law]," she says.

They pay no attention to Ajit and Jasmine. Ajit puts the dinner bag on the table and stands quietly. Mrs. Khan finally takes out bars of Dove soap, and several bottles of body lotion and perfume, thus lessening the weight. Sighing with relief, she gets up and hugs Jasmine, crying. Arshid quickly eats a few bites of dinner, puts the rest in the refrigerator and they leave for the airport.

Back down in their apartment, Ajit gets busy with his studies and Jasmine sits with the composition book trying to brush up on her grammar, but she is unable to concentrate. The thought of something happening to her mother or father deeply disturbs her. *If, God forbid, something happens to my father or mother, I would not be able to go home as quickly as Mrs. Khan*, she worries to herself.

She knows Ajit's work-study program provides only enough money to make ends meet. Once in a while, when Ajit needed extra money, his brother has reluctantly agreed to send some from England where he lives with his British wife and two-year-old son. Jasmine realizes that unless she starts to earn and save money for her airfare, she will not be able to visit her parents any time soon.

After tossing and turning in bed for some time, Jasmine goes to sleep. Around midnight she wakes up shivering and sweating, roused from a terrible nightmare. In it, somebody was screaming. "*There is a dead body on the rooftop!*" Immediately a policeman came and arrested her brother as a murder suspect. Her mother and all members of the family looked for her father but he was nowhere to be found. The neighbors were saying that the police would not have dared to arrest her brother if Mr. Kishan Singh, her father, were present. Her mother was crying and begging the police to wait until her husband returned, but no one knew where he was.

Climbing out of bed, Jasmine collects herself. *Is the dead body my father's?* She thinks. *Is this dream giving me a hint of bad news? Nay, don't be silly; dreams are nothing more than the fears of the subconscious mind.* She drinks some water and tries to go back to sleep, but she is very much shaken by this dream. She gets up again and starts to work on her grammar so that the boredom of the book may put her to sleep. Her mind drifts again. *Tomorrow, I must start looking for a job*, she tells herself. *Mrs. Khan says I could get a job in a factory for the time being, or I could take training in typing to work in an office. I have learned to type but I need practice to build up my speed... but we do not have a typewriter!*

She knows she would need western clothes to work in such a job. On their way to the United States they had stopped in London and stayed with Ajit's brother for a week. Her sister-in-law gave her some western clothes. She wants to wake her husband to tell him her plan, but decides not to disturb him.

Jasmine puts the composition book back on the shelf and starts to read a book from Ajit's bookcase, Sigmund Freud's *Interpretation of Dreams*. She does not find an easy answer to her dream in the book, but her attention is drawn to a page with the heading "The Stimuli and Source of Dreams." It mentions that behind this concept lies a theory: dreams are a result of sleep disturbance. The view makes some sense to her so far, but as she reads further, Sigmund Freud's dense writing thoroughly confuses her. She puts the book back on the bookshelf after reading only a few pages.

Jasmine looks at the clock; it is only 2:00 a.m. She wants this night to pass quickly. The tick, tick of the clock, and the tick, tick of the heater never bothered her before, but tonight is different. Mrs. Khan's father is no more, and in her dream they could not find her own father. The thought of her father not being there disturbs her so much she is unable to go back to sleep. The clock appears to be standing still. Every sleepless moment is beyond endurance. She looks at her husband who is sound asleep. *He is so lucky*, she thinks. *The sad news has not at all disturbed him.*

Jasmine wants to wake him to tell him about the nightmare, and that she wants to work in a factory. About a month ago when Mrs. Khan had suggested that Jasmine could work in a factory, Ajit had rejected the idea, saying that he would prefer she learn English and typing to working in a place where she would have no chance to improve herself. Now she decides to look for a factory job without telling her husband. Finally, she dozes off and when she wakes it is 10:00 a.m., and Ajit has already left for the university.

The western dresses her sister-in-law gave her turn out to be too long and slightly loose on her petite body. Jasmine considers waiting for Mrs. Khan's return from India, for she had offered to give her some dresses which no longer fit. She misses her Shaloo *didi* terribly and thanks God she will be back in two weeks.

# 3

# New Experiences

Mrs. Khan works as a marriage counselor and loves to discuss American culture with Ajit. When they get together, they get deeply involved in discussions, but Jasmine is not confident speaking in English; therefore she listens to them quietly. When they talk in Punjabi, however, she participates. The past four months have been great. Almost every weekend the two couples go sightseeing, and Dr. and Mrs. Khan have taken them to many interesting places in their car. Once they all went to New York to purchase Indian spices and groceries. The Khans knew that Indians buy electronics from 42nd and Canal Street because they are cheaper and they are available with 220 volts, compatible with electrical power in India. The Khans purchased a typewriter and Ajit wanted to buy one also, but could not afford to. They all enjoyed lunch at an Indian restaurant. One time in New York they even went to see an Indian movie.

Some evenings Jasmine and Mrs. Khan cook together and talk for hours, waiting for their husbands to get back from the university. One day, while they are in the kitchen, Mrs. Khan starts talking about her marriage.

"Arshid was my classmate in college. He was a great singer, very intelligent, and a serious student. I could not help but fall in love with him. I knew he was a Muslim and I am Hindu, so my father would never agree to our marriage. We both loved to sing, especially Urdu songs; it seemed the more my parents and brother objected, the more our love grew stronger."

"Wow, didn't you get scared of your brother? My brother would have killed me," says Jasmine in amazement.

"My father had arranged my marriage with someone without my knowledge… that was the trigger point for my drastic action," Mrs. Khan shares. "Only one day before my marriage to a stranger, Arshid and I eloped."

"Where in the world did you disappear to?" Jasmine interrupts. "I remember one girl eloped from my village; the police punished them harshly."

"We reached Bombay and got married in the court," Mrs. Khan continues. "Arshid's brother was living in Singapore and we were able to get passage on a ship and reach him. Luckily, it happened that we both had our Bachelor of Science degrees and, with his brother's help, we both got admission to postgraduate courses at Singapore University."

"You were smart to go far away quickly before the police could find you," Jasmine says.

Mrs. Khan nods. "I wrote a letter to my parents informing them about our court marriage and gave them our address in Singapore. Arshid and his brother lost their parents in a train accident at early ages. A Muslim lady adopted the boys, but she died when Arshid was in high school. Both brothers were very bright and kept up with their studies while working in a hotel as waiters, and later as drivers," Mrs. Khan explains. "My father was so furious that he prohibited my mother and siblings from keeping up any relationship with me. I kept mailing letters to my mother via my friend, who tried hard to convince my mother to forgive me. Initially my mother, being scared of my father, was reluctant, but finally my sister and mother agreed to respond secretly to my letters. My older brother remained as angry with me as my father."

Mrs. Khan pauses her potato-peeling and sighs before continuing, "I kept in touch with my mother, sister, and my *bhabi*. I completed my masters in psychology, Arshid got a degree in medicine, and we came here in 1956 when Arshid started his residency."

Jasmine thinks Mrs. Khan sounds as though she has told her story many times before and she detects no bitterness in her.

"Is your father still angry with you?" asks Jasmine.

"No, not anymore," Mrs. Khan replies, smiling. "When he realized that Arshid had become a medical doctor, he wrote a lengthy, affectionate letter to both of us. So did my brother."

By the time Mrs. Khan's story is finished, Ajit and Arshid have come back, and they all have dinner together. "I want to hear *your* wedding saga next time," Mrs. Khan whispers to Jasmine.

At the dinner table, Ajit asks Mrs. Khan, "Tell us about the American marital problems you encounter with your clients, and what kind of advice you give them."

"Well, I say that if you don't love each other, and if you have no children, get out of a nasty marriage. But, if a couple comes to me really sad and desperate to patch things up because they think their kids will suffer if they divorce, I listen to both sides and help them work it out. I believe when kids are involved, parents should compromise for the children's sake. Usually their problems stem from superficial wants and needs. In my experience, Americans are very self-centered, especially in a marital relationship. It is always 'what can you do for me?' rather than 'what can I do for you?' Most of the couples are dissatisfied because they do not make love as they did before a baby came into their lives. They are unable to adjust to the changed circumstance."

This conversation goes on for a while; Jasmine quietly listens to the three of them, as always. One sentence sticks in her mind. The next day she asks Mrs. Khan, "Last evening, when you were talking about marital problems in America, you said something about love-making. I thought love is not some 'thing' that is made; love is an 'emotion' which is expressed. I was wondering, what do you mean by it?"

Mrs. Khan bursts into laughter. "Oh, my *bholi* [innocent] sister," she says, hugging Jasmine. "I understand why you are confused. In Punjabi, there is no such distinction, but in English, *lovemaking* means you are in love and have intimate relations. But to have intimacy without love is lust, which in our language is called *kaam*," she explains.

Jasmine also laughs and says, "You know, when I was in high school, I asked my father what is *kaam*… his face turned so red with embarrassment! Luckily my uncle walked in to interrupt the conversation and afterwards my mother explained it to me."

Mrs. Khan gives Jasmine an understanding look as a big sister looking affectionately at a little sister. She says, "I feel like eating something Indian, something sweet…what can we make? Any ideas?"

"We can make *halwa* or *kheer* [rice pudding]," Jasmine suggests.

"I want something quick," Mrs. Khan replies. "*Halwa* takes very little time, but I don't have any cream of wheat, and *kheer* takes three hours — how about making *jalebi?*"

"*Jalebi*? Really? That's my favorite sweet," Jasmine says as her mouth waters. "But in America, is it possible to make it?"

"Necessity is the mother of invention, my dear, let us experiment. We know the basics, and whether we succeed or not, at least it will be fun," Mrs. Khan says with her usual optimism.

They are in the kitchen, gathering ingredients. Mrs. Khan mixes one cup of flour with half a teaspoon of dry yeast dissolved in warm water, and puts it in the warm oven for a while. She cleans an empty catsup bottle. In one pot she boils equal amounts of water and sugar until the mixture starts to make three threads.

"I know this much because I watched my sister-in-law making *jalebi* in Singapore. In India, I think they use yogurt in place of yeast, but yogurt in America is hard to find," says Mrs. Khan. "They have yet to learn what is good."

She adds more water to thin the batter and puts it in the clean bottle. When the syrup is ready, she starts to squeeze the batter into the hot oil, making twirls in twisted and round shapes. She fries them for a few minutes, puts them on a paper towel to drain the oil out, and dips them in the syrup.

"Wow! They are ready to eat!" Their faces gleam.

So, this is how the two women spend their time together. Almost every other evening they prepare dinner, experimenting with making Indian dishes by using whatever similar or limited ingredients are available. Jasmine tells her Shaloo *didi* that she used to roll *chapatti* with a bottle until she found a rolling pin. They miss Basmati rice terribly, and agree that Uncle Ben's sticks to their teeth and has no flavor. They go to the Reading Terminal to get Indian spices, *moong*, and lentil beans from the International Market, but the market does not carry Basmati rice or Indian *chapatti* flour. The *chapatti* they make from whole-wheat flour from the grocery store turns out quite hard. Mrs. Khan mixes it with pastry flour and milk to make it softer. One day they try to make *samosas* (a triangular stuffed pastry).

"Thank God, we have all the right ingredients to make this snack," Jasmine says. "And I know the recipe—I learned it in my cooking class in school."

Lacking mint and coriander, they mix red pepper, salt, and catsup with chopped onions and a little lemon juice to concoct chutney to go with their samosas. Inside the four walls of this apartment, they have created a make-believe little Punjab, and they are happy. Jasmine writes to her mother about the Indian dishes they experiment with, and her mother writes her back, astonished at the complicated dishes they can prepare. Mrs. Khan writes to her own mother in a more amusing tone. She explains, "Here in the land of milk and honey, your daughter is a *dhobi* [clothes washer], *halwaie* [sweet maker], *bhangie* [cleaning lady], *rasoiya* [cook], and a *mundu* [dish-washing boy]."

These four months have passed so quickly, yet Jasmine has not mastered her English. In spite of Ajit's desire for her to practice speaking English with Mrs. Khan, Jasmine always converses in Punjabi with her. She hesitates to speak English with Ajit because she is always worried that she will make mistakes and Ajit will give her another lecture on sounding properly educated.

The first floor apartment of this building is divided into two portions. The landlady lives in one, and a girl from Afghanistan occupies the other side. She is a student at Penn. Jasmine rarely sees her and admires her for being brave enough to live alone in a foreign country.

Mrs. Stevenson, the landlady, is always in a wheelchair. Her apartment is just one big room where she rolls around all day. In one corner she has a small kitchen and a refrigerator. Across the room, she has a small bathroom and a single bed. Mrs. Stevenson often sits in her wheelchair in the hallway, hoping to chat with her tenants during the day. Mrs. Khan and Jasmine feel sorry for her, and stop and talk to her several times a week. Jasmine used to give her cooked food once in a while, but Mrs. Khan has stopped her, saying, "If something bad happened to her, her son would sue you for killing her. This is America, my dear." Whenever they meet Mrs. Stevenson, she has just one story to repeat:

"I love Indian people. I lived in India for two years during the British Raj. I was a nurse in the army. One day, a lieutenant, a very, very handsome young man, was brought to the hospital for treatment. We fell in love and got married after only two months. I tell you, my husband was a doll, God bless his soul! We lived in the foothills of Kashmir, and let me tell you, that was real heaven on earth. I lived like a queen. We lived in a big red stone bungalow. We had servants for every chore. You know, I gave birth to a little girl in that bungalow. Even today, I relive those lovely moments of my life and I will never let them go. That heavenly time was short-lived. My dear husband died in a car accident. God bless his soul!"

Because it is such a long story, Jasmine and Mrs. Khan always leave in the middle, and the next time Mrs. Stevenson resumes her story.

"I met my second husband in London. He was a merchant from Boston. I admit to you I married him only for his money. And God punished me for that. My daughter did not like him and stopped talking to me. We had one son. You see him coming here once in a while. My husband always drove; he never let me drive even when he was drunk as a skunk. Late one night we were coming back from a party, and we got into a horrible, horrible accident. He died on the spot and I became paralyzed. I inherited this apartment building; the rest of the property he left for our son." And she ends her story, only to start it all over again.

Today Jasmine is relieved that Mrs. Stevenson is not in the hall as she is not in a patient mood. Checking her mailbox, she is excited to receive a letter from her mother, and as always, opens it immediately. To her surprise, her mother writes about Mrs. Khan's visit to their house:

> Your Shaloo didi came to meet us yesterday; it felt as if a part of you had come. She talked so much about you that we were so happy to draw a good picture of your life. It made us feel so good. She is such a great person, loves you so much, and takes such good care of you. Now we do not worry about you as much as we did before we met her. You do not write as many details

*as we came to know from her. She is very jolly too; she
made us laugh so much. She brought a nice wool shawl
for me. I gave her a sari and a salwar kameez for you—
peach color suits your fair complexion very much. Send
me your photograph wearing this outfit.*

*This world is so small, her grandmother and my
mother were teachers in my school and her mother was
my classmate. At first we did not recognize each other
but when it was mentioned about her mother being
a teacher in Moga Primary School, at once, all the
memories came to us.*

*Mrs. Khan told us that America is very clean and
there are no dirt roads anywhere to be seen. She tells us
that American vegetables and fruits do not have good
flavor or sweetness because they are stored in refrigerated
warehouses. The grocery stores also must store them, and
when people buy, they also put them in refrigerators for
several days. Oh! How we wish you were here, sitting
with us, eating all your favorite fresh foods.*

At the end of the letter, her mother mentions that Mrs.
Khan wants to surprise Jasmine about the visit; therefore,
should she receive this letter before Mrs. Khan's return, she
should act surprised when she tells her.

Jasmine wants to start working as soon as possible, but
she needs Mrs. Khan to give her the American workplace
outfits she had promised before she left for India. Although
she got back from India last night, Jasmine does not want to
disturb her right away. She has asked Ajit if she can work in a
factory, and this time he has agreed, though reluctantly. "Only
if you find time to practice your typing to improve your
speed," he told her.

Finally, Jasmine meets Mrs. Khan and tries on the clothes. She tells Jasmine that she was only 99 pounds when she came to this country and now she is 115. Jasmine is happy to find that all the clothes fit. "Watch out or you will gain weight too," Mrs. Khan says. "This country's food is very rich, plus during the winter you are stuck inside the four walls, unable to go out for a walk. Now let me tell you about my visit to your parents' house."

"Really? You went to visit them? I can't believe you." Jasmine acts surprised.

Mrs. Khan tells her the whole story and gives her the things Jasmine's mother sent back for her. They eat the sweets brought back from India. To Jasmine's surprise, Shaloo *didi* also managed to bring some yogurt in a small plastic container as a yogurt starter.

"Now we will be able to make yogurt on our own," Mrs. Khan says. Then, as she watches Jasmine pick up and examine a red wool skirt, she asks, "Hey, when are you going to tell me your wedding story?"

"Mine is a love story but one-sided," Jasmine says. "I was in my second year when Ajit started to teach economics at my college. To me, he was just a professor, but he fell in love with me at first sight. Of course he kept it to himself and never gave me or anyone else any hints. He promised himself that I was the only girl he would ever marry. He wanted me to complete college, get a degree, and then he planned to ask my father for my hand. He was a Hindu and his name was Ajit Kumar, but since I was a Sikh, he grew a beard and wore a turban. He even changed his last name to Singh, so that my father would not know that he was actually a Hindu."

"Wow, what a deep love he has for you! Changing one's religion is quite a big sacrifice."

"Unfortunately, I think, he got admission to a Ph.D. program a bit too soon. By the time I took the finals for my third year, he was already set to leave for America. He approached my father via a matchmaker and my father was convinced in a minute. As soon as the matchmaker told him that this Sikh, a professor who is highly accomplished, does not smoke, does not drink, and moreover, is going to America for higher studies, my father agreed. My jaw dropped when my mother told me about my engagement. All my friends thought I was so lucky since Ajit is tall, fair, and handsome. Within days, my wedding took place. My mother wanted me to stay back to complete my college, but Ajit would not agree. He told me that he did not wish to spend a single day without me."

"Wow! What a love story. He is so much in love with you!"

"But I wish I could shake the professor image of him from my head."

"You will. Trust me, love begets love. He loves you and I am sure your love will grow stronger day by day."

"Tomorrow I am going to look for a job," Jasmine tells Shaloo *didi*, changing the love topic.

"In the morning I will take you to the Job Placement Office. You should be ready to leave by 8:45."

Jasmine wants to finish writing two important letters tonight. After tomorrow, if she gets a job, she will be too busy. She has not responded to her best friend's letter for too long. She quickly completes a letter to her parents and tries to

finish the one she had started writing to her girlfriend back in
October.

*My dear Simran,*

*It is the month of October. There is a soft drizzle*
*outside and it's extremely windy. I can hear the howling*
*sound through the bay window. Where I am sitting, I*
*can see a beautiful Girja Ghar (church) across the road.*
*The architecture is simply gorgeous. Almost on every*
*block, there is a Girja Ghar. Ever since I moved to this*
*apartment, I have started to appreciate this country*
*much more. Yesterday, we came across spectacular scenic*
*beauty while driving through the mountains. It is the*
*fall season and leaves have changed colors. The trees*
*looked like Indian brides wearing multihued outfits. We*
*had a little picnic on a nearby lake. You wouldn't believe*
*how much I missed you — how much I wished you were*
*here with me — we would have walked and talked in*
*the drizzle. Autumn here is just beyond description. I*
*was so mesmerized that I wrote a poem last night and I*
*want to share it with you. This is my maiden poem so do*
*not make fun, just read it.*

*Leaves, leaves everywhere*
*Moving nimbly on the road*
*Dancing swiftly in the air*
*Enough to ponder,*
*Enough to stare.*
*Let this moment stand still*
*Let the sunshine peep through*
*Multiple hues, awe-inspiring,*
*Pinkish, purple, yellow, blue.*
*Aztec gold, fiery crimson*

*Let me not go anywhere*
*Let me ponder; let me stare.*

*My dear Simran, I wish you were also destined to find someone soon who would bring you to America. If you were here you would certainly paint this fall scene so well and we could enjoy our life as before.*

*I am sorry — I should have completed this letter months ago. I hope you will forgive me for my laziness. A lot has happened since last fall. I met a really nice and affectionate Punjabi lady — I call her Shaloo didi. Truly, these few months in her company have given me an anchor in this foreign land. But, no matter how busy or how anchored I am here, our memories stay fresh in my mind all the time. I miss everyone so much, especially you, that sometime I avoid writing you just because I do not want you to become depressed hearing about my loneliness.*

*How are your studies going? I wish I were there to complete my studies. I do not like having no college degree. It seems everyone in the world except me is a college graduate. Even my nice new Punjabi friends, Shaloo and her husband, Arshid, have advanced degrees. You want to know something funny (and sad)? Ajit is 24, Arshid is 32, Shaloo is 31, and I am 18—a mere teenager among educated, sophisticated, and intellectual people. They discuss various topics in English and I sit and listen for hours like a dummy. Sometimes I feel so immature, inadequate, and diffident. Shaloo didi is very mindful of it and tries to speak in Punjabi to include me in the conversation. Well, don't get me wrong, I am very happy. Ajit loves me so much and we enjoy a lot. I don't want you to start worrying about me.*

*I wish you had met Shaloo didi. You would have liked her. Bibijee wrote in the letter that you were out of town that day. Dr. and Mrs. Khan (Shaloo didi) are a unique couple, and have a good sense of humor. They are jovial and very entertaining. He addresses her as 'madam' and she calls him 'janaab' or sometimes 'janabe-ali.' Initially, her family was against the marriage because he is a Muslim and she a Hindu — her father had arranged her marriage with a Hindu. But you know what? They were so much in love that they eloped! I admire their relationship with each other, so free, so unpretentious, and so unafraid. When they argue, Ajit calls it 'bickering' but I call it natural communication. They never seem angry at each other. All three of them sing Urdu ghazals so beautifully. In front of them, I am so untalented that I hate myself – why didn't I learn anything?*

*In your last letter, I liked your philosophical note: 'arranged marriage is like a seedling, ready to sprout—the more you water it, the more it grows—and, with hugs and kisses, it bears the sweetest fruit'. Okay, philosopher jee, I got the hint.*

*I could write you for hours, but I must go to sleep because tomorrow I should get up early to look for a job. In my next letter I will tell you why I must work. Write me soon; do not follow my habit of procrastination.*

*With lots of love,*

*Jasmine*

# 4

# Job Hunting

This morning Jasmine gets up a bit early. She tells her husband not to worry about her in case she finds a job and comes home late that evening. "I doubt they will offer you a job right away; they will interview several candidates to select from," Ajit says as he leaves for the university.

Jasmine, dressed in a black skirt, white blouse, and high-heel golden sandals with her long hair falling down her shoulders, opens the door for Mrs. Khan. "Wow, nobody would think you are an Indian; in this outfit you look like any American girl with your hazel eyes and fair complexion," she tells Jasmine.

Mrs. Khan takes her to the University Placement Services Office and shows her the notice board full of various job advertisements. "Here is one," she tells her. "It's just across the river. It does not require work experience. Take a bus from Chestnut Street. I must go now so I'm not late for my client appointment." Mrs. Khan leaves.

Riding the bus gives Jasmine a chance to observe the city traffic and she passes the time by reading the carmaker names which are starting to become familiar. She says to herself, *Chevrolet Bel Air,* and *Ford Thunderbird,* but she doubts she is pronouncing the words correctly. She does not want to ask Ajit, but she thinks she will ask Mrs. Khan. She tells herself to remember to also ask about the song she hears coming from nearly every passing car radio, something about "a hound dog crying all the time." Jasmine is grateful to have her Shaloo *didi* to help her understand so many mysteries, especially for helping her in her job search.

Jasmine gets off the bus and notices three old, dirty-looking skyscrapers on her right. The area is kind of run-down and secluded. She goes to the first building and looks at the paper in her hand; the address is Suite #1105, Building B. She goes around the building to read the address but does not see it. All of a sudden, she is startled to hear a voice with weird pronunciation, "Aye, pretty lay–deee…" She notices a strange-looking man sitting in a corner. Her heart starts pounding as she remembers Mrs. Khan's warning her about vagrants and hobos. She quickly enters an open elevator and goes up to the first floor, thinking #1105 must be on the first floor.

The first floor is totally quiet, and filled only with boxes. She takes the elevator back down quickly. She feels relieved seeing a man in business clothes waiting for the elevator. Nervously, she shows the paper to him, points to the address, and asks, "Sir, where is this?"

"Oh dear, go to the next building. This is A, that one is B – and go to the 11th floor." He looks at her from head to toe, perhaps wondering what this well-dressed foreign girl with golden sandals is doing in this area.

At the next building she takes the elevator to the 11th floor. She reads "Happy Publishers #1105" on one of the doors and slowly opens it. A gentleman takes her to the manager's office.

"Good morning sir," she says as Ajit had coached her a little this morning for the interview.

"Good morning," the man answers as he looks up from the work on his desk. "Do you have a resume with you?"

"No, no college degree sir." She hands him a paper with her name and address.

"Oh, your name is Jasmine Singh. I bet you are from Punjab, India. We have a student working here with this last name. His name means 'winner of the heart'… and what does your name mean? Mr. Singh told me all Indian names mean something."

"My name meaning '*chambeli* flower' sir," says Jasmine, pulling her skirt down to cover her legs.

"Oh, that is a very appropriate name for you, I must say."

"Thank you sir."

"So, Jasmine, what brings you to the United States?"

"My hus —ah —British Airways," Jasmine replies.

"Hmm. Do you have any job experience?"

"No sir." Jasmine shakes her head left and right.

"Never worked? Indian teenagers are so lucky. Mr. Singh tells me students do not work unless they are very poor. Their parents want them to concentrate on school. I've been working my butt off since I was twelve," the manager says. Then he asks, "Do you know what 'collate' means?"

"No, sir." Jasmine shakes her head again.

"Let me explain the type of work you will be performing if hired. What you have to do is – put these booklets in a binder in page order. You first spread the pages in number sequence, then pick up one page at a time until you reach the last page. Then make holes with this hole punch and put it in this binder," he demonstrates. "You cannot take a lunch break until all your boxes are empty. We are already behind schedule. Whatever workload is given to you, it must be finished by the end of the day. I mean, you can't leave until you are completely done. Now, do you think you are able to do this job?"

"I can do it," she shows her eagerness.

"Are you able to start right now?"

"Yes, sir."

"Very good, I will give you a trial period. So you are hired!"

"Thank you, sir."

"Just call me Bob from now on."

Bob gives her a form to fill out and takes her to a workstation. While walking, he tells her that she will be paid $55 for 40 hours a week with a one-hour lunch break and two 15-minute coffee breaks. "There is a cafeteria on the 6th floor. If your work does not meet the deadline, you may have to work extra hours without additional pay. The hours are from 8:30 a.m. to 5:00 p.m., five days a week."

"Okay, Jasmine, this is your workstation; the work you have is in these boxes. Do you want me to explain it again?" asks the manager.

"No, I know what to do," and she starts working immediately.

The boxes were supposed to be empty by noon, but it is already after one o'clock. Jasmine skips her coffee breaks as well as lunch, and continues working without getting up. Her stomach is growling, her lips are drying, but she is determined to finish the required work before she leaves. Her coworkers on the left and right look at her and give her a smile occasionally. She smiles back with a stressful face. She looks at the boxes and feels relieved; she is almost at the last page. But then her manager brings new boxes, empties out the previous ones and says, "These boxes must be done before you leave – we're on a deadline."

Glancing up at the wall clock, Jasmine sees that it is 3:00 p.m. She tries to speed up. She is starving. The coworker to her left, understanding her plight, comes over and puts a banana and an empty cup on her desk and points to a coffee pot in a corner far away. Jasmine thanks her, takes the banana, but gives her the cup back because she does not drink coffee. This sympathetic gesture makes Jasmine feel good. *Americans are so compassionate*, she thinks. *The manager does not shout at me for being so slow, and now this lady is so kind.*

It is 5:00 p.m., the boxes are half done, and she is afraid to ask to leave. She calls home to tell Ajit, but he is not at home. She continues working; some employees are still working, and she thanks God for that. After a while, Bob walks by and shakes his head in disappointment. He is clearly annoyed, and tells her to leave for the day.

By the time she reaches home it is half past six. "Where were you? You made me worry myself sick. Thank God for Mrs. Khan who told me your whereabouts and brought down dinner for us. If every day you will be coming home this late, what are we going to do about dinner? Mrs. Khan is not cooking for us every day!"

Jasmine has no energy to talk back. She goes straight to the kitchen and drinks down a full glass of water. On an empty stomach, the water creates a tidal wave, giving her rumbling gas pains. She holds her stomach as tears start to stream down her cheeks. Ajit notices her discomfort and brings her a hot water bottle, saying, "That is it, you are not going to work anymore. I will manage our expenses without your help."

But he does not know that she wants to work so she can make money for her airfare to India. She does not want to tell him for the simple reason that she will have to explain this in English; she does not have the stamina to sit and listen to his lecture tonight.

The next morning, as she gets ready to go to work, Ajit admires her western dress and hugs her. He wants to know why she insists on working.

"I tell you tonight the reason to work; I must be timely," she says as she walks out of the door.

This morning is better than yesterday. She is a bit more confident to walk to the building. She starts to work immediately and completes yesterday's unfinished work before her lunchtime. She brought her lunch today, but as soon as she gets up to go to the cafeteria, a load of boxes is dumped in front of her desk. A note on one of the boxes says these "MUST be completed by 4:00 p.m." She takes only five minutes for lunch and works on the boxes, but at 4:00 p.m. she is only halfway through. Bob comes to her and tells her politely, "I am sorry, Jasmine. I need someone faster than you. There is no need for you to come back to work. I will mail the check to your address for the hours you have worked so far." He has another woman with him, obviously to replace her.

She goes straight to Mrs. Khan and tells her what happened. Mrs. Khan tries to cheer her up, saying, "Oh, good! I was missing you. Who needs that kind of job, anyway?"

They cook their dinner and wait for their husbands, as usual. At the dinner table, Mrs. Khan suggests that Jasmine can take their typewriter to practice typing so as to bring her speed up to qualify for an office job. Ajit does not believe in borrowing, but the next day he buys a second-hand Smith-Corona typewriter. After a few months of practice, Jasmine wants to look for a job again.

This time her husband takes her to an employment agency downtown. The lady at the desk is very polite. She prepares a resume for Jasmine to take to the Mountain View Hotel for a job interview on Monday. She tells her not to wear the golden sandals because they are more suitable for a party. "Or are they fancy bathroom slippers?" she asks Jasmine.

"Our agency charges are your first week's salary, so with luck, I'll see you again soon," she tells Jasmine, giving her the necessary papers and the address of the hotel. The manager of the hotel interviews her and hires her immediately to fill the temporary position of his secretary who is on maternity leave.

"Your job duties include typing, filing, and handling my phone calls when I am not in my office," he tells her.

"Sir, I can type and file, but I am not good in understanding Americans in telephone."

"Now I am definitely interested in hiring you because someone needs to give you a chance to practice. Don't worry, you will learn slowly but surely."

He takes her around, introduces her to the other employees in the office, and brings her to his office. "This is your desk," he points to a small desk in one corner.

The next day, Jasmine starts working. Her manager is very nice. For a few days, he takes her to the cafeteria in the basement at lunchtime. She tries to befriend other employees, however, they do not seem interested, especially the young ones. They hardly look at her because she is different. Only one older lady is very nice and helpful, so Jasmine starts to accompany her to the cafeteria for lunch and coffee breaks. Employees are allowed to eat free in the cafeteria. There is such a variety of dishes and especially desserts to choose from. Jasmine loves working there; the first week passes so quickly. On Friday she gets her first paycheck which she takes to the employment agency.

A couple of weeks later, she tells the manager, "Sir, I need to stay home tomorrow." Jasmine does not realize this should be a request.

"For what reason?" her boss asks.

"It is our wedding anniversary, sir."

"Last week was my wife's and my anniversary – we have been married for twelve years," he tells her.

"We marry only a year ago," stammers Jasmine.

"Then you must take a day off. First few anniversaries are special. Later they become routine, and slowly are forgotten. Are you going somewhere special?"

"No sir, we do not have money."

"Call me 'John'. This is not India – you don't have to address me as 'sir'... are all Indian girls as beautiful as you?" His gaze makes her uncomfortable.

Jasmine does not answer and starts to blush. She is not flattered; she is rather taken aback and confused. In India, a strange man is not supposed to admire someone other than his own wife or beloved in this manner.

"Thank you sir – ah – John," she speaks after a long pause.

When she gets up the next morning, Ajit has already left for the university; obviously, he does not remember their anniversary. Jasmine has invited Dr. and Mrs. Khan over for a special dinner to celebrate. She wants to cook everything all by herself without Mrs. Khan's help.

Soon, Mrs. Khan knocks on the door. She hugs Jasmine, wishes her a happy anniversary and tells her not to cook because they are taking them out to dinner.

"Let us go shopping instead of worrying about cooking," Mrs. Khan suggests.

They go to the Wanamaker Department store. Mrs. Khan buys an avocado-green, three-quart pot and a baking stone as anniversary gifts. She knows that Jasmine wanted these items, but could not afford them.

They all had a very nice dinner in Chinatown. As always, Jasmine was quiet while the other three talked a lot. When they came back home, the three of them were singing songs as Jasmine made tea for them. After an hour or so, Mrs. Khan said, "Let us leave these love birds alone…it is their anniversary, you know."

The next day when Jasmine reaches her office, there is a small, wrapped gift from her boss lying on her desk. Jasmine thanks him for the anniversary present and opens it, finding a bottle of perfume.

Back home, Ajit admires her manager's generosity and suggests that she should give him a gift too, or invite him over for dinner.

"But why would he give me perfume?" she wonders.

"Perhaps to make you smell nice; Americans think all Indians smell like a mixture of onion, garlic, and spices. I think he has given you a hint." Ajit is serious and from now on Jasmine wears the perfume every day to work.

Jasmine has been working for almost a month. Her boss is a gregarious man. Jasmine does not hesitate to talk to him because he encourages her to keep speaking whether her English is poor or correct. He tells her, "All Americans are foreigners except the American Indians. They are the true natives of this land. I am Polish, and my wife is Irish. America is a melting pot. We all have accents, so talk freely; no one is going to kill you for innocent mistakes."

Jasmine feels very much at ease in the office. Her boss, John Stanislavsky, is very lenient. He looks about forty years old and is tall, husky, and partly bald. He has dreamy green eyes and laughs loudly. He has a deep voice though his sneeze is like a high-pitched door squeak.

Late one afternoon, John is explaining to her a hand-written report she is unable to read. All of a sudden, he puts his hand on top of hers and she slowly slides it away, thinking he has done it accidentally. He tells her that this report must be typed by the close of business. Until today, he has never given her a deadline like this. At five o'clock the report is not yet completed. She keeps on typing although all the other employees have left. She is afraid to leave the letter uncompleted. After a while, John comes up from behind and puts his arms around her shoulders and says, "Mmmm... you are wearing the perfume." When she looks up he is leaning down to kiss her. She jumps up with full force, bumps her head into his chin, and runs out of the office and all the way out of the hotel. Her heart is beating wildly as she runs to catch her bus. When she comes home, she tells Ajit what happened. She never goes back to John Stanislavsky's, and her paycheck arrives in the mail a few weeks later.

After a couple of weeks, Jasmine receives a phone call from the employment agency. She is told that she is scheduled for an interview on Monday. Jasmine is beginning to feel more confident going out on her own and finding places.

This building is also downtown. When she arrives for the interview and opens the door, she sees the sign, "Director of Operations." *Operations? Is it a hospital?* She stands there wondering whether she has come to the wrong place.

The door opens, a gentleman comes out and shakes hands with her, saying, "Come on in."

This time Jasmine wants to make sure that her desk is not in the boss's room; she will only accept the job if she will be sitting out here in a cubicle.

After asking her some questions, he explains the work duties to her.

"You will do some filing and typing, eight-thirty to five. The pay is fifty dollars a week."

"Where I am sitting, sir?" Jasmine asks.

He takes her to a cubicle outside his office; she thanks God. The next day she starts work, only some filing and light typing. Since there isn't much work, she is quite bored. One week passes and the workload still has not increased. She feels lonesome, with hardly anyone around except occasionally when someone comes to meet the director. His secretary, Mary, assigns the work to Jasmine. She is a strange, glassy-eyed woman, always chewing gum, wearing ridiculously high heels and a very tight skirt. *Quite unprofessional*, Jasmine thinks. The next week, Mary gives her a typing assignment and a machine she says is a "dictaphone." Jasmine looks at her, baffled.

"Hon, it's easier than typing from a paper," Mary says.

"Okay, I will try." Jasmine starts listening and typing, hearing a weird conversation full of four-letter words; she assumes she is having a problem understanding American pronunciation.

"Can I take the dictaphone to my house? So I finish at home?" she asks Mary, thinking that Ajit will listen, talk, and she will type.

"Oh no, this work is confidential. Didn't Mr. Johnson explain that to you and have you sign confidentiality papers?"

"Yes, I signed papers," she replies, but she has no idea what they contained.

So Jasmine sits there doing almost nothing, not daring to just type what she is guessing she hears, since it sounds so inappropriate. *What if I am just completely misunderstanding the words?* She can neither bring herself to type what she hears nor ask Mary about it.

In the evening, Ajit receives a phone call from an Indian gentleman. "Hello, I am from Kerala. Today I saw your wife working in an office that is not a suitable place for her. I can't tell you any more, but I think it will be better if she finds a job somewhere else."

"I appreciate your call. Thank you very much for making us aware. What's your—" Ajit wanted to talk to him more, but the gentleman immediately hung up.

Ajit tells Jasmine to stop working there.

"I was thinking the same too. That place is strange, and the dictation—I mean dictaphone—had some strange dialogue, I think." Jasmine sighs, then says, "I am not working in this country anymore." The next morning she tells Mrs. Khan the whole story.

"I think that employment agency is not a good one. Start looking in the newspaper advertisements for job openings. I am sure you will find an appropriate one, just be patient," Mrs. Khan reassures her.

Ajit brings home Tolstoy's novel, *Anna Karenina*, from the library for her to read. He tells her not to worry about finding another job. But she does not give up; she keeps on looking in the newspaper. One day, she sees an ad and shows it to Ajit.

"It is volunteer work for the mayoral campaign. It will be a good experience but they won't pay you," Ajit warns her.

"I will tell them to pay me," she says innocently.

And that is exactly what she does. During the interview, she tells the lady that she wants to work because she is in dire need of money. In her broken English she tells her the whole story of her job search and office problems. Somehow, the lady (either likes Jasmine or out of compassion) agrees to start Jasmine on the job immediately with a pay of $1.50 an hour, but reminds her that the job only lasts until the election, which is in three months. Jasmine finds the work very easy, cutting and pasting articles from various newspapers and magazines. One employee reads articles, marks them with a marker and forwards them to her. She loves this job.

That same day Dr. Khan comes home and tells his wife the good news. He has been accepted for a fellowship in cardiology at the San Francisco University Hospital. His program starts in January, but they need to move there in early November.

"Oh my God! It is indeed good news, but so far from here. How are we going to break this to the Singhs, especially Jasmine? It will be earth-shattering news for her." Mrs. Khan does not sleep well that night. She hopes and prays that Jasmine gets a job now; it will make it easier for her to adjust.

Dr. and Mrs. Khan decide to put off telling the Singhs for a while, but they forget to ask the landlady not to mention it to anyone. While chatting with Jasmine, Mrs. Stevenson shares the news that another Indian couple has rented the apartment being vacated by the Khans. The earth moves under Jasmine's feet; she feels dizzy. She cannot believe her ears. She goes straight up and knocks on the Khans' door. As soon as her Shaloo *didi* opens the door, Jasmine blurts out, "Tell me it isn't true what I have just heard from the landlady, tell me it is not true!" and she starts crying.

"Oh, my sweet sister. We could not muster the courage to tell you so we decided to wait for some time. I couldn't sleep all night when Arshid broke this news to me," Mrs. Khan said, hugging Jasmine.

"Some good news is that a Punjabi couple is moving into this apartment. I have already met the woman. She is very nice. You will like her. Who knows, she might turn out to be so friendly that you will forget your Shaloo *didi*," Mrs. Khan says to try and make her feel better.

Jasmine keeps quiet, tears rolling down her cheeks.

"You know, Arshid applied to all the area hospitals but nothing was available. He was only accepted to the San Francisco program."

"San Francisco is so far away. How can we get together? It is like visiting England."

"No... it is good, it is not another country, only a phone call away. We can talk every week," Mrs. Khan consoles her.

"What is her name?" Jasmine tries to control her tears.

"Your new friend? She is Deepika and her husband's name is Sanjiv. Their last name is Verma. And what a coincidence! He is a medical doctor and will be a resident at Penn just like Arshid. She has a master's in psychology just like me, and she may get my position after her maternity leave. She's expecting a baby. We will walk over to her place someday soon so you can meet her."

"Oh, I forgot to tell you," Jasmine changes the subject. "I got a job at the mayoral campaign."

"Hey, that sounds like an interesting job – I think you'll love it. You will get to meet so many people. And it will keep you so busy that you won't have time to miss your Shaloo *didi*."

"I will always miss you."

They hug each other and Mrs. Khan says, "Me too."

After a while, Jasmine goes down to her apartment, telling Mrs. Khan that she should get used to preparing meals without help from her Shaloo *didi*.

"Why this sullen face? What happened to you?" Ajit asks her that evening.

"Dr. and Mrs. Khan are leaving for California in November," she says as she starts crying again.

"Yes, I came to know about it a week ago, but I promised Arshid I would not tell you. People come and go, you know; that is the way of life. Be strong and stop crying." Ajit embraces her. "You know, I learned my lesson very early in my life," he continues. "Do not cling to anyone in this world. I was always clinging to my mother, and she died when I was very young. After her, I started to cling to my grandmother and she left me too."

Jasmine is surprised that Ajit is opening up a little today. He has always avoided talking about his family. All she knows is that after his mother's demise, his father married again, and his stepmother mistreated him and his brother. She had never prodded him to bring up his painful memories from the past.

"I will never go away from you whether you cling to me or not," Jasmine says.

"You dare not…you are my life. I will shatter into pieces if you ever leave me."

The two months pass like a breeze. Jasmine enjoys her work very much. Her coworkers, David and Betty, are very talkative, mostly about their dates, music, and movies. One day Betty asks Jasmine if she's seen the new Rock Hudson movie yet. Jasmine says, "No, not yet," even though she has no idea who Rock Hudson is. It is surprising to Jasmine to hear David and Betty talk about their personal lives so openly.

"I broke up with John last night," Betty tells David.

"I had a big fight with my girlfriend this morning," David tells Betty.

Such conversations go on almost every day. They also like talking with Jasmine about India because they are curious about her country. Sometimes she is astonished at how little they know.

One day while David is scanning the newspaper, he comes across an article on the custom of *sati* (widow-burning) in India.

"Hey Jasmine, you are lucky you are in America. I'm reading about *sati*...do you have any girlfriends who got burned alive?"

"Hey Jasmine, do you have swimming pools in India?"

"Hey Jasmine, I hear your Indian mud houses stay warm in the winter but they stay cold in the summer...is that true?"

*These two are college students—yet they think all Indians live in mud houses and widows often get torched. Utterly amazing,* she thinks.

When she tells Ajit, he says, "Perhaps they like to tease you. I am sure they know the *sati* custom was abolished a century ago and all houses are not made of mud." And when she tells Ajit that she responded to their pool question by saying, "Our pools are so big that even our cows and buffalos swim in them too," Ajit scolds her a little for giving such a silly reply.

Her last days of work are very interesting. Jasmine, David, and Betty are given pages from the Philadelphia telephone directory to start calling people, urging them to vote for their candidate. Jasmine has learned so much during these two months of campaign work. She tries not to think about how much she will miss her job and her coworkers.

The Election Day is exciting and tense. Ajit joins Jasmine at the Civic Center Hall and they both marvel at the hundreds of red, white, and blue balloons. All the volunteers and employees are watching televisions stationed on desks throughout the Center. Their candidate wins and gives a victory speech followed by a gala bash. Ajit and Jasmine are glad to be present to witness an important American political event.

# 5

# The Khans' Departure

After the Election Day, the Khans are ready to leave. Jasmine helps Mrs. Khan with the packing. They have sold their car to Dr. and Mrs. Verma, the new tenants. They will buy a new car in California instead of having it shipped from here. Last week Mrs. Khan introduced Jasmine to Deepika. "This is my little sister, Jasmine," Mrs. Khan said with great affection.

"Take care of my little sister," she tells Ajit as they are leaving for California. "I will give you a call." Mrs. Khan hugs Jasmine one last time.

Parting from good friends is always difficult, but for Jasmine, this one really is almost as sad as it was when she left her childhood home. She wants to talk and share this grief with Ajit, but he is not home yet. Anyway, he is a very private person. Either he is not bothered about the Khans' departure or does not want to talk about it. Even when he is in pain, he suffers quietly, but Jasmine, on the other hand, likes to tell the whole world of her feelings. It is now five o'clock, but she does not feel like preparing dinner. She is sad, very sad indeed.

When Ajit comes home, he looks at her and says, "You have been crying as if someone had died. Come on, cheer up. We will visit them soon. Let us go to the cafeteria and you will feel better."

"I do not want to speak English with you anymore," Jasmine blurts out in Punjabi. "Can't you see that we hardly communicate with each other? For so long I did not mind because Mrs. Khan was here to talk to."

"Okay, from now on we will talk in Punjabi. Are you happy now?" Ajit talks with her as they are walking to the university cafeteria.

They notice that Sanjiv and Deepika are having their dinner at a far corner table. They take their trays to that table to join them. Deepika is due in two weeks. She is wearing a sari. "A sari is the best maternity dress," she says. "It expands along with the width of one's belly." She is worried about having a baby in this country without her mother's presence. "Back home there is so much care available, plus all the relatives are there to pamper you and the baby." Jasmine tells her not to worry and assures her that she will be glad to help.

Deepika is sophisticated, and a typical city slicker. Having lived in Delhi all her life, she does not possess Mrs. Khan's spontaneous, country-like qualities. She is so polite that Jasmine often feels uneasy around her. She is soft-spoken, while Jasmine is loud like Mrs. Khan. She calls her husband "darling" while most Punjabi women address their husbands as "jee." Deepika always wears a sari when she goes out, and at home she wears a blouse with an Indian skirt. Her hair is usually unruly, scattered in all directions with a big bun at the back. She is only twelve years older, but she treats Jasmine like a little girl, not a little sister.

Deepika's husband, Sanjiv, is also citified. He is only a couple of years older, but appears much older than she. Sanjiv and Ajit have some things in common; they like to talk about finance and politics, and they like to play cards. Deepika considers herself an intellectual, and always interjects her expertise in psychology into discussions with her husband and Ajit. They are in their early thirties, just like the Khans.

These days, Jasmine and Ajit converse in Punjabi. At last she is happy to communicate freely with him. One evening at the dinner table, she start to tell him a joke. "In a village, one day a snake came into a house, and the mother asked her ten-year-old daughter to run and find a man outside. She came back and said, 'Mother, there is no man out there, only a *shipaie*—' "

Ajit interrupts, "SIPAHEE not *shipaie*!" He pounds his fist on the table and shouts at the top of his lungs, "Nothing makes me more angry than an educated person speaking like a *gunwar* [illiterate]." His mouth is full with half-chewed food and he is mad, mad, mad.

Jasmine is experiencing her husband's intense anger for the first time since their marriage. She is stunned and starts to cry, her only defensive weapon that comes naturally. Her crying makes Ajit feel bad and he gets up and hugs her, apologizing for his bad temper. From now on, she thinks she has to be careful even when speaking Punjabi. Just then, they receive a phone call from Dr. Verma telling them that Deepika has given birth to a healthy baby boy. The next day, they visit Deepika and the baby in the hospital. They will be home in a few days and Jasmine is ready to help them.

Dr. Verma gets the apartment ready and does the grocery shopping before bringing the baby home. In India, a lady in this condition is not allowed to climb the stairs for six weeks, but unfortunately Deepika has no alternative. This building has no elevator. Her husband and Ajit pick her up and slowly help her up a few steps, rest briefly, and then continue. It is quite an ordeal to take her all the way to their third floor apartment. Jasmine welcomes them and holds the baby while Deepika gets settled in their bedroom.

The first few days are quite difficult for both women, but slowly they become acclimated and the baby begins to sleep more. Dr. Verma is not able to take too many days off from work; therefore, most of the daytime burden of caregiving falls on Jasmine. She prepares light lunches, typically a sandwich and soup. Deepika teaches her how to make a grilled cheese sandwich and heat canned vegetable soups. Jasmine tastes this sandwich for the first time and loves it.

"I am adding grilled cheese sandwich to the list of my favorite foods," she says.

"What are your other favorite foods?" Deepika asks.

"Hot dogs, hamburgers, pizza, corn flakes, milk, and cherry vanilla ice-cream. What are your favorites?"

"I am a vegetarian, so there are only a few American dishes I can eat. In the beginning, it was hard to get used to the flavors; bread and cheese smelled particularly funny," says Deepika.

"I, too, had a similar experience. It took me almost a month to get used to a few food items. One day, we tried hamburger and we both liked it. The following week, while grocery shopping, I was looking for ground ham to make hamburgers. When I couldn't find it I asked a store employee to help me, and she handed me a package of ground beef. Watching my quizzical face, she said, 'Yes, hamburgers are made with ground beef.' At first I felt bad that I had eaten beef, but Ajit told me, 'Don't worry, we have eaten only American beef, not our holy cow,' " Jasmine explains with a tinge of humor.

Deepika listens but does not even smile. It is no fun telling her humorous anecdotes. Jasmine thinks of Shaloo *didi* who would have burst into laughter hearing this.

Every morning, Jasmine goes upstairs around ten and comes back to her own apartment late in the afternoon. In addition to cooking and cleaning, she helps Deepika with the baby's bath. The wet baby, Gautam, is tiny and slippery; he slips from their hands time and again. Although there are four hands rather than two and they don't let him slide through, he occasionally lets out a frantic cry with an insecure shiver. Jasmine loves to hold and cuddle him. Before going downstairs to her apartment, Jasmine always has afternoon tea and chats with Deepika.

"When are you planning to have a baby?" Deepika asks her.

"We can't afford to have a baby until Ajit completes his Ph.D. and gets a job."

"I hope you are careful...I mean taking precautions."

"Well, we get together only once in a while, if you know what I mean," Jasmine says.

"What? Jasmine, that once in a while can get you pregnant. For heaven's sake please do not be careless!" Deepika says, almost crying. "And how can you stay apart like that? Aren't you newly married? Haven't you read marriage manuals or love and marriage books? How can you show your love for each other?"

"No, what is there so much to know?" Jasmine frowns.

"Let me tell you my story. I got pregnant right after our marriage. Sanjiv forced me to abort the baby because we were about to leave for America. I was such a fool and agreed with him. And now, even after having this baby, the emptiness of the lost one still lingers as an open wound, hurting terribly. A woman must listen to herself only, and must make her own decision. I hope not, but if you get pregnant please do not listen to your husband. Take your stand even if it requires a sacrifice." Deepika tells all this in one breath and Jasmine sits there motionless.

When she gets up to go to the kitchen, she suddenly runs to the bathroom, feeling nauseous and dizzy.

"Oh, my goodness! I think you are pregnant, Jasmine. That is what happened to me."

They look at each other and blurt simultaneously, "I hope not."

"Just remember what I told you, and be courageous enough to confront your husband with a woman's strength," Deepika tells her when Jasmine leaves for the day.

Jasmine does not want to tell Ajit until she is sure. Perhaps it is indigestion. She looks at the calendar and sees she is six days late for her period. It has happened many times before, so she is not yet panicked.

Ironically, the next day when she is about to go up the stairs, Mrs. Stevenson stops her.

"I am knitting booties for your baby," the old woman says.

"For *my* baby?" Jasmine asks.

"Yes, in my dream, I saw you holding a pretty baby girl."

Jasmine stares at her in astonishment, unable to utter a word. She goes upstairs and tells Deepika that she felt nauseous again this morning. Deepika gets an appointment for Jasmine with her gynecologist.

Well, Jasmine is pregnant and she is nervous about breaking the news to Ajit. Every day she tries but deliberately delays. Ajit leaves the house before she gets up; therefore, he is totally unaware of her morning sickness. Her nausea is increasing day by day and she can no longer help Deepika. After a couple of weeks, she becomes very ill and is unable to retain any liquids or solids in her stomach. Even the slightest smell of cooking Indian dishes makes her nauseous. Finally she discloses the secret to Ajit. He does not say anything to her, but in the evening he calls his brother Rajiv in London who tells him that he can't afford to send extra money. Even though Ajit tells him that American hospitals are very expensive and Jasmine does not have health insurance, as a matter of fact, he scolds Ajit for being so careless.

After getting off the telephone, Ajit sits on the couch by Jasmine. He tells her he thinks the option of an abortion is best, under the circumstances. Jasmine reacts as forcefully as she can.

"I would rather kill myself than kill my baby!" she screams.

Ajit has never witnessed this side of her personality before. They go to bed unsettled, hungry, and angry.

The next day, Deepika bolsters her strength once again by saying, "Do not relent. Stay firm on your ground…men cannot gauge women's emotional intensity."

That night, Ajit brings up the same topic after dinner. He tries hard to make her understand their financial condition, but fails miserably.

"I can go to my parents to have the baby," she suggests.

"What am I going to do all alone here?" Ajit yells.

"You are so busy with your studies you hardly talk to me anyway…what difference would it make whether I am here or not?" Jasmine's voice trembles with fear.

"What are you talking about? We go out to so many places together."

Every single day they argue about the abortion issue, and every night they go to bed angry and frustrated. But Jasmine is determined to keep the baby whether Ajit likes it or not.

She throws up when she eats any food other than a piece of cheese pizza or corn flakes with milk. She has been practically surviving on these three things. She craves her mother's lemon and mango pickle, and *samosa* with coriander chutney from her college canteen. Sometimes she remembers the tasty snacks she used to eat in her junior high school. Nothing close to all those delectable snacks is available here. She goes upstairs to Deepika and tells about her cravings. Deepika suggests eating some Chinese food; they have some dishes similar to Indian taste.

*What a cold turkey she is*, Jasmine grumbles to herself. She plays with Gautama for a while before going downstairs to her apartment and calling her Shaloo *didi*.

"You know, Shaloo *didi*, I have never come across such a cold-hearted person as Deepika. I went upstairs thinking she would help me make Indian vegetable *pikoras* or *samosas* which I am craving these days. She tells me to eat Chinese food, instead. I miss you so much, I wish you were here."

"Why don't you come here? I will take care of you," Mrs. Khan suggests.

"I wish I could, but it is not possible right now. I must find a job to make some money for my airfare to India. You know, I am going home before my due date to have the baby there," Jasmine tells her. As always she hangs up quickly, mindful of the long distance charges they can hardly afford.

Three months have already passed. She has informed everyone in India that she will come in May, two months before the delivery date. They are excited to hear this news. She must work to make money for her airfare. Since she is feeling better now, she tells Deepika that she wants to find a job. Dr. Verma's hospital needs a keypunch operator's assistant. He takes her to the hospital and helps her to get this job. All she has to do is put the keypunched cards in a sorter and write their counts in assigned categories. The job is easy and there is no urgency of scheduled deadlines.

During the lunch hour, she takes a bus to Woolworth, her favorite store. After eating a slice of cheese pizza, she tries to pick up some gifts for her folks back home. She can't afford to buy expensive gifts; therefore, she gathers a few costume jewelry pieces, clothes for her little nephew, and fabric for an outfit for her mother. She is excited to think that in a few months she will be sitting under the *pipal* tree blabbering her mouth to satisfy their curiosity about America.

In her fifth-month checkup, the doctor tells Jasmine that he hears two heartbeats. She takes it in stride, since she does not understand what it means. After a month or so she mentions it to Deepika.

"Oh, Jasmine, you are expecting twins – isn't that wonderful!" Deepika exclaims.

"What? Oh no, we can't even afford one baby and now two – Ajit will kill me! I am afraid to tell him."

After a few weeks, she informs Ajit and he panics. He calls his brother, Rajiv, and asks him if Jasmine could come to London for the delivery.

"There is no way we could take care of two babies without help. And the hospital will cost so much more here, especially if it turns out to be a complicated case," he pleads. Rajiv reluctantly agrees.

Jasmine is flabbergasted to realize that the plans have been changed. Apparently, Ajit had no intention of sending her to India. She had somehow assumed from his silence that he had agreed with her. When she tells Ajit that her folks are waiting eagerly for her, he insists, "It is better for you to go to England instead of India. Hospitals there are much more advanced, plus it takes only six hours to reach London and my brother is willing to help us."

Unenthusiastically, Jasmine agrees and with a heavy heart informs her folks back home. She writes letters to her family and friends telling them she will come home in about six months, but first she must go to London for the birth of her twins. At the end of her seventh month of pregnancy, she makes plans to travel to England as soon as possible.

# 6

# The Twins

At Heathrow Airport the visitors, sitting in the lobby, are waiting eagerly for their loved ones. Ajit's brother Rajiv, his wife Sandy, and their three-year old son, Stevie, have come to meet Jasmine. "When is Aunty coming? Will she bring me a toy?" Stevie keeps repeating.

Jasmine is relieved when the plane lands. Travelling while in her seventh month of pregnancy and sitting in economy class for six hours has taken a toll. She is dismayed to find she cannot slip her swollen feet back into her shoes which she had removed for comfort at the beginning of the flight. *Oh God, what am I to do?* she wonders. *Alas! If this were New Delhi, I could walk out barefoot.* Coming from one unfamiliar land to another makes her spine shudder. Almost all the passengers have left the plane. The flight attendant comes to her and asks, "Do you need to be escorted in a wheelchair, ma'am?"

"Yes," she says, hardly understanding.

The hostess gives her a pair of socks after noticing her swollen feet and asks, "When are you expecting?"

Misunderstanding, Jasmine replies, "Yes, my brother-in-law is coming."

After the customs clearance, she is taken to the airport lobby where she meets Rajiv, Sandy and Stevie. After a while, Rajiv brings his car to the curb and she feels quite relieved sitting in his roomy back seat.

It is the month of May; a brisk nippy breeze is shaking the delicate buds ready to burst open, giving a passionate message of spring. On both sides of the road, there are rows and rows of daffodils and the sun is shining on them, intensifying their orange and yellow hues. It reminds Jasmine of her college days when her professor of English, reading Wordsworth's poem, tells the whole class to memorize the following stanza:

> "For oft, when on my couch I lie
> In vacant or in pensive mood,
> They flash upon my inward eye
> Which is the bliss of solitude;
> And then my heart with pleasure fills,
> And dances with the daffodils."

Jasmine is exhausted and the car ride is like a rocking cradle. She daydreams herself into the landscape. *No wonder this land boasts of so many romantic poets. The undulating hills and valleys augmented by lush greens and exotic flowers can make a poet out of any lover of nature.* She wants to say this to Rajiv and Sandy but is too timid to speak English.

Sandy breaks the ice. "We are driving through Hyde Park, the largest park in this area."

"It is beautiful," Jasmine replies. As they are approaching London Bridge, Stevie starts to sing, "London Bridge is falling down, falling down."

"You sing wonderfully, Stevie." Jasmine finds the courage to engage him in conversation, but Stevie keeps on singing without paying attention.

Jasmine returns to daydreaming, now recalling the week when she and Ajit had stayed here on their way from India to the United States. During that time, they took an organized tour of London and the outskirts. The most memorable sites were the Victoria and Albert Museum, St Paul's Cathedral, Westminster Abbey, and Trafalgar Square. The National Gallery in Trafalgar Square has the greatest collection of western art, from Leonardo da Vinci to Rembrandt. The Gallery was especially rich in the Renaissance period. In addition to several opera theatres, there stood a house built in the 1830s that was occupied for many years by Benjamin Franklin.

Visiting the Victoria and Albert Museum had been an eye-dazzling experience. It is one of the world's best museums, holding the most valuable treasures from all over the world. Each section was exclusively devoted to one country. Indian, Chinese, and Japanese sections were filled with exquisite pieces and paintings, such as Chinese vases, Persian paintings, and woven tapestries. Jasmine had been thrilled to see a collection from nineteenth century Punjab. She had marveled at how Maharaja Ranjit Singh's golden throne, kept in a glass case, looked incredibly new. In one section there was a remarkable collection of elegant and exotic dresses worn by queens from the past eras.

"This is Westminster Abbey, the place in which most of the rulers were crowned, and many were buried here," Rajiv tells Jasmine as they drive by.

"I think when you came here last you missed seeing many castles and cathedrals," Sandy says, joining the conversation.

"There is so much to see in London," says Jasmine.

Finally, the car enters their cobblestone street, lined with small, brick-front row houses. Stevie points and announces enthusiastically, "There's my house!"

The four passengers leave the car and walk up the steps to the front door. After the small foyer, there is a living room on the left, and a small kitchen with a dining area on the right. There is a powder room in one hall corner, and a staircase in the other.

Feeling the chill, Jasmine wraps herself with a shawl. "Maybe in America you have central-heating, but no one does here," Rajiv tells her as he lights the fireplace to generate some warmth.

After resting a bit, Rajiv calls Ajit to inform him of Jasmine's safe arrival. She talks to him briefly before going to sleep in Stevie's bedroom. Stevie's crib has been moved to his parents' bedroom.

Her sister-in-law, Sandy, is a God-sent angel for Jasmine. She is such a sweet lady and pays close attention to Jasmine's health. In addition to preparing food according to Jasmine's taste, she gets books from the library for her to read. Sandy loves Indian food and wants to learn how to make a few more Indian dishes in addition to the ones she already knows. Due to a large number of Indians living in and around London, there is no dearth of Indian grocery stores. Here, Jasmine can prepare several dishes which were not possible in America. Rajiv's Indian friends invite them for dinner one day, and Jasmine is happy to see *gulab-jaman*, her favorite Indian sweet, after almost two years.

Although the British are known to be reticent, Sandy is quite the opposite. They talk, laugh, and cook together just as she did with Mrs. Khan. Jasmine is happy to be there. Stevie is also good company. She notices that Rajiv mostly stays within himself. Sandy makes sure Jasmine goes out for a walk every day and does some light exercise. She tells Jasmine that physical activity now will help to ease the labor pains and makes the delivery easier.

Sandy has started to collect items for the twins. Since they do not know the sex of the babies, they buy neutral colors. She has one bassinet for one baby and she borrows another one from her sister. After cleaning and disinfecting them, Jasmine and Sandy add beautiful white lace to the bassinets. Jasmine writes letters to Ajit and her parents, filled with admiration for Sandy.

Time is passing quickly and nicely. As her due date approaches, Jasmine gets bigger and it gets harder for her to endure the discomfort, especially at night. She has finished reading *Zorba the Greek*, *The Good Earth*, and a book on parenthood. Sandy gives her many tips on how to lose excess weight after the baby is born. She also buys a girdle for Jasmine and tells her that to get back into pre-pregnancy shape this girdle is really helpful. She tells her that she herself got into shape three months after having the baby. Sandy helps her to prepare her hospital bag. Sometimes Jasmine feels as if Sandy were her friend more than merely a relative. Rajiv, a perfect gentleman, does not interfere at all. He is a chemical engineer and comes home late in the evening.

At Jasmine's checkup with her gynecologist, he tells her he suspects that the twins may arrive earlier than mid-July. Sandy has arranged a baby shower for her, inviting all her own friends and relatives. They bring baby clothes and other essential items. Although Jasmine has recently written letters to her folks, excited over the baby-shower custom and the generous gifts from Sandy's friends, she writes another one again. She has written several letters to Ajit, but feels lonely as she still awaits a response from him. Perhaps he thinks there is no need to write a letter because he talks to her on the phone quite often. Jasmine feels that their phone conversations are limited due to expensive long distance charges.

In spite of Sandy being so friendly, Jasmine feels lonely being away from her loved ones in this miserable condition. It is hard for her to lie down at night; she is uncomfortable in any position. She does not know whether Ajit would have helped her by consoling her, holding her, if he were here with her. Ever since she became pregnant, he has behaved very awkwardly. He has taken no interest in the twins' heartbeats or kicks, but she knows that is how Indian husbands are. And now, being so far away, he does not seem to care what she is going through. Whenever she is perturbed by such thoughts, she writes a letter to her dearest friend, Simran. She is the only one who understands her. After all, they studied together from first grade all the way up to college. She gets up and starts writing:

> *Dear Simran,*
>
> *It is 2 in the morning and I am wide-awake. There are two babies violently kicking inside me. I think they are eager to come out of this little cubbyhole as soon as possible. My doctor thinks they will be born before the due date. Strange are the ways of the mind. At one minute, I wish they were out, but then I get so scared and wish they would stay there until I come home and my mother is there with me. Simran, really, how am I going to survive the trauma of labor pains, the*

excitement of the miracle of life, and feeding two babies
at the same time? One thing has worked in my favor
though. My sister-in-law says since there are two babies,
start feeding them with bottles instead of breast. She says
breast-feeding is considered primitive and mostly out
of fashion. I know my mother will scold me for it but I
think she will understand sooner or later.

Sometimes, I get so mad at God for dumping all
the pains in a woman's lap. Why doesn't God distribute
pain equally between a man and a woman? Why's
there so much injustice in God's court? Occasionally I
wonder whether it occurs to Ajit what his beloved wife
is going through. I have a feeling he sleeps wonderfully
in my absence but I do not blame him. He has no idea
how miserable my nights are. He doesn't even reply to
my letters. You know I feel like changing Shakespeare's
famous line from his play, Hamlet, "Frailty, thy name is
woman" to "Suffering, thy name is woman."

I know my sister-in-law is very helpful, but still
my mind wishes I were with you all. In my mother's
presence I could allow myself to scream loudly, and my
father would make his special masala tea for me in
the middle of the night. You know, during our finals'
preparatory days, he used to wake me up at four in the
morning with a most delicious cup of tea I will never
forget. Here, I feel suffocated and afraid to make noise.
I keep reading novels one after another. I was reading
Tolstoy's "War and Peace" and I liked the two names
Natasha and Sonia, I wrote about these names to Ajit
(if we have girls), but he has not yet replied to my letter.
I guess he is very busy with his studies and it is my fault

*too. I do not write to him about my condition the way I can write to you.*

*You know there is a vast difference between the two cultures—American and British. I notice Americans are extroverts, and a bit free from the nuances of etiquette. They are more like our type—straightforward, but sophisticated to a reasonable extent. One time Ajit invited his professor for dinner and knew the professor loved tandoori chicken, so it was served, prepared along with the bones. We were eating with forks and knives. After struggling for a while, the professor said, "This chicken is finger-licking good. Would you mind if I use my fingers instead?" And if you ask an American, "How are you?" he will reply, "Oh, I am fine," or "I am good," without ending the sentence with "thank you." But I like their natural behavior.*

*Here in England, my goodness! The British make you feel so uncomfortable with their formalities. You have to be so stiff that sometimes my neck starts to hurt. If you meet a British person for the first time, his attitude would compel you to be very polite, soft-spoken, smile unnaturally, and stand erect. The other thing: if you go to a restaurant, dare not make noise. They can make you very nervous with their disapproving looks. Even this little nephew of mine sits at the dinner table like a grown-up. He makes no noise with his spoon, just like his parents when they dissolve sugar without banging the spoon on the cup's sides. There is always a pin-drop silence in the public library and other similar public places.*

*At the time of my departure, Ajit told me three things: 1. When you meet any British person for the first*

*time, shake hands and say 'How do you do?' 2. Talk
with Sandy as much as possible to practice your English.
3. He would miss me very much. Why is he so concerned
about my English? Why is he not concerned about the
babies' and my health? He should have told me to take
good care of my health, to not worry about anything else,
and make sure I do not forget my pre-natal vitamins.*

*One thing is good: the spring season here is
beautiful. In their little yard, there are lilac bushes that
spread their jasmine-like perfume every evening. It
reminds me of our college garden emanating scented air.
Sandy loves to cook Indian food and I have taught her a
few dishes, too. She is such a nice person. She cares about
my health a lot. She insists that I should go for a walk
every day to stay active and strong. Hopefully, if all goes
well, very soon I will be giving you good news. Do write
me soon about the names I have mentioned. Give me
some names for boys, too. I have two names in my mind,
Shawn and Veer. I want to give them names that are
easy to pronounce and spell because they will be growing
up in America. I can go on writing to you forever but I
am getting tired now and will try to sleep.*

*Missing you,*

*Jasmine*

Sandy has been taking Jasmine to the hospital for a class
on exercises to ease the labor pains. Other pregnant ladies
bring their husbands along with them. "Indian husbands
would be a little reluctant to accompany wives to such
things," says Jasmine. Sandy tells her that Rajiv came with her
only when she pestered him to do so.

"Only in India, Indian men have it so easy—not so when they live in the western world. In India, due to the joint-family system, there is so much help available that the men are not expected to do anything for their women and babies," Sandy says. "At least that is what Rajiv told me."

One day while they are taking a stroll in a nearby park, Sandy tells Jasmine that in the beginning of their relationship, Rajiv was very insecure, shy, and detached. She loved him so much that she worked hard to bring him out of his cocoon. Sandy says she would assume both the brothers are quite similar and warns Jasmine that her relationship would suffer if she were not aggressive enough to break the ice and make Ajit exhibit love and affection. "They have suffered so much in their lives that they do not know how to show affection or remorse," Sandy says. "Do you know their mother eloped with a policeman when they were very young?"

Jasmine stops walking and looks at Sandy. "No, Ajit told me their mother died."

"That is what Rajiv used to tell me until one day we had a big fight over our deteriorating relationship and I was ready to leave him. I forced him to accompany me to a marriage counselor. After having some sessions with us, the counselor suggested that Rajiv should see a psychiatrist. At first Rajiv was reluctant to go, but through my persistence, he agreed. Under hypnosis, he cried out the story of his sad childhood. He had this buried resentment toward women and once he got it off his chest, his behavior improved greatly and now he is a loving person."

"Ajit does not show much affection or emotion either, and I always think it is because of my being so submissive, shy, and naïve," says Jasmine.

This conversation makes Jasmine very restless that night. She starts to worry about Ajit. *He must be feeling so lonely; no wonder he is so quiet and irritable. In spite of his love, he is so emotionally disconnected.* She writes another letter to him expressing more affection than she ever had in the past.

Sandy's one sentence, "If you love him as deeply as I love Rajiv, you will persist in curing him, too," rings in her mind.

*Perhaps I have to take him to a psychiatrist too, but he will never agree to it. Sandy is not as meek as an Indian wife. She was able to give Rajiv an ultimatum which I wouldn't even think of…do I really love him or do I feel obligated to love him?* She has no answer for this; not yet, anyway, she thinks.

The next day she receives two letters. To her surprise, one letter is from Ajit and the other is from Mrs. Khan. Ajit's letter is quite dry, filled with general information of his daily routine and his loneliness. He wants her to come back as soon as possible after the delivery and postpone going to India. He does not exhibit any concern about her being alone in this critical and exciting stage of her life. He does not write anything about her going through the birthing ordeal by herself. She is agitated by it rather than feeling happy that she has received his much-awaited letter.

Mrs. Khan's letter is so funny and affectionate. She is expecting a baby too. She writes that Arshid has started to cook because the kitchen smells make her throw up. He does not know how to cook and keeps on burning her pots and pans. She has sponsored her mother to come and help them. Hopefully, she will come soon enough to save her remaining pots and the poor kitchen. *Ah! Shaloo didi is so lucky; her mother will be present at the time of her delivery.* The thought of being alone in the hospital haunts Jasmine.

*Oh, no, Ajit wants me to think of Indian names for the babies,* Jasmine remembers. *Everyone back home will also appreciate Indian names, but nobody understands how difficult it is for western people to spell and pronounce Indian names. I should forget giving any Punjabi name that is spelled with a 't' since that Indian sound does not even exist in English. And I don't want to give a name with the letter 'd' which is supposed to be pronounced like 'the' in Punjabi. Well, I at least have narrowed down my choices a little,* Jasmine thinks as she drifts off to sleep.

Early in the morning she experiences a shooting pain in her lower abdomen. She endures it with deep breathing exercises as she had practiced in her class. She nervously bathes herself, eats her breakfast, and gets ready as if she were going to catch a plane. Then she brings her hospital bag downstairs and tells Sandy that the babies are coming. Sandy quickly calls her doctor who advises Jasmine to stay home until she gets frequent contractions, or her water breaks. Jasmine does not get any more contractions until late afternoon, and then one in the late evening. At midnight, the frequency picks up and the pain becomes unbearable, so Sandy takes her to the hospital.

Jasmine finds herself being wheeled to a large room where there are three other women screaming with pain and cursing the ones who contributed to their condition. Jasmine wonders whether these women hidden behind the curtains are British. She thinks they behave more like foreigners. Jasmine tries to hear them to decipher their nationality, but is unable to decide. As far as she knows, English women are reserved and very private, but these ladies are hilarious. Suddenly, one opens her curtain and slowly all curtains are opened. They introduce themselves to each other. One woman is from Malaysia, one is from Pakistan, and one is from South India.

In between contractions, the Malaysian tries to entertain the others by telling a joke. "One time a group of women took their plea to God and said, 'God, it is not fair that women have to suffer so much pain while their husbands go pain-free; we feel justice should be done.' God realizes that women do indeed suffer too much; therefore, God decides that from now on, when a woman is ready to give birth, the baby's father will suffer the labor pains. The women were very happy at this justice. Several months later, one of them was with her midwife at home, giving birth to a baby… and the man next door was having labor pains. And her husband was sleeping comfortably." Jasmine and her roommates burst out laughing, a violent scream of shooting pain mingling in the laughter.

Jasmine wonders if this room of four non-British women is intentionally segregated. Perhaps the hospital is aware of (or some English woman objected to) the noisemakers and is deliberately keeping them away from those who prefer pin-drop silence.

After a while, Sandy arrives, holds Jasmine's hand and tells her that soon two bundles of joy will make her forget all the pain. "We are in touch with Ajit and he sends his love to you," says Sandy. Jasmine suspects that Sandy has just made up the last sentence to make her feel better.

Her contractions are coming on strong now and only minutes apart. The nurse comes and gives her an epidural, which after some time lessens her pain. By four in the morning, her two beautiful daughters have been born and are lying on top of her soft empty belly. Jasmine is delirious, nervous, and ecstatic. She strokes them, amazed and overwhelmed.

No one is with her to share this joy, and she misses her mother terribly. Her happiness is tarnished by an awful dilemma. Her heart tells her to go to India; her duty tells her to listen to Ajit. He is lonely and wants her to come to America. *How am I going to travel so far away with two babies? How am I going to feed them without a helping hand?* She must go to her parents and hope that Ajit can endure the loneliness for a few more months. She will tell him so, and she starts to think about Indian names. Two names come to her: *Komil* and *Sohil.* Both names mean "delicate" and are easy enough to spell and pronounce.

Sandy returns early in the morning and congratulates her with a bouquet of flowers. Holding both the babies in her arms, she says, "Ah, they are so precious…they are adorable!" She tells Jasmine that Rajiv tried to call Ajit but he was not at home; he would keep on trying until he got him. She assures Jasmine that Ajit will call at the hospital.

After several sleepless nights, today, Jasmine is finally sleeping like a merchant who has sold all his horses and has nothing to worry about. Even if the phone rings, she does not hear because she is sleeping so soundly. The nurse wakes her to hold the babies, but Jasmine tells her to take them back to the nursery. That evening, Rajiv and Sandy visit her. Rajiv tells her that Ajit has tried calling her several times with no luck. Due to the time difference, he will try again tomorrow. She feels guilty that she was not awake to answer the phone. *Tomorrow, I must stay awake. I must tell him about the names I have given to our daughters.*

The next day, she finally talks to Ajit and tells him the Indian names she has chosen for the girls, thinking he will be quite pleased. Ajit shows no reaction, and he does not seem eager to see his daughters. He shows no regret about not sharing this important time of their life. He only emphasizes how lonely he feels and how much he wants her to come back soon. Jasmine remembers how Sandy described the deep emotional issues of the two brothers and thinks she must pay more attention to Ajit's needs; therefore, she decides to go back to America instead of flying to India. So she tells Ajit not to worry, she will be there as soon as she is able to travel.

As soon as Jasmine is off the phone she starts to panic. *How in the world will I tell my parents, friends, and cousins that I have changed my mind again? They will be devastated.* She is in a quandary and starts crying; she doesn't know what to do.

Although she is supposed to be released today, when the doctor checks her, she is running a fever. "You can't go home today, Mrs. Singh. You have a fever due to infection and it's best if you stay here a few more days."

Jasmine can hear thunder and a heavy downpour; it makes her nostalgic. This is exactly how the monsoon season back home sounds, but the reaction here is different. Back home it generates an unforgettable thrill — you can sense the excitement in the birds, the cattle, and the children splashing in the rain. How splendid are those days when mothers prepare special sweets to celebrate the rainy season! After a storm, the puddles are crystal clear; you can see your face just as in a mirror. The seven-colored rainbow, sometimes two of them, the peacocks dancing, the birds chirping, and the intensity of the unfathomable joy in the entire atmosphere — are all beyond description. What a difference! Here, she feels nothing except the haunting sounds of thunder-burst.

Jasmine thinks about her mother's last letter which describes everyone's excitement at hearing about her coming during the monsoon season. *"How much we miss you,"* she wrote, *"especially in the afternoon when we all sit down to eat mangoes one after another."* Jasmine closes her eyes. She wants no more of this nostalgia nonsense. She is tired of feeling torn apart. She wants to go back to her husband in America and think no more of her parents or friends. Her life is where her husband is; after marriage it is her duty to be with her husband and her daughters. That is what God has chosen for her and this is what she is going to base her life on. Relieved and happy with this decision, Jasmine tells Sandy about it when she comes to her hospital room that evening. Sandy brings her two letters that came a few days ago. Jasmine does not open the letters immediately as she has always done before, but puts them away. Nothing will come between her life and her decision; she goes to sleep.

The next morning, she sees the letters lying on the table and quickly opens the one from her mother. It was written before the girls' birth. Her mother is obviously excited to see her very soon. She is concerned about her being uncomfortable and alone during her delivery time. The other letter is from her friend Simran, which she is eager to read.

> *Dear Jasmine,*
>
> *By the time you receive this letter, I am sure your bundles of joy will be lying on top of your tummy instead of inside, and I am sure all that pain you endured will have flown away like a cuckoo bird. The pains that bring tremendous joy, that create a miracle of life, are much better than those pains that keep recurring to make one miserable. I think a woman's life is so much better than a man's life. I read your letter and felt bad*

*that you could not sleep at night due to the discomfort. But I know that this discomfort is temporary; and as they say, 'there is no gain without pain.'*

*You changed Shakespeare's line from 'frailty, thy name is woman' to 'suffering...' but I would like to change it to 'sacrifice, thy name is woman.' Truly Jasmine, I don't know about western women, but the word 'SACRIFICE' is written on an Indian woman's forehead in capital letters. Right from the age of puberty, a girl learns how to sacrifice herself for the happiness of her parents and her siblings; she forgoes her yearning for love for the sake of her parents' honor. She lives like a stranger in her parents' house because one day she will leave that house to go to her in-laws. And there too, she is considered a stranger.*

*But no matter what her fate is, she does not shy away from spreading happiness around her. If you compare a woman with a man, all the delicate and beautiful things are used to describe a woman — such as delicate as a flower, as emotional as a flowing river, as dedicated as a musician. On the other hand, a man is compared to rough things — such as solid as a stone, as emotional as a parched land, and as dedicated as a wrestler.*

*Ideally, I would wish you to have one girl and one boy. But if that is not realistic, then I hope that you have two beautiful daughters instead of two boys. Girls' names are like poetry, their clothes are so beautiful, and one can dress them in so many fashions. Give them Indian names that have beautiful meanings. As a matter of fact, the same thought crossed my mind when I was reading 'War and Peace' — I like 'Natasha' and 'Sonya' but not for Indian girls. For boys, I like the names Veer, Vijay, or Nishan, and for girls, Sita, Komil, and Gita are easy ones to pronounce and spell.*

*Oh, I forgot to tell you, I am in LOVE! You want to know with whom? In our Punjabi class, we are studying the Punjabi Sufi poets. Sufis take (within Islam) a particular spiritual path to recognize that man is incapable of grasping God. 'The inability of understanding is already to understand' is their mantra. Their poetry reveals celestial experience and humanistic philosophy. They address God as their lover. At present we are reading the poems of Baba Bulleh Shah, Baba Farid, and Baba Kabir. I wish I could write all what I have read so far, but I realize you are too busy to read my craziness. I am totally wrapped up in their philosophy and unable to sleep at night.*

*Aren't all these symptoms of a lovesick mind? So I am in love!*

*We all are waiting for you, please do not change your mind again, and come soon. I have so much to tell you when you come back.*

*Sweet, sweet remembrance,*

*Simran*

Both letters emphasized her coming to India soon. Ajit is pressuring her to come to America soon. What a dilemma! She doesn't know what to do. She feels torn in two. She looks over the babies, sleeping soundly in their bassinets. *They are so lucky,* she thinks; *at this age they have nothing to worry about.* She picks them up and holds them tight. *Let the girls decide for me. Where would they be happier? In America they would be cooped up in a small apartment, in India they would be loved and pampered by many people; they would be in an expansive courtyard with fresh air and stars to watch at night. Yes, I should decide based upon their comfort. I must sleep now, I will decide tomorrow.* And she goes to sleep.

After a week of hospital stay, Sandy brings them all home. The babies are dressed in white bonnets and booties. They look like dolls and all passers-by stop and look at them admiringly. At home, Stevie's happiness knows no bounds. He is running and dancing around to entertain them. It is hard for Jasmine to keep him away from them even when they are asleep. Sandy is very excited, too. She helps Jasmine with all the daytime chores, but at night she only comes if she hears the babies crying. Time is flying; the girls are now five weeks old and she must make a decision very soon. She asks the girls again and if they laugh she thinks they want to go to India. Every night before going to sleep she thinks she will decide tomorrow.

One night she falls asleep, totally unaware that God has figured it all out for her. At the first ray of dawn, she receives a telegram stating that her father has died of a massive heart attack. She is shocked and speechless. Her tears are frozen; she sits like a zombie.

"Someone has to make her cry, otherwise she will lose her mind," Sandy, quite concerned, tells Rajiv.

Neither of them knows how; therefore, they invite some Indian friends over who have their mothers living with them.

The old ladies have ways to make Jasmine cry. First they start crying, and then they say to Jasmine, "How sad it is for your poor mother who has become a widow at such a young age, and your poor sister who needs him the most. It is so painful to think that you are not able to even see him or attend his funeral." Upon hearing this, Jasmine finally starts to sob. She wants to go home as soon as possible. She informs Ajit that she will go to India now and return to the States as soon as possible.

Sandy buys a second-hand two-seat retractable stroller, very light in weight to make Jasmine's journey easier to handle. She helps her prepare with everything necessary for travelling with two small babies. The next morning, Sandy takes them to the airport and bids them farewell.

# 7

# Home, Sweet Home

The plane ride from London to New Delhi is not bad at all. The girls sleep all the way in comfort and the flight attendant is very caring. Although the journey is relatively smoother than her last one, Jasmine feels the anguish of losing her father and pity for her mother at becoming a widow though she is not even fifty years old.

Her plane lands at midnight. As she stands in the queue for customs clearance, the baby girls wake up and start to cry frantically. The airport is very hot and humid. There is no air circulation and the line is pathetically long. There appears to be no priority line for mothers of infants or old folks.

Luckily, one lady standing next to Jasmine, says, "They must be hungry – let me help you feed them." She holds one girl while Jasmine prepares two milk bottles. As soon as the girls start to gulp down the milk they calm down. Jasmine wipes her forehead dripping with perspiration. Just two years of luxury living in the West has made Jasmine so delicate that a little heat and humidity becomes unbearable. Her brother and sister have come to receive her and Jasmine feels better just seeing them as they admire her baby girls. The journey from New Delhi to Punjab is another five-hour ordeal by a taxi with no air-conditioning. But in the company of her siblings, the travel is as smooth as one can hope for in the intense heat of August.

At last the taxi arrives. Their house, called "Red Rose *Haweli*", is made of red brick with a *chubara* (room) and a *barsati* (rain shelter) on the roof. These rooms are connected with an open large rooftop space surrounded by a five-foot high railing of decorative red bricks. The *haweli* has a big courtyard surrounded by eight-foot high walls, with a beautifully carved rosewood door fitted into a gothic style arched gate. The gate opens into a spacious verandah where all the mourners are sitting on the floor. It appears as if the whole village is present to mourn her father's untimely departure. Jasmine's heart throbs with excitement as well as with grief. Where everybody's embraces and kisses would have been a thrilling experience, today they end up in tears and sobs.

The mourning period continues and people, especially the ladies, come and go all day long. They cry and hug Jasmine, saying, "My poor child, you have been separated from your father for two years and it is so unfortunate that you could not be present at his funeral." Jasmine does not like the way they continue to put on such an act almost on a daily basis. It breaks Jasmine's heart to see her mother's face drenched in pain and her sixteen-year old sister's immense grief.

The babies remain upstairs and Jasmine's mother has already hired a woman and her teenage daughter to look after them. After a month or so, the mourners stop coming and the family life slowly gets back to normal. Now little Sohil and Komil are taken everywhere in the house. Jasmine is pretty much free from the daily care of the girls. Shanti, the nanny, washes their diapers, clothes, and bathes them every evening. When they are asleep, she even gives Jasmine a massage. Shanti's daughter, Sita, feeds the fast-growing girls and rocks them in their swings. The swings look like small lightweight bassinets that the local carpenter has made to hang on one of the trees in their courtyard. Jasmine's friend, Simran, stops by every day on the way back from college. They giggle and gossip the way they used to do in their school and college days. Simran holds both girls in her lap, but as soon as Jasmine's sister, Dilbeer, comes home, she tries to snatch them from her, creating quite a fun-filled scene.

Bibijee enjoys the happy noise her granddaughters create around her home and is becoming accustomed to accepting her life of responsibility and loneliness. In a joint-family household, usually a mother lives like a queen when her husband is alive, but this changes drastically when she becomes a widow. A daughter-in-law and an older son begin to challenge her authority.

Once day the postman hands a letter to Dilbeer and Simran as they are walking back from college, and they come running home excitedly. *"Didi, didi! Jeejajee's* [brother-in-law's] letter has come." But Jasmine shows no excitement until she reads it.

> *Dear Jasmine,*
>
> *I am very sorry about Bapujee's untimely heavenly abode. It must be extremely hard for Bibijee and Dilbeer who needed him the most. How are the girls? I miss you very much. Although I want you to come back soon, it has occurred to me that since you are already there, why not finish your college education? Also the girls will*

*grow up a little. Here we won't have any help in raising them. I have written a letter to the college principal and my friend, Professor Mohan Lal, to get you belated admission, and asked that you be tutored at home to catch up with any missed lectures. I know it is hard for me to live alone for so many months, but I feel your bachelor's degree is also important. You will complete it by next July, which is less than a year from now and I am busy in my studies anyway. Let us sacrifice our happiness for the sake of our children. If you obtain a degree, you will be able to get a professional job, then we both will earn well and give the very best to our daughters.*

*Nothing new here except that the Vermas are leaving in a couple of months. Dr. Verma has accepted a fellowship program somewhere in Florida. I have made a couple of new friends so don't worry about me. Weather is very pleasant here. I don't like staying alone in the apartment; therefore, most of the time I stay in the library, in classes, or on the university lawns.*

*Professor Mohan Lal will visit you at your house soon to tell you about your admission and tuition schedule.*

*Affectionately,*

*Ajit*

Ecstatically, Jasmine tells Dilbeer and Simran about her admission to the college, and like young schoolgirls, the three of them jump up and down screaming with joy. Her mother comes running from the kitchen to find out what is going on.

"Bibijee! *Didi* will be staying for almost a year to complete her college," Dilbeer tells her mother. All of a sudden, rays of happiness shine upon their faces and they all feel uplifted after so many days of sorrow.

"Ah, my dream comes true. How much I wished you were here with me, sitting in the classes as we used to, walking in the drizzle, singing songs, laughing, talking, oh! Is it really true? I can't believe it!" Simran exclaims with delight, hugging Jasmine.

Komil and Sohil are sleeping in complete comfort under the tree. The swings are covered with a net to keep the flies away from them, and the morning breeze lulls them to sleep. There are so many people to take care of them that Jasmine has to grab them to have her own time to play, talk, and make them smile. At night, one baby sleeps with Bibijee and one with Dilbeer. Jasmine wants them to sleep alone, but the custom here is to keep the babies close to a loved one.

Bibijee explains, "The infants dream about their previous life, and at times they remember scary incidents; therefore, they need to feel very safe and secure." She wants one girl to sleep with Jasmine, but Dilbeer insists on sleeping with one, at least on the weekends.

"Bibijee, how do you know that?" Jasmine snaps at her mother.

"We know this from our experience. We have looked after so many infants! Such things do not have to be rationalized," Bibijee and her *bhuajee* (paternal aunt) reply simultaneously.

"Okay, okay, we are going to the bazaar," says Jasmine, getting up. She calls to Dilbeer and Simran to leave now. They travel to the nearby town market to purchase some outfits for college. Jasmine does not want to give any clue that she is a married woman; she wants to look and behave as the girl she was in her college days. Even Simran reminds her,

"Remember that married lady who was in our second year and always wore a sari and heavy makeup – and they made her feel as if she were from a different planet. That is what they will do to you."

"Oh yes, I remember, and I definitely don't want to give that type of impression." So Jasmine fills her wardrobe with pastel cotton outfits just like Simran, Dilbeer, or any girl in her college. The latest fashion is a *kameez* so tight that it literally clings to the body's contours and a *salwaar* with an opening so narrow that to slide a foot into it needs expert maneuvering. Jasmine tries these on and looks beautiful in the outfit. Sandy's advice has helped her lose all the excessive weight of pregnancy, which is unbelievable. She looks and feels like a girl, not a married woman at all.

Her mother is thrilled for her to get a chance to obtain her college degree, but her brother does not like the idea of leaving Ajit alone in America where there is so much social freedom. He tries to persuade Jasmine that she should go back now, but she is too excited to listen to him. For now, she wants to forget all that has happened in the last two years of her married life and live as a carefree student.

Since their father is no more, the responsibility of land management falls upon her brother, Amar, the only son. Jasmine's *bhabi* (sister-in-law), expecting a baby, has gone away to her parents' house, as is the Indian custom. She will stay there for quite a few months after the delivery, but Jasmine's home is still full of relatives. In addition to Jasmine's grandmother, her *bhuajee*, a widow, lives with them because she has no son to take care of her. Her *masijee* (mother's sister), who is also a widow, comes to stay whenever she has a tiff with her daughter-in-law. At times, she does not go back for several months. And especially in the afternoons, the village women come to chat with them too. So, the house is always full of people generating a lot of *raunik* (hustle and bustle).

There is a well in front of their house, and all day long the women come to fetch water. Some of them also stop by to gossip. They look at the babies and always make negative remarks, which makes Jasmine very upset. She remembers how much her daughters were admired in England, but here it is quite the opposite. She tells Bibijee about this and Bibijee says, "No, my child, don't you remember the custom? They deliberately make these remarks to save the girls from the evil eye. These illiterate women believe in rituals that do not make sense, but just remember they are actually caring for and admiring your beautiful daughters. Who would not?"

Jasmine's father was the *Sarpanch* (mayor) of the village and now her brother takes over until the next election. He is extremely busy with two big responsibilities and comes home quite late at night. Bibijee worries about his health and shares this concern. "My poor son, he has lost his father's support at such a young age, all the responsibilities have fallen upon him." She cries to the neighborhood women who also love to show their sympathy, usually with crocodile tears.

"You know, Bibijee, when I was in America I thought how unemotional and unconcerned those people were during their mourning. But after seeing these women make you cry all the time, I think the American way of condolence is much better. Here people can drive you nuts with their drama. They come, they cry, they make you cry; why such nonsense?"

"Look at you, oh my God! In a couple of years of living over there, you have stopped liking our way of life. I am so disappointed at your comments," Bibijee says, shaking her head in despair.

Professor Lal has started to tutor Jasmine at home. She knows him very well. At their marriage, he was Ajit's best man and he was her history professor, too. He is a very jolly person of small stature with big spectacles. She is taking English, history, and economics. The professor has gone over all these subjects and the parts covered so far. Simran has shared her notes with her as well. The history test is scheduled next week and Jasmine has plenty of material to study. She has been so busy that she has not written a letter to Ajit for quite a few days. Normally, she tries to write a letter to him once a week whether he writes back or not.

College is so much fun. Sometimes she thinks she is leading two lives or she has a split personality. When she is in college, she forgets that she is a wife and a mother, but at home her daughters remind her who she is. She and her friends, especially Simran, enjoy their free time. They sit on the college lawn for hours as a warm breeze blows the clouds away. They crack jokes, imitate professors, sing songs, and prepare for the exams. They become hysterical when a moving cloud ruptures right on top of their heads, drenching them. Time is flowing like water in a river; once it leaves it does not come back.

Although it is a co-educational system in Jasmine's college, the boys and girls sit together only in classes. Even there, the boys sit separately from the girls. They do not mingle at all and the tutorial groups are also separate. Every Friday, the girls' tutorial group meets to discuss various issues. Today, they all want Jasmine to tell them about America.

"Tell us about your first impression of America," the professor starts.

"It mesmerizes you. When the plane was landing, I looked down and it appeared as if all the stars had come down to earth. The glittering lights from tall buildings expanded to the horizon in such a way that it appeared an enchanted place. When our taxi was on the road, the other cars moved like a flowing river, with a mild swishing sound, and absolutely no honking of the horns. There are no dirt spaces anywhere; either there are roads, cement pavements, or grass."

"Wow! Tell us about their beaches," a student calls out. "Are there really half-naked or nude people?" Everyone starts laughing.

"I have been to only one beach," Jasmine says. "The ocean was spectacular with shimmering sunrays, waves rolling over my body, and the sand sliding under my feet. Yes, we would call them half-naked, but I did not see any nude person running around."

"Do boys and girls meet freely and kiss or hug in public? Do they date for a long time before they get married?" another student asks.

"Yes, but I noticed more public kissing in England than in America."

"Did any one kiss you?" someone asks and they all start giggling.

"Yes, a kiss on the hand or the cheek is sometimes their way of welcoming you."

"Tell us more about their living standard; are they all really very rich? How much is India behind? Will India ever catch up to America?" The curious students are all staring at Jasmine, hanging on her every word.

"All Americans are not rich, but even the middle class have cars and live well. Any level of job is considered respectable, which is very admirable. Oh, yes! America truly is a land of milk and honey. Food is inexpensive and available in abundance. Americans eat a lot and waste a lot, too. They do work very hard and are always on the move to find better jobs. Here the people just keep on living in the same house for generations. I think India is behind by anywhere from fifty to eighty years. I hope it catches up sooner than that."

"Wow!" And they are speechless after that.

The college is about four miles from their village: they commute by auto-rickshaw. They are the only three girls from their village who are studying there. Most of the village girls stop their education after completing the local primary school. Jasmine and Simran's mothers, having had high school education themselves, are adamant about educating their daughters in spite of their fathers' lack of enthusiasm.

Jasmine and Simran are in their final year and Dilbeer is a sophomore. Due to serious illness last year, Simran was unable to sit in the finals; therefore, she is repeating her final year and Jasmine has caught up with her now. Jasmine still wears a girdle to smooth her belly that stretched during pregnancy. She looks slim and trim.

"You know Jasmine, it appears as if God deliberately made me ill last year so that I could be with you again," Simran says.

"Yes, Simran, I don't believe much in destiny but I definitely have faith in deepest desire," Jasmine says. "Oh, how much I wished to be with you, only God knows. Now, it is my greatest desire that you marry someone who can bring you to America."

"I hope it comes true," Simran sighs.

"You know, Simran, no matter how many splendid places I have seen in England as well as in America, the most excitement, and also tranquility, I feel are right here. Nothing surpasses our tiny trips and picnics together. Why is that?"

"Because you have spent seventeen years of life here and only a couple of years away, and here you have a friend who loves you very much."

"Oh, I forgot to tell you something very interesting. You remember my writing you about Deepika Verma who moved to the Khans' apartment after they left for California?"

"Yes, that weird psychologist you wrote about."

"Exactly. One day while we were having lunch, I sighed and said, 'I haven't received a letter from my friend for so long and I miss her very much.' Rather than saying something similar so that we could start to communicate on a human level, she asked me, 'Are you a lesbian?'"

"What is a lesbian?" Simran asks, frowning.

"That is exactly what I asked her, and she told me that when a female is romantically involved with another female it is called 'lesbian' and when a man is in love with another man it is called 'homosexual.' I was shocked to hear her say that a large percentage of high school Indian girls are lesbians. I told her that you and I are childhood friends and we love each other very much, but do not belong in that category. And I told Deepika that there were only a couple of such rumors in our school, but she did not believe me."

"And you still helped her; you should have told her to get lost." Simran is angry at such baseless comments. "You should have told her that the Indian teenage girls in romantic relationships with other girls are not lesbians. Since they are not allowed to meet boys, they find this outlet relatively safe at an age when they are on emotional roller coasters." Simran continues, "And homosexuality in adolescence is considered by psychologists as a normal and passing phase."

"Wow! How do you know so much? You amaze me with words of wisdom. I remember you used to ask such deep questions about God, life, and religion that our Punjabi teacher, Mohan Singh, would look at you in astonishment. And one day he told your father that you were not an ordinary student," says Jasmine. Simran smiles a little and squeezes Jasmine's hand.

Normally, the end of August cools down when the monsoon season sets in. But this year the scorching heat is unbearable and there is no sign of rain. The ponds are completely dried up, leaving no damp ground for the cattle to lay and cool down. The farmers try to keep their farms irrigated with well water as well as the allotted water from a nearby canal. The dry ponds are a treasure for brick makers. They create deep ditches by digging in the ponds for clay and mortar. The turtles try to hide themselves in the cool clay, but the poor creatures must scurry away from the digging spades of the brick-makers.

By mid-September, the monsoon finally starts. When the sky is pitch black and the clouds are heavy with water, the tiny black rain birds start to sing and fly in all directions. One can feel the ecstasy in the air. Expectation of rain drives animals and birds into frenzy. The peacocks start to dance and the children come out into the courtyards to bathe in the rain. Women put wide buckets under the downpour to catch rainwater, and they celebrate the monsoon season by making sweets. Sometimes the dark clouds gather, raising everyone's hope for rain, but the cruel wind blows them away, allowing the scorching sun to pierce through.

At night they all sleep on the rooftop. The girls love to look at the stars and play for an hour before they go to sleep. Since it is monsoon season, a passing cloud can burst open right in the middle of the night, forcing them to jump up and run to take shelter. They can always sleep in these rooftop rooms, too, but they love to sleep out in the open air so much that they are willing to risk being disturbed in the middle of their sleep.

Early in the morning one can hear the crowing of the rooster and the musical jingles of the bells around the bulls' necks when the farmers plow their fields. The flute they play and the churning sound of butter-making are simply intoxicating. Occasionally, there is a wedding celebration going on which involves the whole village. The songs and the marriage ceremony played over the loudspeakers at night and very early in the morning soothe everyone to sleep.

The months of September and October are known for weddings, newborn babies, and a special dancing festival in which all the girls gather in a park every evening for fifteen days. The newlywed girls also visit their parents to celebrate this festival. They dance, gossip, and swing on the swings for two or three hours every evening. Jasmine, Simran, and Dilbeer also go to the park and take the baby girls too. It is so much fun that Jasmine forgets everything but the moment.

******

In Philadelphia, the month of November gets chilly in the evenings, but sunny afternoons are very pleasant. Ajit often sits on the university lawns and studies, or just sits on the bench with his face turned upward to enjoy the warmth of the sun. One student always notices him sitting there and is drawn to him for some unexplainable reason. One day she is in no rush to get to class and stops to talk to him.

"Hi, my name is Susan, may I sit down?" She points to the bench space on his right.

"Please do. My name is Ajit – I am a Ph.D. student."

"Me too," Susan says, smiling. "I am working on my dissertation in Philosophy."

"Philosophy always intrigues me…sometimes I wonder why did I major in economics," says Ajit.

"Why did you?"

"Well, philosophers usually starve and I wanted to live well, to tell you the truth."

"Yes, we Americans are more foolish in this sense – we always follow our hearts, not our brains, and then we struggle to make a living," Susan says. "Which part of India are you from?"

"I am from Punjab State, in northern India. Are you familiar with India?" asks Ajit.

"Just a little…I would like to learn more about India from you, if you don't mind. I have read E.M. Forster's *Passage to India* and I loved it. I also know an Indian classmate but she is leaving soon," Susan tells Ajit.

"And I would love to talk to you some time about philosophy, my favorite subject." Ajit shows his eagerness.

After some more conversation, Susan gets up, saying, "Ajit, it was very nice talking with you – we'll meet again. I have to go to class now."

Ajit sits on the bench for a long time, going over the encounter in his mind. A girl with beautiful blonde hair, blue eyes, slim and tall, about his age, talks to him as if she had known him for ages. He walks home; her image is walking with him and does not leave him alone even if he tries to forget.

******

Monsoon season is over and the chilly months of winter are approaching. It is already November, the most pleasant month of the winter season; the icky, sweaty days of October have passed. The babies, now toddlers, are growing very fast. They have chubby cheeks and big beautiful eyes. They have started to sit up and any funny little action makes them chuckle uncontrollably. Each of them has four teeth now. Sohil likes to poke Komil in the eye and Komil puts her finger in Sohil's mouth. Sohil bites her finger and they both start to cry. When anyone tries to make them sit away from each other, they come crawling near each other. The neighborhood girls from school always stop by to play with them. Jasmine often feels immersed in perfect bliss and believes life could not be better than this. Other times, she misses her father, or worries terribly about Ajit, so far away in another world.

The fields are brimming with soft white cotton and the women, everywhere, are busy with cotton-picking. Jasmine loves to accompany her mother whenever she goes to the fields to supervise the workers, and she usually brings along Komil and Sohil. The girls are very attentive to their surroundings. They can give a pretty good idea of what they like and what they don't. The colorful women workers pick them up, or start singing and dancing to charm them. The jingling of the oxen's bells as they move to plow the field also fascinates the girls.

As they are identical twins, the only way one can tell the difference is from their behavior and different colored hair ribbons. Komil is more aggressive, quick, and possessive than Sohil. They have different food tastes. Komil likes rice and *daal*; Sohil likes *roti* and chicken curry. They have been eating table food for quite some time.

Although the November nights get pleasantly cool, everyone (including the girls) still likes to sleep under the stars on the rooftop. There is nothing like sleeping under a cozy comforter and the cool starry night, especially early in the morning when dewdrops tickle one's face. The rooster crows at the top of his voice, and you hear the sounds of people awakening on other rooftops.

Jasmine's *bhabi* has come back from her parents with a three-month-old baby girl and her four-year-old boy, Arjun. Bibijee is happy to have two more little ones in her home. Now the house is full of babies and Arjun to entertain them. He sings and dances around them when they are awake.

Jasmine writes to Ajit that her decision to bring Komil and Sohil to India has proven very beneficial. They are growing up in such an expansive and emotionally rich environment. Since everyone talks to them, they are learning to speak Punjabi very fast. They look so adorable when they crawl and smile, Jasmine wishes for a camera to catch all their actions. But Ajit does not write her back with similar excitement. *Is Ajit worried that he is burdened with two daughters? I think he would have preferred two sons,* she worries.

"Why don't I miss Ajit?" She shares her concerns with Simran while sitting on the college lawn. "Why does my world start here and end here? Why doesn't it go beyond the four walls? Why can't I only think of my husband as I should?"

"Because, he does not seem to miss you or the girls."

"No, he always writes me that he misses us a lot. I mean whenever he writes – which is once in a blue moon."

"I wish he had opened his heart to you before you and he got married. He never gave you a chance to idealize or fantasize about him. I am sure you would have fallen in love with him, if this were a forbidden love." Simran's wisdom speaks again.

"You know when you were not here last year, it appeared as if the time stopped, but this year is flying by and soon it will be time for you to go back. That thought pierces my heart. Please this time take me with you." Simran squeezes Jasmine's hand tightly.

"I wish I could find someone who would marry you and take you to America. Why don't we look for someone?" And they both look at each other in excitement.

Coincidentally, just then one of their male classmates comes near them and hands a notebook to Jasmine, saying, "Jasmine jee, you left your notebook in class."

"Oh, thank you very much, I appreciate it," Jasmine tells him and he goes away.

"Maybe this is the boy for you, Simran. He is a singer like you, belongs to a rich family, and is tall, fair, and handsome. You know he was staring at you while giving me the notebook. Perhaps he was trying to tell you something. He looks to be the type who would love to go abroad."

"Hey, I do not want to fall in love based on conditions, my love has to be spontaneous," Simran says, and Jasmine agrees.

At home, Jasmine's *bhabi* is creating a scene almost every day.

"Ever since your *bhabi* has given birth to this baby girl, she has become vicious, irritable, and obnoxious. She used to be nice, bubbly, and humorous, I do not know what has happened to her," Bibijee expresses her concern to Jasmine.

"Bibijee, you should take her to a doctor; perhaps she suffers from postpartum depression. When I was in London, my sister-in-law told me that some women suffer from this after a baby is born and they never realize it. Here in India, it would not occur to a woman to seek help." Jasmine asks her mother if she knows of a psychiatrist.

"Oh my God! My daughter-in-law is not so crazy that she should go to a *Pagal Khana* [mental institution]; keep your western wisdom to yourself." Bibijee is outraged and goes to the kitchen shaking her head left and right.

******

One afternoon when the campus is crowded with students heading to class, throwing a football across the lawn, or just sitting down with open books, Ajit notices Susan coming toward him and he feels his heart start to beat very fast.

"Oh, Susan, where have you been all these days? I missed you," he blurts out.

"My grandpa was ill and my grandma is too old to look after him, so I stayed there for a week. Now he is okay, thank God."

It had only been a week, but for Ajit it seemed as if she had been away for months. Since they are in a hurry, they eat their lunch, and leave immediately for their classes.

"Oh, by the way, I was wondering if you like bowling," Susan asks as they walk rapidly together. "We can meet there this evening," Susan says without waiting for his answer.

"Yes, certainly, I will meet you after dinner," Ajit answers.

These days, Ajit and Susan meet frequently here and there around the university. They like to discuss various subjects, especially philosophy. The more they meet, the closer they get to each other. They both like bowling, reading, and music. Susan plays the piano and Ajit loves to sing. Although Susan does not understand his language, she likes to hear him sing.

One day she invites him to her apartment so she can play the piano and he can sing to the tune. The combination of Ajit's singing and Susan's playing music is a soul-stirring experience. They are drowned in immense delight merging into each other's souls utterly unaware, unconcerned about the classes they were missing at the time. They get up and embrace each other tightly. Time stands still and their souls mingle. Ajit plants a quick kiss on her cheek, and suddenly steps away. *Oh no, what am I doing? I am a husband and a father. I have no right to ruin so many lives.*

Susan is standing there with closed eyes and lips ready to receive his kiss. He remembers his wedding night with Jasmine. He tries to stop, but a memory flashes of how he sang a romantic song to Jasmine, hoping she would embrace him in excitement; instead, she kept her arms to herself, shy, submissive, sitting like a statue…trying to be a perfect Indian bride.

Ajit puts his hand lightly to Susan's cheek and brushes his thumb across her lips as his answer, for now, to her invitation. To his relief, she just opens her eyes and smiles.

"Oh, I forgot to tell you that my grandparents would very much like you to join us for Thanksgiving dinner next Thursday. They have a house on the beach," she tells Ajit, as he is ready to leave.

******

Jasmine's tutorial group has arranged a trip to Bhakhra Dam, about three hundred miles from her college. This time the boys and the girls are going together in a chartered bus, but of course the boys sit at the back of the bus separately from the girls. There are two professors accompanying them. A male professor supervises the boys sitting in the back. The girls, sitting in the front portion of the bus, are singing religious hymns, while the boys are making fun of them and playing charades. Professor Ramchandran tells them to stop and listen to the songs the girls are singing, but they pay no heed. After all, they have come to enjoy the trip sitting in the bus, not in the temple. For the first time, Jasmine and Simran have ventured out of their cozy environment. In the past, several such trips had been arranged, but they were not allowed to go. Since Simran's older sister is now a professor in their college and is the girls' chaperone, they can go.

The bus stops at a Punjabi *dhaba* (roadside eatery) for lunch. They all sit on cots, chairs, as well as on the ground. It feels like a picnic. One boy stands up. "Attention, attention please. Gagan wants to recite his poem, and all talented people be prepared – when your name is called, you are not allowed to refuse."

The poem Gagan recites is about a *diwana* (one who is love-stricken) who reveals how deeply he is in love with a girl and that he is unable to sleep the whole night.

"Did you notice, he was looking toward you the whole time?" Simran asks Jasmine.

"Nay, I think he was looking towards you!" They tease each other, laughing.

The boy who came to give Jasmine her notebook last week comes over. "I wish I could write such a poem for you," he tells Simran with a long gaze. Their eyes meet and Simran blushes as he returns to the other boys.

Simran squeezes Jasmine's hand and whispers nervously, "I think he loves me, he is so handsome, I could die. I like him a lot."

"I am scared for you, Simran, please don't fall in love," Jasmine murmurs.

"Why not?"

"Because I know how easily you get carried away."

In the evening, their bus arrives at the *Gurudwara Anandgarh Sahib*, a large Sikh Temple. The Sikh Temples always provide free food and shelter to anyone who comes; therefore, they all are free to eat at their kitchen any time they feel hungry and sleep in their sleeping halls. Boys and girls stay in separate buildings with their respective chaperones. Early in the morning, the most beautiful religious music begins and the girls go down to sit in the *Gurudwara* to pray. The misty hills and trees around are magical. Simran tells her that she could not sleep all night and she wishes to see that boy.

"Why don't you pay attention to these soul-soothing hymns and look at nature's beauty rather than think of that unknown person," Jasmine scolds her. "You don't even know his name."

"I do know him. His name is Tanveer Singh. Everyone calls him Veer, and he is a son of the magistrate recently transferred from Amritsar."

"He has to make his move first if he loves you. You don't give him any hint; promise me," Jasmine says.

Their trip has reached the final destination, *Bhakra Nangal Dam*, situated near the Bhakra village of Bilaspur in Northern India. It is one of the highest straight gravity dams in the world. People from far and wide come to visit this most ambitious engineering project in India. The view of the dam, as well as the green woods around, is very scenic. While returning, they make a stop for lunch on the bank of a canal. There is a beautiful park with food stalls and tables. They buy their lunch and sit down to eat. After a while, a boy gets up and asks Simran to sing. When she hesitates a little, Veer gets up, saying, "While Simran is getting ready, I will sing."

Finally, they both sing a duet from a film in which a hero and heroine express their love for each other. By the time they get back home, the rumor of their love story has spread fast.

"This trip has written your destiny, Simran," says Jasmine.

"Destiny is written at the time of one's birth and whatever is written will happen," Simran answers. "All I know is that this trip has carved Veer's initials deep on my heart and there is no turning back."

******

Thanksgiving has finally come and Ajit and Susan are at her grandparents' beach house having a turkey dinner. On their way there in the car, Ajit asked Susan about her family.

"Well, my father left home for another woman when I was six years old. My mother remarried shortly after that and I hated my stepfather. It was a very stressful situation, so my mother took me to go and live with my grandparents. They've been very good to me."

"My life story is somewhat similar to yours," Ajit confides. "My mother died when I was five and my father remarried. My stepmother mistreated my brother and me so much that my father put us into a boarding school. After high school graduation, we cut our ties from our folks for good."

Although Susan has never asked or suspected, Ajit feels compelled to tell her that he is a married man and he blurts out, "Susan, I want you to know that I am a married man. My wife and two baby daughters are in India these days."

"Ajit, are you kidding? How come you don't wear a wedding band?" Susan asks.

"What is that? Indian men don't wear them, I guess." Ajit looks at her and Susan keeps silent for the rest of the drive.

At the dinner table, there isn't much conversation because Susan's grandfather is still not out of the woods. The illness has made him very weak. Her grandmother tells Susan they can clean up the dishes the next day, as she and her husband are tired and ready to go to bed. Ajit and Susan go out to walk on the beach but soon come back when storm clouds suddenly bring a stinging wind. Susan's room is next to the guest room, which is occupied by Ajit. She can feel his presence on the other side of the wall that divides their rooms.

Ajit reads on the wall, '*Wait a minute Ajit – you are a husband and a father – what you are thinking about doing will ruin so many lives.*'

The wall on her side is free from social taboo; Susan can look through the wall and tell him that she is in love and adores him.

After tossing and turning, Ajit goes to sleep. In his dream he sees Susan coming to his room and asks her quizzically, "The wall is no more...who made the wall disappear?"

The Angel of Love appears, looks at Susan, and whispers, "You, my dear."

"Me? I did not even touch it," Susan speaks.

"Your love, the love that is unconditional, soul-stirring, and divine, can break walls, cross oceans, and climb mountains. This wall is nothing against the power of love," the angel tells her.

"But what about Ajit...he is a father and a husband?" Susan asks. "He fell in love with his wife and they married..."

"His love was conditional, my dear. His purpose was to marry a beautiful girl so that people would admire them as a handsome and lucky couple."

Hearing this, Ajit protests, "No, no, that is not true, I married her out of love."

"That was infatuation, the love of superficial beauty, and beauty does not last forever." With that, the Angel flies away. Ajit wakes up at the crossroads of confusion, dilemma, and helplessness.

******

The winter season starts with a lot of excitement due to several festivals. It begins in November with *karva chauth, Diwali, Lohri,* and *Gurupurab.* Before *Diwali,* married women keep a one-day fast to wish for the long and healthy life of their husbands, which is called *karva chauth.* Jasmine is fasting today but her husband is far away. He is supposed to break her fast by feeding her the first morsel in the evening after the moon's appearance in the sky. But she isn't sad that he is not here; she is performing this ritual only because her married friends persuaded her to.

Traditionally, the *Lohri* festival is to celebrate newlyweds and newborn baby boys (not girls). Jasmine's mother is an educated and quite progressive lady and she shuns all these orthodox beliefs. For her there is no difference between girls and boys. She distributes sweets in the whole village and invites neighbors to participate in the *Lohri* celebration for her three granddaughters in the evening. The month of January gets cold, and they encircle a heap of burning wood, dancing, and throwing sesame seeds into the fire. They say "*eesar aa, dalider jaa*" which means let happiness shower upon us, and let pain and strife go away. Bibijee prays for Jasmine's happiness every time she throws sesame seeds into the fire and Jasmine prays for her own daughters' future.

After just a few months, a pleasant spring season arrives with the deepest colors of flowering sweet peas, zinnias, moss roses, pansies, petunias, and various vines. The college is known for such beauty, as it is fortunate to have a gardener who works with passion to cultivate and grow exotic flowers. Simran and Jasmine are sitting on the lawn, preparing for their examinations. The boy who recited a poem comes by and motions for Simran to come to him. He hands a notebook to her, telling her that he is in love with Jasmine and that this book of poetry is written for her.

She returns and hands the book to Jasmine, saying, "I told him that you are a mother and a wife, and you know what he said? Ah, it was so romantic! He said that he already knows but it makes no difference; that he loves you and that is the only truth he knows…that he would live and die only for you." Jasmine starts to speak but Simran continues, "Oh Jasmine, please don't break his heart. I feel he is genuinely in love with you; he will die if you reject him."

"Simran, wake up. I am a mother, a wife, and foreign resident. Oh my God! Why did I behave like a teenager? I can never forgive myself for ruining someone's life, even if unintentionally. You return this book and tell him I am leaving for America soon."

"Let's at least read his poetry, we will return it tomorrow." Simran starts to read:

> *"Two birds sitting on the*
> *Branch of heartbeat*
> *Singing a song of love*
> *Unaware, unconcerned,*
> *That the cruel winds can*
> *Blow them away."*

"Here is another one, oh how sweet!" Simran is excited.

> *"Oh fragrant evening*
> *Put this garland on*
> *My beloved's neck and*
> *Wish her the best*
> *And kiss her on my behalf."*

"Here is another one, oh, how deep…" Simran is getting emotional.

> *"I see her face in every flower*
> *I see her face in every moon*
> *I see her face in every dream*
> *She walks with me when I walk*
> *Then why do I miss her?*
> *Is it love? I ask*
> *Yes! Yes! My heart says*
> *With a loud scream!"*

Jasmine snatches the book from Simran's hand and puts it away, scared, baffled, and shaken. That night she has no appetite and can't sleep. Her stomach feels full and she cannot digest even a sip of water. She tells her mother about the poet. Her mother takes it very lightly and says, "Just ignore him, and do not respond. He will get over it sooner or later."

The next day Simran tries to give him back the book, but he refuses, saying, "This book belongs to Jasmine – the poems are written for her. Please tell her to accept my words of love. I would be forever grateful for just that gesture."

"She will be going back to America after the finals and she wants you to forget her and move on with your life," Simran says as she tries to close the opened chapter of his love.

It is the month of May and the finals are drawing near. Classes are finished, so the students can prepare for the exams. Veer comes and hands a note to Simran, telling her that he loves her and he will miss her very much. Simran's happiness is beyond description. She breathlessly tells her friend, "Jasmine, he loves me, he loves me."

"If he loves you, tell him to send his mother to your house after the finals to make a proposal. You must stay within limits. I wish instead of Veer, you and The Poet had fallen for each other. You both are equally crazy, impulsive, and love-sick."

After a while, they notice The Poet is coming toward them. (His name is Gagan, but "The Poet" is what they like to call him.)

"This time *you* are talking to him. I am not soliciting for you any longer," Simran says, encouraging Jasmine to get up.

"Jasmine jee, I wish you the best for the finals, and I wish you a long and happy life. May God add my life's years, which are useless without your love, to your life," The Poet says, wishing her good-bye with teary eyes.

Jasmine looks at him, speechless; their eyes meet, a lonely tear trickles down his face, and a song is playing on the gramophone which translates to English, "I hope someday, you too, fall in love with someone who rejects you and stays away from you…only then will you understand the pangs of love."

# 8

# The Power of Motherhood

In mid-May, Jasmine's final exams begin. Jasmine has written several letters to Ajit, but she has not yet received a single reply. Since there is no telephone service in the village, her mother, being worried, sends a telegram to Ajit to inquire after his health. His response comes immediately; he is fine and there is no reason other than being tremendously occupied with his studies. Jasmine, feeling relieved, can now concentrate on preparing for finals. She expresses her desire to plan her journey back to America immediately upon completing her tests, but everyone wants her to stay until the girls' first birthday, July 15, and she agrees to that schedule.

Having no electricity in the village, Jasmine studies under the light of a lantern, and during the day she sits on the rooftop in the sunshade. Usually the male students go to farms and sit under the trees to study, but the female students are not allowed to roam about as the boys do.

Their neighbor's aunt has come for a visit and she is a palm-reader. One day she comes to their house, studies

Jasmine's hand and says, "I see a dark cloud ahead. Your daughters will not meet their father soon. You will need a lot of courage to overcome the hurdles in your immediate future…" She is about to tell more, but Bibijee quickly pulls Jasmine's hand away and says, "No, no, we don't believe in fortune tellers; no one can claim to know the future. Why don't you sing a song, you are such an acclaimed singer, everyone would love to hear you sing."

So she starts to sing, and Simran and Dilbeer chime in after a while. The women at the well also come to listen to them. Some of them start singing folk songs, and so the women spend the entire afternoon singing and drinking hot tea on the front verandah. That night, Jasmine, disturbed by the prediction for her future, tosses and turns. Her mother, sensing her restlessness, comes to her bed and tells her that these claims are baseless and she should put her mind at ease and go to sleep.

Finals are going very well. Jasmine and Simran are so happy that in a few days they will be free from the strenuous ordeal of day-and-night studies and examinations. One evening before her last day of exams, Jasmine receives a registered letter from Ajit. She opens it and while reading, she faints, falling against the wall and down to the floor. Bibijee quickly calls the village doctor to examine her. She takes the letter from Jasmine's hand, reads it and hides it away. The doctor gives Jasmine an injection and tells her mother, "Your daughter is under a lot of stress and this will help her relax and sleep."

"Doctor, please make her well overnight so that she doesn't miss her last exam tomorrow," Bibijee pleads. She does not reveal the contents of the letter to anyone because she, now more than ever, wants Jasmine to pass her finals to acquire a college degree. She is praying to God, hoping that when Jasmine wakes in the morning she will not remember Ajit's letter and will not miss her finals.

At dawn, Bibijee wakes Jasmine, bringing tea as she normally does. Jasmine sits up, holding her head. "Ma, my head is so heavy; why do I feel so groggy?"

"You had a nightmare, my dear child, and I gave you a sleeping pill since you were not able to rest after that. Drink this tea and take a bath and you will feel better. Today is your last day of finals, and then you'll be free to relax all you like," she says, hoping her optimism is contagious.

Jasmine remembers the letter and asks her mother about it; she starts to cry.

"You are my brave daughter and crying is not going to help you," Bibijee says. "Right now the most important thing in your life is to get your degree. This is your one last trial and I want you to concentrate and pass the exam. Be strong and think only of this! We will take care of the letter when you come back from the college."

Jasmine looks over at her sleeping daughters and says, "Yes ma, I must pass my finals," and she goes to her college with Simran.

On their way back, she tells Simran about Ajit's letter. She cannot stop her tears as she shares the news that her husband has asked for a divorce.

"No, it must be a joke," Simran responds. "I can't believe it. Let's go home and read the letter again."

They read the letter carefully, but it does not say much except that there is an enclosed divorce form for her signature. Ajit wrote that he is madly in love with an American girl,

Susan, and wants to marry her. He begged Jasmine "to understand his condition and forgive him." There is no mention of their daughters.

"Oh my God, I think he has lost his mind! No sane person behaves like this," Simran says, holding her forehead.

"It is all my fault. I left him alone for so long. He was begging me to come back from England because he was feeling terribly lonely. Oh, Simran, I feel so guilty," Jasmine starts to sob.

"There is always a bright side to things," Simran innocently tries to cheer her up. "You can free Ajit and marry The Poet, and you will save two burning hearts by doing so."

"I do not love The Poet, I think he is a lunatic! He is not even good-looking."

"Well, Ajit is very handsome but I have never heard you say that you love him."

"Simran, he is my husband. He is the father of my girls! That is the only truth I know – my daughters need their father."

"And what about you? Don't you need someone who loves you?" Simran asks.

"What if someone who loves me does not love my daughters? Besides, I do not know what love is. I feel some people are not fortunate enough to fall in love or to be loved."

Bibijee and Amar walk in and her brother reads the letter to make sure this news is true.

"I think he has gone insane and I am going there to beat the insanity out of him!" Amar says. "Son of an owl— bastard!" He is spitting out his angry words, his rage filling the air like a dark cloud heavy with water.

"I blame Bapujee," he says. "He did not check Ajit's family background before arranging the marriage. He did not follow any rules of arranged marriage. The first thing to check is if there is any history of mental illness in their family tree. And how was this dog brought up? How come he had no relative except one brother? Bapujee just fell in love with his credentials." And Amar goes upstairs spouting anger.

"Oh, ma, it is all my fault! I should have listened to Ajit when he was begging for me to come," Jasmine sobs.

"Don't be hard on yourself, my dear child, it is not your fault," Bibijee says calmly, though she is a bit shaken by Amar's violent outburst. "These men belong to a different planet; they behave like roosters and do not think with their brains when it comes to their libido. I want you to be a brave woman and rather than crying, which is not going to help you, go there and teach him a lesson. Throw that *kanjari* [whore] out of your house."

"Oh, ma, I am no one to manage that," Jasmine says.

"Let me tell you my personal story, which I have kept to myself all these years. I tell you now because you may draw some courage from it," Bibijee goes on. "When I was expecting you and wanted to go to my parents' home for delivery, your grandmother did not permit me to do so. Anyway, after you were born, I was not allowed to climb the stairs to sleep in our bedroom for many weeks of recovery, but your father still slept upstairs. I started noticing something fishy going on."

"Oh, please, ma, I don't wish to hear anything against Bapujee." Jasmine covers her ears.

"No, it is not against your father, dear…it is the story of every woman on this planet and I only want to make you aware that you are not alone. The men have always inflicted this injustice onto their women; history reveals how men kept concubines, harems, and mistresses without feeling any guilt because women were weak. They were not educated and were totally dependent on men. Unless women educate themselves, and start working side by side with men, most men will take advantage of their vulnerability."

"Anyway, let me continue my saga. Your father's behavior around me was unusual, and he did not show much emotion toward me. His changed attitude concerned me. I started to pay attention to his nights by staying awake. Each night I could hear footsteps on the rooftop. One night, I slowly made my way upstairs and saw a woman sleeping beside him. I quietly picked up her clothes, threw them in the tandoor still red with hot ashes, and covered it with a lid. Early in the morning before dawn, I hid behind a chair outside his door and as soon as she came out wrapped up in a bed sheet, I grabbed her by her braid and gave a big jerky pull. She started to beg me to keep this as a secret. I recognized her, and promised her that I would never reveal her name if she would stop seeing him. She never came back, and your father was so ashamed of himself that until his death he stayed a faithful and loving husband to me."

The whole story embarrassed Jasmine, but she couldn't help finding humor at the way her mother had thrown the woman's clothes into the tandoor oven, and had covered it so that the smoke would not wake anyone in the house or the neighbors.

The next morning, Amar is ready to go to New Delhi to get himself a visa and passport. He plans to go to Philadelphia and confront Ajit. Jasmine tells him that to obtain a visa he needs an affidavit of support from someone living in America.

"Moreover, if Ajit has any spark of decency left in him, only the innocent faces of his daughters will ignite it; therefore, I should take the girls and go there myself. I can get my affidavit of support from Mrs. Khan," Jasmine says with determination.

She immediately writes a letter to Mrs. Khan, explaining the whole situation, and asks for an affidavit of support so she can get a visitor's visa. Her student visa had expired. Bibijee starts praying hard every day to grant some wisdom to senseless Ajit.

Just to take Jasmine's mind away from the turbulence, Simran suggests that they go to a movie. In the theater, they see Veer sitting in the front row. Simran's heart starts to beat fast; excitedly, she squeezes Jasmine's hand so hard that she lets out a little cry. The noise makes Veer look back. He smiles and exchanges a glance with Simran. At the intermission, he comes out to the lobby. Since Simran wants to talk to him, she walks out also. Jasmine follows her because she does not wish Simran to be seen alone with Veer. If Jasmine is with her and talking to him in a group, people will not look at them with suspicion. When Simran talks to him briefly, he tells her he wants to see her once more before he leaves for the Simla hills to escape the hot summer of Punjab.

"Simran, please do not meet him alone. I will accompany you, otherwise people will spread rumors," Jasmine expresses her concern.

"It is no longer a rumor – it is a fact that we love each other and we are not afraid what anybody says. *Jab pyar kia to darna kia'* [why be afraid of people, when in love], but I promise you I will never allow him to touch me before marriage," Simran assures her.

Back at home, Jasmine sees Sohil and Komil outside chasing after the baby chicks; the eggs hatched only about two weeks ago and the hen is still very protective of them. Their cousin, Arjun, is teasing the hen by picking up a chick and she pecks at him. The girls laugh and clap along with him. Copying everything their older cousin does, they are learning the Punjabi language quickly. Jasmine's heart aches and her stomach churns when she thinks about taking them away to a strange and lonesome place. Here, they are as free as birds in the expansive courtyard and have affectionate people around them all the time.

"It is good you are taking them to America; their upbringing will be in the land of freedom and opportunity." Bibijee tries to cheer her up whenever she notices Jasmine's sad face. "Make sure they study hard and become doctors or lawyers. At the same time, teach them our culture and values so that they can take advantage of the best of both worlds."

Mrs. Khan promptly sent an affidavit of support along with a long and a sympathetic letter. She writes that she and her husband both are shocked to hear of Ajit's intentions and hope he comes to his senses soon. Jasmine wants to go to America as soon as possible. Her brother goes to New Delhi to get her a visitor's visa, an updated passport that includes her daughters' photographs, and the tickets for them. Getting everything done takes him almost three weeks. After the girls and Jasmine receive the required vaccinations, they are ready to plunge into the unknown.

Before leaving for America, Jasmine wants to visit her college again. She wants to stroll the garden, sit on the lawn once more, take a last look at the colorful flowers, and she wants to tell The Poet to forget her.

Simran and Jasmine walk half-way to the college and ride a rickshaw the other half. When they reach the campus, Simran sees Veer sitting under a tree. She abandons Jasmine standing there and runs to him like a crazy person. Jasmine leaves them alone and goes a little farther to sit on a bench to wait for her. After a while, The Poet comes and she gets up.

"Jasmine jee, I want to give you this gift, please do not reject it." He hands her a book of his poetry.

"I came here today to tell you that I am leaving for America soon. I do not want to go there unless I put closure to this. Please do not waste your life on me. Life is God's gift and it is one's duty to respect and live it to the fullest. Please get married and lead a normal life. You must forget about me," she says, taking the book from him.

"I have heard that your husband wants a divorce. If that is true, please count on me, I am willing to marry you."

"How did you hear about this?"

"Well, they say walls have ears too," says The Poet.

"What you have heard is not true," Jasmine lies.

"I am glad to hear that, and may God bless you with a long, happy life together. I will always love you." He leaves quickly, hiding his tears.

Simran comes and Jasmine starts to sob on Simran's shoulder. She feels sorry for The Poet, feels guilty for her husband, feels helpless, and utterly confused. She wants to cry so hard that her river of tears will wash away all the pain from her. Her anguish pierces Simran's heart, but there is nothing she can do to make her friend's pain go away.

"What did The Poet say?"

"He heard about my divorce…I do not know how it got out. He said that he would always love me and would be available to marry me."

"I wish you could leave that good-for-nothing Ajit and marry The Poet to simplify your life. Your visit to America is complex and full of uncertainty," says Simran.

"First of all, why are you so sure that The Poet will marry me the minute I tell him I am free? I do not know anything about his parents; they could vehemently oppose this marriage. Secondly, how can we know that he will not become another Ajit after marriage? They say love is blind and marriage is an eye-opener. Moreover, love based upon surface beauty is just as fragile as glass; it can break with a tiny tap. Such love lives forever in novels and movies, but in marriage, the intensity dissipates in due time. One needs compatibility and adjustability to nurture the relationship."

"Oh, Jasmine, my dear, dear Jasmine, at what crossroads God has brought you to stand. Both paths lead nowhere. I wish God had given me all the pain instead of you. I can't bear seeing you in this grief-stricken condition," Simran says, and hugs her.

After a while, they come home and Simran starts to play with the girls. No matter how much Jasmine tries to be brave and follow her mother's advice, inside she is shattered like glass. She has lost her appetite and her enthusiasm to be here in her enchanted childhood world. The only thing that keeps her going is her ambition and love for her two precious daughters. She will go through any hardship and strife to give them the best in life they deserve.

Jasmine is supposed to play a part in a skit on campus the next week. She does not wish to go back to the college and wants to withdraw her name, but her mother prompts her to stay engaged. "My child, do not disconnect yourself from life. God has given you so much beauty and a compassionate heart, our duty is to respect and love God for giving us such a wonderful gift."

Simran chimes in, saying, "Giving up on life is not the answer to one's problems. The path of life is always full of stones and splinters; only a brave and determined person can navigate it successfully. One can not pick a flower without getting pricked by a thorn." Simran continues to persuade her to participate in the skit and Jasmine agrees, half-heartedly.

"Okay, but I want to practice my part at home. I do not want to face him again," Jasmine insists.

"You mean The Poet? He has already gone home. I heard he withdrew his name from the list of participants," Simran tells her.

Just then Dilbeer walks in and says, "No, that is not true. He asked me about the rumor. He had heard about your divorce and I told him the truth, so now he wants to meet Bibijee to ask for your hand."

"Is that so?" Simran is excited.

"But I told him not to come because I was afraid Amar would beat him to death. And you know what he said? He would rather give his life for his love than be afraid and not help her in her time of need," reports Dilbeer.

"Oh no, please Simran, go to him and tell him that I do not love him, and that I am definitely going to America. He should not come to our house." Jasmine is adamant.

"I can go and tell him not to come, but I don't want to break his heart by saying you don't love him. That would completely shatter him. You will live in his memory forever if he thinks you love him too. I think it is better to let him keep this delusion," Simran says.

"Let's ask Bibijee what to do," Dilbeer suggests.

Bibijee decides to meet The Poet at the college rather than have him come to the house. She tells him that the first step for Jasmine is to try to make up with her husband, and if that fails, she will come back and marry him. Without consulting Jasmine, she has brought the situation under control.

Jasmine has lost her peace of mind. Her thoughts wander back to her wedding day and it all feels as if she has passed through a dream, a dream having no connection to her innocent life. Now, her daughters have become a source of energy and give purpose to her life; she will not fail them at any cost. At night, under the starlit sky, she counts the stars until one breaks away and gradually disappears. She makes a wish and starts counting again until another one catches her eye as it streaks across the heavens. She pushes away memories of Ajit on their honeymoon; strolling on the bank of a river, visiting the museums and gardens, or watching movies together. It pains her terribly to think that she had felt so little connection to Ajit, and now feels responsible for ruining their marriage.

Jasmine holds her head which aches with painful memories. Her mother, lying next to her, senses Jasmine's turmoil and prays out loud as she rubs pain-balm on her daughter's temples.

"Ma, why do you keep on praying? God has nothing to do with it. It is my fault! I was so dumb...I could not understand Ajit's love for me, and left him alone for too long," Jasmine cries.

"Enough of this nonsense, I do not want to hear about your guilt anymore. Everyone is responsible for one's own deeds. He never allowed you to love him back. Now be brave and stop weeping on others' shoulders. This world laughs with happy-go-lucky people, but no one cares for crying people. If this is the way you want to live your life, one day you will find yourself utterly alone." Bibijee scolds her to bring her out of her misery.

The next afternoon, Dilbeer and Simran walk in, laughing and talking. They have come back after meeting with their cultural program director.

"I have a brilliant idea for our skit. Mrs. Gupta, the director, liked it very much. She told us that the competition is based on originality, creativity, and costumes. The skit time must be between five and ten minutes." Simran is thrilled.

"Moreover, *didi,* you won't have to practice any dialogue," Dilbeer jumps in.

"Well, tell me about the skit, don't keep on babbling your mouths off." Jasmine tries to show a bit of excitement.

"The theme is love's bittersweet pain. The story is about a lovesick bird, named Thornbird. Far away in a mountain valley, there is a blue lagoon, and on one side there is a small tree full of beautiful flowers. One flower is absolutely gorgeous. Thornbird is struck by its delicate beauty, falls in love, and tries to kiss the flower. As soon as he bends to kiss it, a sharp thorn hidden behind it pricks his cheek where it catches hold. The blood trickles down and mingles with the tears rolling down his face. He coos in spite of the pain and the valley resounds with the melody. People are entranced by the emotion of the music and come from far and wide to experience it. They take pity on the bird and wonder why he does not try to free himself from the thorn. But these innocent people do not know that Thornbird wants to live in this pain, and wants to die in this pain. They do not know that although he is in excruciating pain, he is in perfect bliss, in a union of body, mind, and soul."

"Wow, Simran, what a philosophical romance! It is very original and creative, but how are we going to make costumes for these characters?" Jasmine asks.

"As a matter of fact, that is the easiest part. You are the tree, and your legs will be wrapped with brown cloth, and we'll cover your head and face with green cloth. On top will be a large, beautiful flower made of colorful tissue paper, surrounded by tiny flowers. And you will be standing on the edge of a blue cloth with painted white water waves. For me to dress up as a bird is easy, too," Simran tells her.

"The difficult parts are to create an echo of the bird's cooing with pain, and to find some girls to play the people gathering around. Actually, they will be the ones who will need to practice a little dialogue," Dilbeer adds.

"We have only seven days to do all this," Simran says, taking the lead.

"We could get Bibijee and *Masijee* [Simran's mother] to help us," Dilbeer offers.

While Dilbeer and Simran are conversing with so much excitement, Jasmine does not wish to dampen their enthusiasm. She pretends to be with them too, but her mind is far away, thinking about her uncertain future. *Am I really up to the task of fighting with Ajit for the girls' sake? What if he closes the door in my face and we end up on the streets, begging for food and shelter? How dare you become so pathetically weak?* Quietly, she scolds herself.

Bibijee is a genius at reading her mind and tells her to stop worrying and to be brave. Her one straight look into Jasmine's eyes tells her the condition of her daughter's mind. Bibijee is such a positive and tenacious woman that she will not rest until she instills confidence and courage into Jasmine's sinking spirit. She draws her out with stories of great women of history. "Have you read about Jhansi Ki Rani, how bravely she fought with the enemy when she was left with no choice? She had to fight to save her people from being killed." Or she says, "It all boils down to sacrifice. Women know how to sacrifice their own happiness for the sake of others – think of Maharani Jinda, Mata Gujri, Florence Nightingale, just to name a few out of many."

Bibijee appears strong and determined on the surface, but inside she is as worried as Jasmine. Sending her daughter to a faraway land without a predictable outcome is scary and almost irresponsible. At times, she wakes up sweating over this feeling and starts praying to God to show her the right path to guide her daughter. *What if Ajit is so determined that even seeing his daughters' innocent faces doesn't melt his heart? Where would they go for help? Mrs. Khan would be the only ray of hope within this realm of the unknown. She would definitely help my daughter, God bless her.* And this is how she soothes herself every day and every night.

"Bibijee, can you come with us to Simran's house?" Dilbeer asks. "We want you to help us make our skit a success. We want to defeat the other team, the team of those arrogant boys."

"Where are the children? I have not seen them for quite some time," Bibijee wonders aloud.

"They are in the barn, playing with our newborn calf. They love to go there, it is like visiting a zoo," Dilbeer answers.

Jasmine jumps up, saying, "Oh no, they shouldn't be playing in that place, full of germs, full of mice…what if they get sick?"

"*Didi,* they have been going there quite often for several months. They love to watch and feed the animals. Don't worry, they are immune to the place," Dilbeer says.

In the barn are two buffaloes, two cows, one horse, two bulls, and some calves. In one corner, there is a room filled with crunched-up wheat residue to feed the animals. In another corner, there is a heap of dry cotton plant sticks to be used to make a cooking fire. A large, multi-colored lizard lives in the cotton sticks. The children get very excited when they see this creature. The barn also houses a tractor, a bull cart, and mounds of organic mulch and dried cow dung.

Beside the barn, children gather to play under the shade of a berry tree. Since they have grown out of their wooden cradles, the carpenter has turned them into regular swings, which the kids love to use.

The girls are thriving in this open environment, and every time Bibijee thinks about their leaving soon for America, her heart sinks and a surge of pain shoots through her chest, even though she knows it will be best for them.

"Ah, they have come back." Bibijee sees the children come towards her.

"*Daadi, daadi* [paternal grandmother]," they cry, racing to her.

Komil and Sohil mimic the four-year old Arjun. Bibijee corrects the girls, "Say *naani* – I am your *naani* [maternal grandmother]. I am Arjun's *daadi* and your *naani*."

Komil and Sohil hug their *naani* and chant together, saying *naani, naani, naani.*

"You love them more than me!" Arjun blurts out. "Why don't they go to their *daadi*?" Arjun, feeling jealous, starts crying.

"Their *daadi* lives in the stars; she can't come down," Bibijee hugs and kisses him.

"Their Papa lives in the stars too, and now we all have only one papa," says Arjun innocently.

"No, their Papa lives far away in America and they will be going to see him soon," Bibijee tells him.

"No, I don't want them to go! I don't want them to go – if they go, I go too," he says.

"Ma, why did you tell him? Now he is so upset." Jasmine makes a face.

"We better start preparing him as well as the girls, for the day is coming soon they will be separated."

"They are too young to understand all this," says Dilbeer.

"No, they are not. They understand much more than any other children their age."

"No, Ma they don't," Jasmine insists.

"You want to bet – let me show you," Bibijee challenges.

"Sohil, Komil, soon you will be taking a plane ride to go to meet your Papa."

"No, no, my Papa here, no Papa there," they move their heads left and right. They speak Punjabi, the only language they know.

"But 'Papa' here is Arjun's Papa, not yours. Your Papa lives far away. He is missing you and he wants you to come."

"No, no, *uthe nahin jaana* [I don't go there]." They both start crying.

"Ma, see what you have done, you have made all of them cry." Jasmine looks at her mother.

"But they need to…" Bibijee persists.

"No Ma, no, they will end up crying more. I will tell them when they are sitting on the plane, not before," Jasmine says with conviction.

"Okay, okay, let's go to Simran's house soon…you always contradict me." Bibijee is a bit annoyed.

As soon as they reach Simran's house, her mother greets them and tells the servant to get samosas and gulab-jamans from the snack shop to serve with tea to everyone. As per Indian hospitality, if a guest drops in near dinner, lunch, or teatime, he/she is always served accordingly, without inquiring.

Simran describes the details of her idea and the script for the skit. Her mother, being very creative, makes a suggestion. "It will be good to show the gathered people in outfits representing different states. That will enhance your costume competition."

Everyone is assigned a task or two to have ready by Friday. Jasmine has to practice standing up with her hands folded above her head, holding a green cotton cloth studded with paper flowers. She will make all these flowers and attach them to the cloth with one flower bigger and more beautiful. Simran's role is to dress like a bird. A hidden tape recorder will play musical lyrics similar to the bird's cooing. Dilbeer has to enlist six girls to represent the people from different areas to hear the enchanting song. Both mothers will help put together costumes for these girls.

Jasmine is not enthused about the cultural program or the skit; however, she keeps her chin up just to please everyone. With the date of her journey approaching, she is getting nervous. *What if Ajit is not moved when he sees his daughters? What if he is angry at our surprise visit and makes the girls feel unwanted and unloved? What if he does not reconcile at all? Where could we go?* All these thoughts cross her mind day and night but she tries to ignore them. For the sake of her daughters' future, she is willing to take this risky path.

"You have no idea how lucky you and your daughters are. People envy you! They wish they could find a way to go to England or America. Ajit will be fine once he sees Sohil and Komil, I am pretty sure about that." Her mother continues to strengthen her wavering determination.

Poor Jasmine, she came to India with a heavy, grief-stricken heart, and now she is going back to America with looming uncertainty and despair.

"Find a match for Simran in America," Simran's mother suggests.

"Yes, I will keep my eyes open, but maybe you can find someone here who is willing to go to America for higher studies." Jasmine looks at Simran, with Veer in mind.

"I want to study further for my masters before I think of getting married," Simran objects.

"Your father is determined to get you married soon. He would never agree to send you away to a university, so give your studies a rest until you get married," says her mother.

"Why? Ma, why are there different standards for daughters? The sons are sent far away to schools to become anything they wish. This is not fair!" Simran is angry.

"This is the unkind truth of our society, my child, but there is improvement in every generation. Yours is much better than mine, and surely the day is not far off when girls and boys will be considered equal."

"Tell her I got married when I was only ten," Jasmine's grandmother says, and starts to talk about her own generation. "In those days many girls were killed before they even opened their eyes. You want to know why? Because the rich men, the kings, and the landlords would take any one's daughter by force. The poor fathers were utterly helpless to fight against these powerful, evil men."

"That was the reason the veil came into existence," Bibijee adds. "It became necessary to cover up the girls, especially the beautiful ones, to hide and save them from those nasty, evil eyes."

The day of their cultural program has arrived and they are ready. The evening starts with excited expectations and thrill. As the sun goes down, the crescent moon, along with the evening star, appear in the sky. Simran looks at the evening star and makes a wish for her team's success on the stage. She is determined to win this competition. The skit goes well and their resounding success wins them the trophy. They are thrilled and relieved after many days of hard work.

The girls' birthday party is scheduled in early June, a little early since they will be leaving soon. All their relatives have come to celebrate as well as to say good-bye to them. Jasmine and the girls' departure for America is just a few days away. All day long the visitors come, hug Jasmine, kiss the girls, and express their sadness over their going so far away to a foreign land.

Finally, the journey must begin and Jasmine and the girls get into a taxi and wave good-bye through dusty windows. Jasmine sweeps her tears back to show her mother her courage, but Bibijee is aware that the swept-back tears are flowing into her heart.

# 9

# The Journey

Through the village, as the taxi drives over the dirt road, children run behind all the way to its outskirts. At every alley and every corner, women carrying water vessels on their heads stand still to watch the procession and wave good-bye to their village daughter and offspring who are going abroad. Jasmine waves her hand, holding back her tears, not knowing when she will be able to return. Simran and Dilbeer, along with Amar, are accompanying her to the airport. Little Arjun's relentless screams compelled them to bring him along, too. The girls are happy to be with them in the taxi. It is a five-hour ride to the Indira Gandhi International Airport in New Delhi. Jasmine has forgotten how hot the summer can feel and squints her eyes from the dusty, hot, June air blowing into her face as the car speeds up.

"Oh, no, I forgot to bring their carriage. How am I going to carry the two girls in the airport?" Jasmine is concerned.

"That little rickety carriage you brought from London? I remembered to bring it, although I am pretty sure the girls won't sit still in it," says Dilbeer.

"Oh, thank you…you're probably right, but they have no other option. I feel so sorry for them; all of a sudden they will have to behave like grown-ups."

"Ah, look at them…they are sleeping like little angels, so unaware that all of us will be leaving them soon," laments Simran.

"Oh, Simran, please hush! I can bear this thought no more. My heart is drowning in a deep ocean and it is becoming hard to breathe," Jasmine says and they both start crying.

Her brother tries to console them, saying, "These little girls are very lucky to get to see the western world at such a young age. Look at the positive side and be happy."

"But I see only dark clouds in our future." Jasmine wipes her tears.

"Don't be so pessimistic; every dark cloud has a silver lining," says Amar. "They will be growing up in a rich country with all the modern facilities. Here they might be happy in their innocent childhood, but what would they gain growing up in such a poor country? If and when I have a chance to leave India, I will do so in a minute. Nothing gets done here without bribing someone, even at the lower level. Just to get your passport and visa done on time I had to grease their palms, starting from the doorman all the way up. I hear so many good things about western countries." Her brother tries to cheer her up.

"*Veerjee* [brother], no doubt you are right, but how can you not love your birthplace? Your country is like your mother, whether it is poor or rich, you must love it and show the utmost respect," Simran says.

"Of course, I love my country as I love my mother but that does not mean I cannot see its shortcomings."

Suddenly, a truck comes toward them at full speed. It would certainly have crushed their car, had the driver not quickly swung to the far right, almost entering a field. They all thank God for saving their lives and are especially grateful for the driver's expert maneuvering. They even make a stop to pray at the next temple they see.

"The road system is terrible here," their taxi driver says.

"The problem is that there is no road system, no highways, no traffic rules, and this is only a narrow single lane," Amar says. "Everyone survives only due to one's good deeds in a past life, I think. We don't know when this country will wake up to make progress, especially, much-needed roads. These are the reasons people try to get out of here." Jasmine's brother vents his frustration.

"My friend just came back from Malaysia," the driver tells Amar. "He told me how impressive their roads and bridges are. The automatic traffic control system is fantastic." The driver's talk only makes Amar more disenchanted with India.

The sudden stop of the car jolted everyone and the children woke up from their deep sleep. All of them are hungry and decide to eat at a small roadside restaurant.

"*Didi*, eat as much as you can – you will not have our wonderful Punjabi food in America," Dilbeer sighs.

"I worry about the girls, that they won't eat anything other than their favorite Indian dishes. I think I should at least pack a few chapattis for them. Other dishes would go bad."

"You know Bibijee has packed rice, spices, pulses, pickles, and a little bit of yogurt as a starter," says Dilbeer.

"Yogurt will definitely go bad due to the heat. When Mrs. Khan packed some yogurt, it was during the winter season. It soured but stayed good enough to start the yogurt-making," says Jasmine, and takes the yogurt out of her luggage.

For the rest of the journey, the children are restless from being cooped up in the hot car. After reaching the airport, they all get permission to go inside. Their luggage is checked in without any problem. Sohil and Komil are hugged and kissed by everybody before they are made to sit in the stroller. Arjun starts to cry and the girls can't understand why. Jasmine hugs everyone with a smile, pretending to be strong and brave, as she does not want them to be worried about her. Pushing the girls' stroller in front of her, she enters the security gate. The nearby passengers look at the identical twin girls admiringly and some try to make them laugh and talk. Sohil sits quietly, but Komil responds laughingly. Jasmine sighs with relief that they are not crying or trying to climb out of the stroller.

Jasmine gets the front seat with two small baby-sleepers, a fantastic arrangement made available by British Airways. The girls, after the long, uncomfortable journey from Punjab to Delhi, slumber deeply in the air-conditioned plane all the way to London. Jasmine, although tormented and worried, tries to find solace in seeing her daughters' faces, so peaceful and divine. She thanks God for giving her this greatest gift, which has become a reason for her to live and fight for their rights and well being. They give her enormous courage to confront Ajit. Without them, quite possibly she would have signed the divorce papers.

There is a change of planes at Heathrow Airport and a four-hour layover. She manages to disembark with the help of a flight attendant who gets the twins into the stroller while they are still sound asleep. Sohil wakes up and starts to cry. The girls did not eat for the past six hours and now they are starving for the food they always eat in the mornings, *roti* with yogurt. Jasmine opens a wrapped-up pack and tries to feed them roti with the butter she brought in her bag. Now the girls sense their strange surroundings. Seeing no familiar faces in the airport, Komil starts to cry and says, "*Naani house Jana, Arjun naal khelna.*" They both refuse to eat the cold roti without yogurt. Jasmine controls her tears and tries to cheer them up by drawing their attention to a large fountain.

An Indian lady, working as a sweeper in the airport, notices them and asks Jasmine, "Why are they crying? I know why, they are missing their grandparents back home," she answers herself.

"Yes, and they want *roti* with yogurt and I do not have yogurt," says Jasmine. "I should not have left it behind."

"Oh, I have yogurt. I always bring it with my lunch. I'll give it to you." And she opens her lunch bag, taking out everything to share.

They all sit together on corner chairs, and the woman begins to feed the girls with rice, daal, and yogurt. Jasmine saves a few spoons of yogurt in a butter container to bring with her. After a while they start to smile and call her *naani*.

Jasmine hugs the lady and says, "Aunty, you are so nice, I will never forget you and your kindness."

At six in the evening, they are ready to board the plane for Philadelphia International Airport. After six hours, the plane will land in the world of uncertainty. Jasmine does not wish to think about it, for now she just wants to sleep in peace, which she may not have again. The girls are wide-awake, well fed, and it is their playtime. They are unaware that it is a plane with restrictions; all they know is to run around freely. Jasmine tries to hold them back in the seats in vain. She looks around and sees all the passengers who seem to be from many different countries. No one appears to be bothered by the noisy, wiggling girls. Eventually, the twins go to sleep.

As the airplane approaches its destination, Jasmine's nervousness grows very intense. *What if Ajit has gone away? Where would we stay? What if Ajit opens the door, but refuses to accept us? No, he would not dare to do that; his daughters would not allow him to be so cruel. I must plan wisely, just in case he is not home.* She thinks of the landlady, Mrs. Stevenson, but her apartment is so depressing and dark, with no windows. The girls would feel scared and suffocated. She remembers an acquaintance, Marianne, a very fine lady, who had invited them to her house for dinner, but she does not know her last name or address. The only people she can count on are Dr. and Mrs. Khan. But how would she get to California to stay with them? *Oh, God, please help me.*

Jasmine starts to pray hard. She keeps on repeating the mantra from a *gutka* (small prayer book) given to her by her mother at the time of her departure. Jasmine remembers when Bibijee had said, "My child, do not be discouraged.

Remember, God helps those who help themselves. Chant this prayer and God will show you the right path."

At five in the morning, their plane lands. By the time she clears customs and claims their luggage, it is half past six. The girls are sleeping in their stroller and she is sitting on a chair to wait for the dawn. Somehow, perhaps from being extremely tired, she also dozes off into deep sleep and does not wake until almost nine. She quickly gets up to find out how to get a taxi.

Whatever little English she had practiced speaking when she was in America, she has somewhat forgotten. She approaches a porter, saying, "Sir, I want car."

He brings his cart, loads the luggage, and starts walking towards the door. Jasmine nervously runs after him, pushing the stroller. "No, no, sir! Taxi...stop, stop...a taxi car!"

The porter takes her near the taxi stand, gives her a smile, and puts his hand out for his tip. She gives him one dollar as she watches the taxi driver put her bags in his trunk without being asked. She gets into the taxi with Sohil and Komil, handing a written address to the driver, saying, "I want to go here."

After about twenty minutes, the taxi stops at the given address. He puts the luggage out on the entry steps of the building and Jasmine tells him to take the luggage inside.

"Oh, no, lady," he says, shaking his head. "I can't leave my car unattended." And he takes off after getting paid.

Jasmine has no option but to leave the luggage out on the steps. She looks around to ask for help, but realizes this is not India where so many would have gathered around to assist her. She manages to bring the girls' stroller inside the corridor and rings Mrs. Stevenson's doorbell, hoping to leave them under her watch while she brings in the luggage.

After a while, a man opens Mrs. Stevenson's door.

"Mrs. Stevenson home?" Jasmine asks.

"Oh, my mother…she is in heaven."

Jasmine feels as if a bucket of cold water had been poured on her head. She puts her hand on her mouth to stop a cry, and looks at him with teary eyes. She is unable to speak. *Hi rubba (oh God) – what an inauspicious beginning*, she thinks. The girls start to cry as soon as they see their mother's tears. Jasmine gives them a fake smile to quiet them and tells Mr. Stevenson, "I want help." Her body is shaking and her voice trembles as she says, "You see them, so I go out for my bags."

While he is standing in the open door trying to figure out what she had said, Jasmine goes out to fetch the luggage, leaving the girls at his side. Then, leaving the luggage in the hallway, she carries the girls, one on each arm, up the stairs to the familiar second floor apartment, as she and Ajit had done so many times. She repeatedly knocks on the door, but no one answers. Jasmine does not know what else to do, so she waits and knocks again. A woman opens the door. They stare at each other and Jasmine asks, "You are —-?" Jasmine doesn't know her name.

"I'm Susan and you must be Jasmine," the woman says, glancing down at the girls. "And they are the most beautiful girls I have ever seen." Susan admires the girls with a smile.

"You live in here, with my husband?" Jasmine asks her.

"No, I don't live here, though I come here quite often. Please come in, I was just about to leave," Susan lies.

The girls cling to their mother even when she sits on the sofa; they feel shy and somewhat scared. Whenever she tries to leave them in order to bring her luggage upstairs, they start to cry.

After a long silence, Susan goes into the kitchen and brings back some cookies and milk for them. They take a bite and start to smile.

*She sleeps in the same bed?* Jasmine is suspicious, noticing the double bed where she and Ajit always slept. She squints her forehead with anger and rebukes Susan as a *besharum kanjari* (shameless whore) silently in her mind.

"You marry my husband?" Jasmine asks, holding her throbbing head between her hands. She remembers her mother's tale and feels like grabbing Susan by her hair and giving it an angry jerk.

"Oh, no, I will never marry your husband. I love him and I will love him until my last breath, but I will not marry him," Susan tells her with peculiar sadness in her eyes.

Jasmine feels a little relief and tells her, "He send me divorce form for me to sign."

"He did not mention that to me. Had I known, I would have told him not to divorce you. I am glad that you have come."

"Why, you are happy? Me here make you sad that I take him away from you?"

Jasmine asks her innocently.

"No, I am going away from here...far away." Susan tries to control the tears welling in her eyes.

Jasmine feels sad to see Susan's face and says, "These girls bring me here. They need him, but I do not want separate you from him."

"God is separating us, not you," Susan smiles a little, camouflaging her grief.

"Why God separate you…God always like true love like you have." Perhaps Jasmine does not understand Susan's meaning.

"I have breast cancer. The doctor has given me only a few more months to live." Susan gets up from the chair with a tortured breath.

Forgetting that Susan is her rival, Jasmine grabs her and starts to cry, "*Hi rubba*! How can God be so cruel? You so young and pretty, I ask God why?"

"You can be happy that I am getting out of your way. Please do not shed crocodile tears," Susan says, unaware of the fact that Jasmine is a simple, compassionate, and sincere girl.

"Poor Ajit. What does he say?" asks Jasmine.

"He doesn't know, and I don't want him to know until after he submits his dissertation. Actually, I never want him to know about my illness. My plan is to break up with him and move out of town. I'll stay with my friend until—until it's over. My grandpa passed away, and my grandma has dementia and has moved to a nursing home. I have no other family."

"You tell the truth to Ajit," pleads Jasmine. "You want me to live with this secret all my life? Not possible for me to carry the guilt. Plus, you break his heart…you must tell him!"

"You don't know how he is these days. He will shatter like glass, and I am afraid he could have a nervous breakdown," Susan says.

"Breaking up with Ajit is *zulam, paap* [torturous, a sin]. I think you stay with him until your last breath," Jasmine says, frustrated that she does not have the English words at hand to say everything she wishes.

"Our immediate problem is to keep you and the girls away from him for a couple of months—I mean until the day his thesis is submitted," Susan says. "Surely you agree it is important he stays focused on that."

"Where we to go? I know no one here."

"Before Ajit comes back, I will take you to my apartment. He must not know about your arrival for a while—if you want him to obtain his degree."

By this time the girls have fallen asleep and Jasmine agrees with Susan. She loads the luggage in Susan's car and quickly gets them out of Ajit's apartment. Susan lives only five blocks away, in a second-floor unit. It has a big bedroom, dining room, a small kitchen, and a very well kept living room. Sohil and Komil, seeing a cat, jump with excitement and start to run after it.

"Oh, that is good, they like to play with my cat." Susan brings the cat over to the girls and tries to talk to them, saying, "Her name is 'Fluffy.'" They touch the cat gently and giggle. They are no longer shy or scared. Susan brings chocolate candy for them and soon after, they start to call her "Aunty." Jasmine is relieved to see them getting acclimated to this new environment easily.

It is about lunch time, so Susan takes Jasmine to the kitchen and shows her whatever she has in the refrigerator and the pantry. Jasmine remembers the grilled cheese sandwich she used to make, and she makes one. She gives a bite to Komil, who makes a face, spitting it out crying, *"roti khani ai, naani ghur jaana* [want to eat roti, want to go to grandmother's house]." They are very hungry and Jasmine doesn't know what may be to their liking. She makes plain toast with lots of butter and puts a little bit in Komil's mouth. She likes it and so does Sohil. Jasmine thanks God and feeds them a couple of slices of buttered toast. Luckily the girls have no problem with the taste of American milk and are happy to drink it with Susan's cookies. Jasmine eats a grilled cheese sandwich and has a cup of tea. Susan shows her how to turn on the television and how to take care of the cat. She gives her the phone number where she can be reached.

"Where you stay? Not here? I live alone here?" Jasmine asks her because she has never lived alone in her entire life and she is panicked.

"I can't stay here. There is only one bedroom and I have my grandparents' beach house to look after until it gets rented or sold. There is no need to worry. This building is very safe."

"But I never live alone." Jasmine is apprehensive.

"You are not alone. Look, you have your daughters with you! I will visit you once a week to help you with the grocery shopping. And you can call me during the day in my office whenever you need to," says Susan, turning on the television. The twins sit down to watch a cartoon with interest; however, once in a while they remember Arjun and start to cry.

As it gets closer to sunset, Jasmine feels suffocated in this small, closed apartment. In spite of her daughters, she feels utterly alone and miserable. She wants to run out to see Ajit, to tell him that she can never live alone. Everything in this apartment is staring at her. She feels terribly sad for Susan to die at such a young age, not even thirty. She is worried about Ajit, thinking how he will handle the shock. At least, to her relief, the girls seem to be happy; they do miss everyone back in India, but at the same time they are excited to see new things.

She opens her luggage and takes out the rice, pickles, yogurt, and spices. Putting a small pot on one burner with two cups of milk, she starts to prepare her dinner of rice and *moong daal* on the other burners. Having no expertise in multitasking, especially cooking on a gas stove, the milk boils over when her attention is on the rice. She quickly picks up the milk pot and sets it down onto the laminate countertop. The hot pot chars the countertop and smells like rubber burning. She holds her head, closing her eyes in despair.

That night, the girls start to cry. They want to sleep with their grandmother and aunty. They want to hear stories from them and wish to play the star-counting game with their cousin. Finally, they cry themselves to sleep.

Jasmine calls Mrs. Khan to tell her that they have reached Philadelphia safely and explains Susan's sad news. Mrs. Khan feels sorry and tells Jasmine to stay strong to confront the inevitable situation.

"Susan wants me to keep this secret of her cancer to myself forever, but I cannot do it. I think Ajit must know the truth, what do you think?" she asks Mrs. Khan.

"I concur with you, he must know the truth. You tell Susan that you won't be able to keep it from Ajit forever. After he submits his thesis, she must tell him."

Jasmine asks her how and where she should go to send a telegram to her mother.

"I will send it on your behalf tomorrow morning, when I go to my office. So don't worry, I go right by a telegraph office," Mrs. Khan insists, and obtains the necessary information from Jasmine.

It is almost midnight but Jasmine is wide-awake; she is not used to such solitary and silent darkness. She looks at the sky through her window, and is shocked to see literally a starless sky. Back home the sky was always full of stars and there was always some kind of noise present twenty-four hours. In her imagination, she hears melodious songs playing on the neighbor's radio at the loudest volume until late into the night. The songs used to be so enjoyable, and early in the morning there were sounds of the villagers starting their chores, along with the cock's loud crows. Here, even the rain does not make its normal sounds. She does not want to turn on the television because the girls are sleeping.

She sits in the living room and starts to read a magazine she picked from a heap belonging to Susan. An article catches her attention, *"Can this marriage be saved?"* The problem for this couple is that the husband has no interest in his wife ever since their baby was born. The wife feels jealous that all the time he is home, he is kissing and holding the baby. In the beginning, she did not mind, but now the baby is a year old and her husband shows no intimacy to his wife. The husband complains to the counselor that his wife has become very irritable and cold, and this puts him off. His daughter, on the other hand, soothes him by smiling and giggling. At the end of the discussion, the marriage counselor comes to the conclusion that the wife is suffering from postpartum depression and the husband, feeling neglected, pays all his attention to his daughter. This case reminds Jasmine of her brother's wife, when she was behaving like this. What a difference in the two cultures, she thinks. In her sister-in-law's case, being in a large joint family, it never became such a big issue that their marriage was on the rocks. A marriage counselor was unheard of in India in the late fifties. Her sister-in-law became back to normal on her own after several months.

Komil's cry awakens Jasmine and she realizes that she has gone to sleep right on the sofa while reading the magazine. It is eight in the morning and she opens the window curtain. It is drizzling softly on the leaves of a maple tree in front of the window. Across the street, there is a beautiful church. She feels a little better than being in the lonesome darkness of the night. Although this morning is not bright and sunny, it is far better than last night. She gives milk to the girls and makes a cup of tea for herself. The tea does not taste as good as back home, but sooner or later she has to develop a taste for the American kind. After a while, she remembers that she used to like corn flakes. She looks in the well-stocked pantry and finds a box of crispy rice cereal. She puts a little in the bowl and when she adds milk, it starts to make a popping sound that entices the girls to eat it, of course with a sprinkle of sugar.

Soon after eating, the girls start to play with the cat. Jasmine fills the bathtub half-way and makes the girls sit in it and play with two sponges. They love this expansive, smooth-surfaced, white tub, so different from the narrow metal one back home. Every time the girls like a food item, Jasmine feels relieved. Now they enjoy the bath, the cat, and watching cartoons on television. Yet not an hour goes by that they don't cry for someone or something they miss in India. They want to get out of the house and run wild as they used to. Jasmine is afraid to take them out for fear of their getting out of her control and running under a car. She is not familiar with this neighborhood, but they keep crying to get out. When they cry, she starts to cry too and curses Ajit for putting them in this misery.

It is only eleven in the morning and she does not know what next to do to entertain the girls. After a while it occurs to her to take them out in the stroller. She waits until they have eaten lunch — a grilled cheese sandwich for her and buttered toasts for Sohil and Komil. This time she tries giving them apple juice, and they love it. She makes them sit in front of the TV while she takes the stroller downstairs, and tells them she will come right back to carry them down. As she steps out, closing the door, it automatically locks. Jasmine had no idea that the door would lock just by closing it, but when she comes back, and finds the door handle won't budge, she panics. Frantically, she goes downstairs, knocks on the neighbor's door, but no one opens it. Then she runs upstairs to the third floor, knocking on the doors. No luck. Confused and hysterical, Jasmine tries to open the door of Susan's apartment once again, but it still does not open. She runs outside in the street, but sees nobody passing by. Like a mad person, Jasmine starts to knock on each and every door on their cul-de-sac street. Finally, an old lady opens her door.

"I want help. My children inside and I am not opening the door," Jasmine says in a very desperate manner. Furthermore, in her Punjabi outfit, she looks strange to the lady.

"What do you want?" the lady says in an irritated tone. "Who are you?"

"I want help, please open the door, my girls are in there."

"No one is here. Go away, you don't make any sense." And the lady shuts the door.

Jasmine closes her eyes and prays. *Oh, God please help me. Please do not let the girls go into the tub and turn on the hot water…please, please God help me.*

She waits for someone to pass by, but having no patience, she runs out to the main street and asks several different people for help; they shrug their shoulders and move on, not understanding her. Instinctively, she thinks of going to Ajit; she no longer cares about what Susan has told her. Her only priority right now is to save her daughters from an accident. She runs to Ajit's apartment since she has no money with her to take a taxi or bus. Drenched by the slow drizzle, she reaches the building, races up the stairs and pounds on the door. As soon as Susan opens it, Jasmine collapses in her arms, "Please help, and open the door, my girls inside."

Susan at once understands what has happened. She quickly wraps a dry shawl around Jasmine, grabs her keys, and drives them hurriedly to her apartment.

Inside, the twins are sleeping on the floor near the television, a crust of tears on their cheeks revealing that they cried themselves to sleep. Jasmine runs to them, scoops them up in her arms, and kisses them, the tears trickling down her cheeks and dripping onto their heads. Susan sits down, touched to see such a deep bond.

"It is my fault. I should have told you about the door, I am so sorry," Susan laments.

Jasmine does not respond; her eyes are closed and she is at peace with the whole world. Her precious daughters are safe and sound. After a while, she lies down on the carpet with the girls cradled in her arms and falls asleep.

Susan looks at her innocent face and curses herself for being the cause of this poor girl's agony. *She is so young, so simple, and such a caring girl.* Susan does not feel like calling her a *woman,* as she appears so child-like, even for a teenager. *Just like her name, she is a blossoming flower of indescribable beauty,* Susan thinks. Sitting quietly, she continues to gaze at the sleeping girls, reflecting that another kind of wife than Jasmine would have had no mercy. She would have been pushed out of Ajit's apartment, her things thrown out mercilessly, in spite of having knowledge of her terminal illness. Jasmine, on the other hand, had cried with sympathy for her, and even thought about how Ajit would suffer after his beloved's demise. Susan sits there motionless. After a while she writes some tips for Jasmine on a note pad:

1. *At night, lock the door from the inside and bolt it.*

2. *Do not open the door until you first look through the peephole, and not unless you know the person who is knocking or ringing the doorbell.*

3. *In an emergency, call my office or my friend, Terry. The numbers are on the blue card I am giving you to always have with you, even when you go out.*

4. *There is a kid's playground one block down Baltimore Pike.*

5. *A pediatrician (children's doctor) is on 42nd and Baltimore Pike, and a hospital is on 34th and Walnut.*

6. *Grocery and pharmacy stores are on 45th and Spruce.*

Susan puts the note and blue card on the kitchen table along with some cash and leaves without disturbing the girls. Jasmine is exhausted from the effects of jet lag and her emotionally frantic day. She and the girls sleep the rest of the day. Late in the evening, Komil and Sohil wake up, crying—they are famished. Jasmine quickly gives them toast with butter, and cereal with milk to fill their tummies for the time being. (These are the only food items they have liked so far.) Although Susan's pantry is full of food, the refrigerator has only milk, bread, butter, and cheese. Jasmine has some leftover *daal* and rice to feed them for dinner.

The next morning, she walks to the grocery shop, pushing Komil and Sohil in the stroller. She buys corn flakes, hot dogs, ice cream, bananas, wheat flour, vegetables, chicken, and a rolling pin. The girls, to her surprise, sit calmly in the stroller and enjoy having a ride. The next day she dares to take them to the children's playground. They play freely and happily with other children of their age.

When they get back to the apartment, Susan comes by and drops off some toys and spends a few minutes playing with the girls and Fluffy. Jasmine begins to find some solace in the midst of her tumultuous circumstances.

A week passes, but there are seven more weeks to go until Ajit will find out about them from Susan. Jasmine has started to speak with the girls in English. They are learning fast, partly from watching kids' shows on television. Slowly, they are building their taste for a variety of foods. Now they love hot dogs, french fries, and orange juice. Still, they often say, *"Naani ghur Jana* [want to go to grandmother's house]" and every night they cry before going to sleep.

For Jasmine, too, sleeping inside without the tranquil blanket of stars and moonlit nights is unbelievably painful. The girls express their frustration by crying miserably. Jasmine, at such times, feels broken, defeated, betrayed, and asks her mother in her imagination: *Why, oh my mother, why have I spun my life's thread so weak that it keeps on breaking and I do not know how to make it strong? Tell me how can I strengthen the thread which was woven in your courtyard.* She imagines her mother responding with words of encouragement, "*It is okay, my dear child, if you have woven a weak thread, because a weak thread can be made strong in due time. An already strong thread is hard to mend because it has no flexibility.*"

Jasmine has prepared chicken curry and rice. The girls are happily enjoying the meal while Jasmine tells them, "Oh, I wish your Papa were here at the dinner table this evening," and the girls start to sing, "Oh Papa, oh Papa come."

"You will see your Papa very soon, let us count the days and sing." She counts one, two, three, and up to forty along with the girls. "Yes, in forty days, you will meet your Papa."

Susan visits them regularly, once or twice a week. She plays with Sohil and Komil and they have started to feel very close to her. Jasmine treats her with much affection and always saves Indian food for her.

"Good news! Ajit has been offered a teaching position in Lewisburg and will be moving there by the end of August," Susan tells her.

"When you tell him you are sick and not marry him?" asks Jasmine.

"Well, I have decided to tell him the truth after he submits his dissertation. And I will take you to your husband soon after," Susan promises.

Jasmine keeps quiet, not knowing whether she should thank her or feel sorry for her, or should tell her to live with him until her last breath. She is overwhelmed with grief, relief, and confusion. She feels relieved at the thought of being reunited with her husband, she feels grief for the dying girl, and she feels confused about her relationship with Ajit and her daughters' future.

In the middle of the night, Komil wakes up crying. She is running a fever and sweating. Jasmine gives her medicine she has brought with her from India. The night passes. In the morning, she takes her to the pediatrician and purchases baby aspirin and the prescribed medicine from the pharmacy. Once home, she gives Komil the medicine and a baby aspirin. She forgets to tell Sohil that the medicine is not for her, only for her sister. Sohil watches her mother as she puts the bottle of aspirin on top of the chest of drawers. While Jasmine is in the kitchen, Sohil grabs the aspirin bottle and eats all of them like candy. Jasmine panics when she sees an empty aspirin bottle in Sohil's hand and tries to reach Susan at the two phone numbers, but there is no answer. She grabs both the girls, puts them in the stroller, and walks as fast as she can to the hospital.

"My daughter ate this," Jasmine says, and shows the empty bottle to the emergency room doctor. She is out of breath and her hands are trembling.

"How many, and at what time?"

"I don't know how many in the bottle. I gave one to my sick daughter at ten this morning. I see empty bottle in Sohil's hand one hour later."

Sohil is taken from the stroller and carried down the corridor by a nurse wearing a white dress, white hat, and white stockings. Jasmine must sit with Komil in the waiting room. After some time, the doctor comes out and tells her that he has done what he can for Sohil, but as a precaution, she should be taken to the children's hospital to be observed overnight.

"Where is hospital?" Jasmine asks, with quivering lips and a stream of tears.

The doctor, gauging her helplessness, says, "I am almost done for the day. I will take you there."

On the way to the hospital, he asks her, "Where is your husband?"

"He is not home and my friend Susan is not home. Thank you very much for help."

"Have you come from India recently?"

"Yes, two weeks."

The doctor parks the car, walks them inside, and explains the situation to the attending physician before he leaves.

While Sohil is under care in the pediatric ward, Jasmine sleeps in the waiting room with Komil on her lap through the night. Her sleep is in short spurts. She feels terribly guilty for not keeping a good watch on Sohil, for not putting the aspirin bottle way above her reach. It never occurred to her that Sohil could climb the chair next to the chest of drawers. With eyes closed, she prays to God as tears stream down her cheeks.

"My daughter okay?" Jasmine asks a nurse as the dawn breaks.

"Your daughter is going to be fine. As soon as the doctor comes in, she will be released."

"Oh, thank you, thank you. I need milk for her, she is hungry."

"There is a cafeteria downstairs," the nurse tells her.

In the afternoon, they all go back home. To comfort herself, Jasmine thinks of her mother's saying, "All is well that ends well."

# 10

# The Uncertain Times

Ajit comes home, throws himself on the sofa and gives a long sigh of relief. He has finally submitted his thesis, acquired an assistant professor's position, and applied for immigration. Life is wonderful! He is definitely ready to talk to Susan about his desire to marry her. Susan, on the other hand, walking to his apartment, is determined finally to tell him about her terminal illness.

"Oh, good, you have come home early, let us go out somewhere," Ajit tells Susan. "The weather is pleasant and I feel as free as a bird."

Susan sits on the edge of the couch and sighs as she tries to gather her strength. "How can you feel so free?" she says. "You are a father of two little daughters and have a wife. Don't you feel any responsibility toward them?"

"Oh, I do, very much indeed. I want to bring them over here to give them the kind of life they deserve. I would, I definitely would."

"And what about their mother, would you bring her along too?"

"Please, Susan, let us go out, let us not spoil this evening," he protests, embracing her. "Let us talk only about us."

"How about going to the beach house and staying there for a few days, since the closing of the house is coming soon?" Susan responds.

"How come? Why are you selling the house?" Ajit asks, dismayed. "Why didn't you tell me? We both love going there."

"I will tell you the reason at the beach," Susan says, trying to keep her voice neutral.

They drive to her grandparents' beach house. Ajit immediately starts to relax as they sit on the porch in the soft breeze and view the many flowers in bloom. Susan wants to explain to him about her illness, but just can't bring herself to spoil his mood. After having a few joyous days together, Susan finalizes the sale of the house for ten thousand dollars, and they pack up to return to the city.

"You look so pale and weak these days, I think you should see a doctor," Ajit says.

"No, I am just tired…I'll be back in a couple of hours," Susan says as she drops him off and goes to her own apartment. Jasmine has been waiting for her for several days. She is anxious, as she has no money left to buy groceries. She had to spend so much on the girls' medical care that she nearly ran out of basic food items such as milk, butter, and bread.

"Good, you come," Jasmine says when Susan walks in. "No money to buy food."

Jasmine tells Susan about the trips to the hospitals and her medical expenses for the girls. Susan quickly takes all of them for a ride in her car to buy groceries and some early-fall clothes for the girls. She persuades Jasmine to buy jeans and blouses; though she doesn't say it out loud, Susan wants her to stop wearing the Punjabi outfits that make her look so different.

Jasmine reluctantly tries them on, and comes out of the fitting room, looking apprehensive.

"Wow!" Susan exclaims. "Jasmine, you look amazing. Once you get used to these clothes and start to feel comfortable, we will buy some more. I think my clothes will fit you, too."

Susan takes her to the bank and adds Jasmine's name to her account, so she will not experience another out-of-money crisis.

Every Sunday, Susan comes to help Jasmine with groceries and take them out for a ride. The girls look forward to seeing her, and if she does not come by a certain time, they start to cry. They call her "Aunty" and cling to her as soon as she shows up. Jasmine is gaining confidence and getting used to her lonely life. She has a hope: a hope to win Ajit's heart back some day. She is learning fast to manage the worst situations while bringing up Sohil and Komil on her own. Although she very much appreciates Susan's help on Sundays, she is worried about her daughters' attachment to her. It pains her to think about the end of Susan's life drawing nearer with every passing day. Susan, on the other hand, is worried about Ajit, Jasmine, and the girls, knowing that her time with them is slipping away.

*Susan looks so frail these days…* Jasmine writes to her folks back home. *She looks older, and tired, but she still helps me so much. She has only a month or two to live. How can God be so cruel? She is so young and so nice to me. She gives me money, and buys clothes and toys for the girls, and we are still living in her apartment.*

Her friend, Simran, feels sorry for Susan, too. She doesn't hate her for taking Jasmine's husband away. Moreover, Jasmine does not blame Ajit or Susan. She writes to Simran that they were destined to love each other, and just as in all romantic legends, true love always ends in separation, to meet in heaven.

Days are passing; it is still hard for Susan to tell Ajit about her condition. Whenever she picks up her courage to talk about it, Ajit diverts her attention to something else. He does not want to hear anything on the serious side; he wants these moments of their life to be carefree. He is very self-centered and rarely mentions his daughters and wife. All he cares about is enjoying his life with Susan, though he is so self-absorbed he does not even notice her rapidly declining health.

The month of August is a crucial decision-making time. Ajit is getting ready to move in three weeks, and Susan is aware of her growing weakness. Her angst is also growing about how to explain everything without destroying Ajit. She is dealing with her fate, but cannot imagine Ajit's handling it. Finally, he decides to pop the question. "Susan, let us get married before I move to Lewisburg," he says enthusiastically.

"What about your daughters and your poor wife?" Susan asks, still putting off what she must disclose.

"I promise you, I will get my daughters here and take care of them."

"What about your innocent wife?" Susan asks. "How will she live her life? I know that in Indian society, a second marriage is unacceptable."

"She will also come here; I will not separate her from our daughters. We will get her married again over here."

"In that case, will you write a letter and send them the air tickets before I agree to marry you? You write the letter and I will make their travel arrangements." And Ajit agrees.

Susan decides to keep silent about her condition for her own peace. She wouldn't have the strength to support Ajit in his misery if he were to know the truth.

Ajit writes a letter and gives it to Susan to include with air tickets to be mailed to Jasmine. She plays this trick on him so he will not discuss marriage again until he receives a response from Jasmine.

It is the third week of August and Ajit is packing his stuff for the big move. Susan has not visited him for several days, but she calls him every day, making false excuses so he cannot see her. She has stopped going to her office and lives with her friend, Terry. One morning, all of a sudden, Susan becomes very weak and almost falls down, catching herself by grabbing her friend. Terry calls an ambulance for Susan, and she is taken to the hospital emergency room. Terry informs Ajit, but forgets to call Jasmine. Ajit, oblivious to the cause of Susan's illness, is concerned, but would never imagine it leading to something so serious as death.

As he is sitting in the hospital waiting room, the doctor comes and puts his hand on Ajit's shoulder, his face grim. "Her end is near," he says gravely. "I am sorry."

Ajit stares at him, not quite believing what he's hearing. His body and voice begin to shake.

"How come? What—what has happened to her? What do you mean? I don't understand."

"Does she have any relatives?" the doctor asks. Ajit stares at him and says nothing.

"Her breast cancer has spread, and she is dying," the doctor says. "Is there a family member who should be called?"

Ajit silently shakes his head, looking at the doctor with frozen eyes, mouth agape. Then his body goes numb.

The night has passed. Ajit is still sitting motionless in the waiting room. His eyes are open as he stares ahead, expressionless. Though many people pass by and a few glance at him, no one stops or checks on him. The hospital staff is busy and focused on the patients. Others have no time to notice his condition; they have come to the hospital with their own problems. Ajit is in shock.

Jasmine is in the apartment with the girls and has no idea what is going on. Every Sunday, without fail, Susan has come to visit and help her with groceries, but this Sunday she does not show up at all. On Monday, Jasmine calls Susan's office.

"Hello, Susan—hello, hello."

"Susan is on sick leave. I'm her assistant," the speaker tells Jasmine.

Jasmine calls Susan's friend, Terry, who informs her that Susan was admitted to the hospital.

"What? Which hospital?"

"University of Pennsylvania Hospital. Are you Jasmine?"

Jasmine utters a hasty "yes," hangs up, and quickly dresses the girls. She puts them in the stroller and pushes them to the hospital as fast as possible. She has no idea how and where to find Susan, so she asks the concierge.

"What is her last name, Miss?" the concierge says, preparing to flip through his patient log.

"I do not know," Jasmine says, wringing her hands. "She has cancer and she dying."

"Who are you? And how do you know her?"

"She is my friend. I must see her."

"You'll have to wait in the waiting room, and I'll see what I can find out."

As soon as Jasmine enters the waiting room, she spots Ajit sitting like a zombie in a corner chair.

"Ajit!" she cries. "Ajit, look Ajit—your daughters are here."

She is so nervous that she forgets the Indian tradition of not calling her husband by his name. She shakes him again and again, but there is no reaction, no word uttered, and no response. Jasmine looks around and then runs to a person walking by to ask for help. He doesn't stop. She runs to the admissions clerk.

"Miss, I need help!" she cries. "My husband not moving—he is like a statue!"

"What do you mean?" the clerk says, squinting.

"Please come with me, help him," Jasmine pleads.

The admissions clerk calls a nurse to help her. When she sees Ajit, the nurse quickly gets a wheelchair and, with Jasmine's help, gets Ajit into it. The nurse wheels him away.

Jasmine glances at her daughters in the stroller and is relieved to see they are preoccupied with their baby dolls. She does not want their first impression of their father to be traumatic. Keeping one eye on them, she asks a different clerk and finds out that Susan is in the Intensive Care Unit. She leaves the emergency room, and pushes the stroller down the hallways as she follows the signs.

"Miss, you can go in, but you have to leave your daughters outside with someone," an orderly tells her.

"I have no one," she replies. "My husband is sick. Can I leave them with you?"

"No Miss, I have work to do. Sorry."

Jasmine asks a woman sitting in the waiting area, but doesn't receive a friendly response. So she sits impatiently in the waiting room, having no knowledge of Susan's and her husband's conditions. The girls climb out of the stroller and run around in the open area of the room while she tries to keep them under control. She thinks of poor Susan, the girls' Auntie; how she wanted to be by her side, holding her hand, if only she were allowed to visit her. After a while, a nurse comes out from Susan's room.

"Are you Jasmine?" she asks.

"Yes," Jasmine says, relieved for the attention. "How is she?"

"I am sorry to tell you, but she has passed away...she left this for you."

The nurse hands her a large envelope. Jasmine stares at it as her hands start to shake and her eyes fill with tears. She sits down, motionless, and clueless as to what needs to be done.

"Are you responsible for the arrangements?" the nurse asks. "Or does someone else need to be informed?"

"No, no, not me," Jasmine says softly. "I do not know what to do. I will call her office."

"Her office has already been informed. I guess we will wait for them," she says, turning to walk back to her station.

Jasmine's eyes follow the nurse's white hat, white dress, and white stockings. She does not want to be left alone with the envelope, with the news that Susan is gone. Komil runs to her and gets her attention. Since the girls are hungry, Jasmine takes them to the cafeteria. She has lost her own appetite completely. She feeds the girls before going to the emergency room to see Ajit.

"My husband okay?" she asks the first nurse she sees. "His name Ajit."

"What is his last name?"

"He has no last name, only family name—Singh."

"Oh, yes, that handsome young man from India," the nurse says. "He had a nervous breakdown."

"What?" Jasmine says, confused and anxious. "Is he awake? He moves and talks?"

"Miss, you can go home. He has to stay here overnight," the nurse says. "You come back tomorrow morning and I am sure he will be all right."

It is about five in the evening and she decides to go home since there is nothing she can do at the hospital. After putting the twins to sleep, she starts to pray for Ajit's full recovery and peace for Susan's departed soul. She reads the prayer book again and again. Susan's presence in her thoughts does not let her sleep, no matter how much she tries. She gets up and opens the envelope given to her by the nurse. Inside is a letter:

*Dear Jasmine,*

*When you receive this package, I will have gone away from your life for good. It's ironic: I feel happy that it will be easier for you to get your husband back, but at the same time, I wish I could be there to see you happy. Life is strange; you have won my heart through your kind and compassionate behavior towards me. I feel as if I have found a sister. The sad part is that I could not live longer to enjoy this loving relationship. And your precious daughters—I wanted to see them growing into beautiful teenagers. The bond you all have with me is eternal. You have enriched my life beyond description.*

*You need not worry about my funeral. I have taken out insurance and my office manager will handle all the arrangements. I know I should have informed Ajit of my fate before this day, but I was not up to it. I am aware of the devastating effect my death will have on him. I am afraid he will be shattered into pieces, but promise me that you will get him out of his shock and sorrow with your loving care. He needs you now; it comforts me to think you will take good care of him, and that his daughters can help mend his heart.*

*I have paid rent for the month of August. You and Ajit can take anything from the apartment you want to Lewisburg or get rid of it. Make sure to return the keys to the rental office on the first floor on your last day in my apartment.*

*The yellow envelope is for Ajit, and the other one is for my lawyer. Please hand-carry it to him at the*

*written address before you both leave for Lewisburg.*
*Give my hugs and kisses to the girls. God bless you with*
*the happiness you deserve.*

*In peace,*

*Susan*

Jasmine is tempted to read the letter written to Ajit. She
opens it half way, and then stops. She is afraid it's not ethical,
so she puts it away and starts to read another note lying inside
the package. It contains general information in case Ajit has
already left for Lewisburg—his address there, the university
telephone number, and instructions for taking the train to
Lewisburg.

Jasmine opens another envelope and finds some cash and
a checkbook with instructions on how to withdraw the cash
and close Susan's bank account. The note reads: *Make sure to*
*inform my lawyer as soon as possible about me. My apartment's*
*lease ends this month. Ajit is moving to Lewisburg on August 31;*
*make sure you go to his apartment before that date.*

It is midnight and Jasmine is worried about Ajit. She
wonders if he were to cry and sob he could overcome his grief.
She recalls a similar situation when she received the shocking
news about her father, and some Indian women in London
were able to induce her to weep. She became normal after
letting it out, wailing loudly. *I should have prompted Ajit to cry*
*before leaving him at the hospital.* Her thoughts torment her.
*What if Ajit never cries? Will he go crazy?*

She remembers a woman in her village who went
completely berserk after her son passed away because she
was unable to cry. She pictures her life with a crazy Ajit and
shivers with fear. She imagines her daughters having a lunatic

father. If necessary, she would take him to the best doctors for treatment.

After a few hours, her curiosity to read what Susan has written to Ajit takes over and she opens the letter.

*Ajit, Darling,*

*When you read this letter, I will be gone forever. Please forgive me for keeping my illness a secret from you. I just could not hurt you with such awful news. Remember the day I was admitted to the hospital for minor surgery about six months ago? It was for a biopsy of a cyst in my breast. The test result changed our entire future when the doctor told me that a malignancy had spread to my lymph nodes. He predicted that I would live only through August. I wanted you to concentrate on your thesis, so I decided to keep quiet. I knew there was nothing we could do. At times I felt like leaving you so that you could hate me. Perhaps such a betrayal would have been better than the shock and pain I have given you today. I guess it was selfish of me just to want our last times together to be wonderful, as they have been.*

*I was in a dilemma for several months—the person who helped me to decide was none other than a most remarkable woman whom I was fortunate to meet. Today I die in peace because of her loving care and devotion. Ajit, this woman is your wife, Jasmine, who is the most compassionate, selfless, gentle soul. She came back to this country, along with your lovely daughters. They have been staying in my apartment. I had planned to break up with you and go away to spare us this ordeal. Jasmine advised me not to betray you by leaving. She convinced me that the divine love you and I have for each other must have truthful closure. She insisted that I continue to live with you until my last breath. What a great soul she is! Ajit, you must forget me and accept your wife back with the full devotion and love she deserves. Do not dwell in the past...*

Jasmine reads this letter and weeps profusely. *What a love story*, she thinks. *Why do such loves always end in separation? Sohni drowns in the stormy river while crossing it to meet Mahiwal on the other side. Romeo kills himself when he thinks Juliet is dead. Ranjha kills himself upon seeing his beloved Heer is dead. Sassi burns to death in the desert heat while following the footprints of Punnu, her lover. And now Ajit is half-dead...*

The dreadful notion of his going crazy scares her. She passes the whole night in prayers. She recites spiritual hymns to calm her nerves, and is a little comforted when she imagines her mother telling her "...be strong my child, it is a blessing in disguise; all will be well."

The next morning, Jasmine goes to the hospital and asks, "How is my husband, Ajit Singh?"

"He is still not talking," the attending nurse responds frankly. "Physically, he is okay, but he is despondent...it seems he has given up."

"Let me better him," Jasmine pleads. "Please let me go to him."

"How will you make him better?" the nurse asks, skeptically.

"Make him cry. Make him scream loud. His pain needs to come out."

"No, no. You have to be patient," she says, shaking her head. "He is under excellent medical care and his doctors know how to treat him." The nurse rolls her eyes as she leaves.

The girls are sleeping in their stroller while Jasmine sits in the waiting room. After a few hours, the nurse tells her to go home because the doctor has decided to keep Ajit under observation for a few more days. Jasmine knows the girls will be crying with hunger soon so she leaves.

Back at the apartment, she finds a letter from Bibijee and starts to read it:

*My dear child,*

*It has been ages since we have received a single letter from you. I start to worry more when I do not know the conditions at your end. Although I am certain you are my brave daughter and would not give up until you succeeded in your mission, I begin to wonder when I get no news from you. I know you are extremely busy but please write, if only a few lines every week. I wish and pray the phone line connections will be established soon between here and America, and we can talk over the phone regularly.*

*Simran stops by every day to find out whether we have received any letter from you. Every day, she becomes extremely sad when she gets a negative response. She has written you several letters, too. Please write us soon even if you have time for only a few lines. Dilbeer misses you and Sohil and Komil terribly and worries about your future. I have a sanguine hope that God will make things work out in your favor. As you know, we say there*

*may be delay in God's court, but justice prevails in the
end. Needless to say, we all miss you very much.*

*Give our hugs and kisses to Komil and Sohil.*

*With lots of love,*

*Your Bibijee*

Jasmine immediately starts to write a letter addressed to
all of them in which she briefly tells them that all is well and
not to worry. She pauses. *How can I write what is actually
happening here? They will be worried sick to know that Susan's
death has affected Ajit's brain. Who knows when he will come out
of this shock? Will he be able to begin his teaching job on time or
lose it altogether?* She trembles with fear and uncertainty. She
folds the letter and encloses it in an envelope after writing
only a few lines about the girls' activities and how they
have adjusted without much trouble to the new foods and
environment. She tells herself that when the circumstances get
better, she will write lengthy letters explaining everything that
has happened to her in these few months.

Early in the morning, she mails the letter to India and
strolls the girls to the hospital. Ajit's condition is not good
enough for him to be released yet, and Jasmine is not allowed
to see him unless she can leave the girls with someone in the
waiting room. She is reluctant to leave them with a stranger,
and moreover, she suddenly worries whether it's a good idea
to see him, as much as she wants to. What if his condition
should worsen after the shock of seeing her? She decides to
stay away from him until he gets better. The nurse tells her
he will be released tomorrow and perhaps will be referred to a
psychiatrist.

"Why?" Jasmine asks, frowning. "Is he crazy?"

"No, no," the nurse says, giving her a comforting smile. "He is just not completely in touch with reality. You can help him by making sure he stays under a doctor's care for some time."

Not sure what she means, Jasmine keeps quiet and leaves. At home, she prepares Komil and Sohil for meeting their Papa for the first time. She shows them her wedding photographs.

The next day, rather than confronting Ajit in the hospital, she watches for him to walk out of the main entrance and then follows him to the apartment. After waiting outside for a while to give him time to get settled, she rings the bell and Ajit opens the door. He stares at them in shock.

"Papa, papa!" the girls cry, clinging to him while he stands motionless.

"Ajit, hug them, for heaven's sake!" Jasmine scolds. "They are your daughters."

Jasmine sounds assured, but is now holding her breath, powerless to do anything but hope the loving spirit of the girls will revive him back to life. He moves his arms a little to hold them with shaking hands. All of a sudden, a flood of tears covers his face and he sits down on the floor holding the girls in his embrace. They start to cry when they see their father crying uncontrollably. Jasmine is happy, assuming that now he will become normal without seeing a psychiatrist. *He needs to let his emotions out, which is finally happening.*

He does not look at Jasmine directly; she thinks he must feel so guilty about his infidelity. He tells Jasmine to hit him over the head with her shoe, as he deserves. "I am so ashamed of myself," he weeps. "If I didn't have the girls to take care of, I would have committed suicide."

"Please do not feel that way," Jasmine says. "It was my fault to leave you alone for so long. I do not blame you for falling in love with Susan, and I am very sorry that she is gone forever. Yes, I know Susan. God bless her soul, she won my heart too. She left this envelope for you." Jasmine gives it to him, but he puts it down without opening it. She hopes he will read the letter soon.

"Ajit, please get up, Sohil and Komil are upset. They will only feel better after seeing you laugh and play with them." She pulls him up from the floor and makes him sit on the sofa. She puts his daughters on his lap. "Tell your papa not to cry and to play with you," she tells them.

They touch his hands, arms, and face as if they have found something precious, and coo, "Papa, Papa." He smiles and hugs them, touching their hair without looking up at Jasmine. He is still afraid to meet her gaze. After a while, the girls go to sleep on his lap. Jasmine thanks God for this turning point in her life, which appears to be in a positive direction. She gathers up all of Susan's belongings including her photographs, and puts them away in a large empty box in the closet. Jasmine hopes to erase all memories of Susan from Ajit's mind to create a new beginning. *Better days are surely ahead.* She goes to the kitchen to prepare some sandwiches. After lunch, she packs up much of the kitchen. There is only one week left before they must move to Lewisburg where Ajit will join Becknell University.

# 11

# The Turning Point

The month of October is over, leaving the trees full of multi-colored dry leaves, hanging proudly on the branches. And as they say, *pride hath a fall*—the cruel winds of early November shake them down to the ground. The bare trees in front of Jasmine's bay window uncover the mystic beauty of the church. She always finds consolation just looking at the architecture and often wishes to take a peek inside one day. The month also ends with the most celebrated fall festival, Halloween, which Jasmine knows little about. In the evening, someone knocks at their door; she is surprised to see three children dressed in funny-looking clothes. The front one looks ragged and has a dirt-smudged face. She goes inside to get some change to give them.

"Beggars, in America?" she asks her husband, frowning in confusion. Ajit is reading a textbook and does not respond.

After a while, there is another knock. To her astonishment, this time it's an Indian woman about Jasmine's age, standing beside her son who is dressed as an Indian prince. Their eyes meet and simultaneously they exclaim, "Oh my God! You're from India!"

Although Jasmine was terribly lonely and missed conversations in her own language, she was hesitant to meet Indians. In fact, she even had seen this particular woman with her son in the park a while ago, and tried to avoid her. But now, the same woman has come right to her door.

"Namaste," the woman says, smiling. "My name is Purnima. You live in this building?"

"Yes, my name is Jasmine."

"You must be from Punjab, I can tell. I'm from Bombay."

"Yes, I am," Jasmine says shyly. "Please, come in."

"How come you aren't taking them for trick-or-treat?" Purnima asks, noticing Komil and Sohil playing in the family room.

"What's that? A few kids came just ten minutes before you and I gave them money, thinking they were beggars."

Purnima laughs, and Jasmine, realizing she must have made a mistake, cups her mouth with her hand in embarrassment.

"I did exactly the same in my sister's home," Purnima admits. "I had just come from India then. It is called *Halloween*—I think it is the celebration of fall colors. The children, dressed in costumes, gather candies from neighborhood homes."

"Ah, it reminds me of the *Lohri* festival back home," says Jasmine. "The kids go door-to-door, singing and asking for sweets." Jasmine quickly dresses the girls in Indian outfits to accompany Purnima and her son for trick-or-treating. They talk as they walk from home to home.

"They look like twins, yes?" Purnima asks. "How old are they? My son, Gautam, is three years old."

"Yes, Komil and Sohil are twins, sixteen months old."

"What is your husband's name and what does he do?"

"He has just completed his doctorate in economics and he is looking for a teaching position," Jasmine says, her lips quivering in mid-lie. "His name is Ajit."

"I love Punjabi food. There are so many Punjabi restaurants in Bombay."

"You speak Urdu beautifully," Jasmine tells her.

"As a matter of fact, my parents are from Hyderabad and our language is *Telugu*. Our neighborhood in Hyderabad was full of Muslims. My parents loved to speak Urdu and insisted that we learn to speak it, too. My father was a poet. He often said that Urdu is as melodious as a romantic song."

"Hindi, Punjabi, and Urdu are similar," Jasmine says. "Although my state language is Punjabi, I can understand and speak Hindi and Urdu to some extent."

"The children seem to get along very well; let us take them to the park every day. You can bring them up to our apartment, too."

"Yes, of course, you do the same, too," Jasmine says as a courtesy.

In actuality, she is perturbed by the thought of exposing Ajit to an Indian family. *What would they think about all that has happened to us, if they come to know? And the fact that Ajit goes to see a psychiatrist? No, no, I wouldn't tell anything to her.*

Later, back home, as she is about to wash her face, she sees her reflection in the mirror. *What has happened to you? You should be thrilled to have met such a friendly desi girl. You are in dire need of a friend with whom you can share your grief. You avoid meeting people here—you avoid writing the truth to your folks for their peace of mind. What about your peace of mind? Your happiness? No, no, go away!* And she smudges the mirror with hand lotion to make her image disappear.

After Susan's death, Ajit became so ill he couldn't report to his secured teaching position at Becknell University in Lewisburg. He showed no interest in contacting them or in seeking another position somewhere else. Jasmine is at her wit's end and doesn't know how to tackle the situation. She tries her best to encourage him to eat, play with, and show affection to the girls, but to little avail. She inherited a little more than ten thousand dollars and the car from Susan, as per the lawyer's letter. They can continue to stay in this apartment for as long as they need to. The kind-hearted son of the late landlady, Mrs. Stevenson, tells her that he understands her plight and is willing to help her in every way. She is grateful that he drives Ajit to the psychiatrist appointment each week.

Something which seems very strange to Jasmine has boggled her mind. She noticed that Susan's belongings are slowly disappearing from the box where she put them. She mentioned this in her last letter to Bibijee, and today she receives her response:

> *My dear child,*
>
> *We were relieved to hear from you that all is well at your end. I thank God every day and pray for your happiness. I asked our yogi about the disappearance of Susan's things. He said that Susan's soul is not at peace, and to help her attain it, you will have to find a Pundit to read Ramayana continuously for twenty-four*

*hours, and also give to charity in her name. I personally
do not believe in superstitions, but your Bibo aunty
is convinced about this. She has done it when their
cattle started to die one after another. She tells me that
after the reading of Ramayana, not a single animal
died. Needless to say, we are missing you all very much.
Simran was complaining that you have not yet replied to
her letter.*

> *With lots of love,*
>
> *Your Ma*

Jasmine is not comforted by the letter and decides to stay
awake one night to find out who is stealing Susan's things.
After several nights, she finally succeeds in uncovering the
mystery. She watches as Ajit gets up, picks up some of Susan's
things from the box, and walks out to their little deck in
the back. She quietly follows him. He digs a hole in the tall
and wide flowerpot and hides them there, covering them
with dirt. Then he walks straight back to bed, apparently in
deep sleep. Jasmine has heard of sleepwalking, and is now
convinced it happens.

The next day she takes Ajit to the deck and uncovers all
the buried things. Ajit's face becomes red up to his ears with
rage.

"Why are Susan's things here?" he demands.

"You buried them here. Don't you remember?"

Shaking his head in denial, he stomps back inside. She
gathers up all of Susan's stuff and puts it back in the box. In
the afternoon, Jasmine goes alone to Ajit's psychiatrist. When
she tells him about Ajit's sleepwalking, the doctor decides to
hypnotize him.

"What is *hypnotize?*" she asks.

"Frequently, the cause of sleepwalking lies in earlier trauma the patient experienced," the doctor explains matter-of-factly. "The subconscious mind becomes protective and blocks out memories which disturb the psyche. Through hypnosis, the patient's buried traumatic memories are brought to the surface, exposing the root cause of the problem. It may require several sessions. It is a costly treatment and I must inform you that with some patients it does not work. You may want to take your husband to the state hospital, which specializes in mental disorders. Then the state takes care of the expense."

"My husband is not crazy," she insists. "The mental hospital is for crazy people. I will not take him there. I want you to treat him."

The therapy is scheduled for two weeks later. A few days before the hypnotherapy, the psychiatrist meets with Jasmine to find out every detail about her husband's habits, hobbies, life story, and personal relationships. As she leaves his office, she stops.

"Oh, one thing important I forgot to tell you," she says. "My husband used to sing a lot. Now he doesn't. The day he sings again, I'll know he is cured."

When she takes Ajit to the office, the doctor asks her to stay. He explains that some patients in regression start to speak the language spoken during that period of their life. "I will need you to translate," he says.

The doctor invites Ajit to sit comfortably in a recliner and begins the hypnosis process.

"Now close your eyes and imagine a peaceful place, and concentrate. Look at the floating clouds. Relax, relax, you are falling asleep, asleep…asleep. Now take two deep breaths. You are now calm and asleep…where are you?"

"It is dark, very dark," Ajit mutters. "I can't see clearly. I can see my Mama…she is leaving, and a policeman is taking her. I am running after her. Ouch! My bare foot is cut…"

Then Ajit draws a sharp breath and his whole face clenches in pain. Watching him is hard for Jasmine. She thinks that he has suddenly left the room and that he is now back in time. He is no longer telling them a story, he is re-living it.

"Mama! Mama!" he screams, speaking in Punjabi. "Do not go! Please! Please do not go!"

Ajit starts crying while he continues, in Punjabi. Jasmine interprets for the doctor, telling him that Ajit is begging his mother not to leave, and is asking his grandmother where his mother is going and why the police have taken her.

"How old are you?" asks the psychiatrist.

"*Daadi, daadi*, where is my Mama?"

Ajit is crying uncontrollably and the doctor puts down his notepad and leans toward Ajit.

"When I count to three, you will wake up," he says calmly, but loudly enough to be heard over the cries. "To find your mother, you will have to be in very good health."

After the count, Ajit wakes up, seemingly back to normal, though his face is tear-streaked and solemn.

"Now, tell me, how old were you when you saw your mother leaving the house?"

"My grandmother told me that I was four and my brother was five when our mother died. We thought she was dead! My father got remarried. But now, I am certain Mama is alive. My grandmother lied to us."

"Well, if you really want to find out her whereabouts, you have to get well first."

"Yes, I want to get better and go back to India to find her," Ajit agrees.

After another session, Jasmine tells the psychiatrist that Ajit's behavior is no longer hostile, but he still does not talk with her.

"He requires additional sessions to heal his grief, not only about his mother but about losing Susan. Only then will he be returned to himself and able to show love to you," the psychiatrist tells her.

Therefore, another appointment is scheduled. In the next session, Ajit's regression is about recent events in his life.

"Where are you?" the doctor asks him.

"I am in the hospital. Susan has left me…why? Why! I loved her so much, but she did not care. Why are her things in my home? I do not want to see them."

"What would you like to do with the things?"

"I wish to hide them."

Near the end of the session, the doctor makes the suggestion to Ajit that he forget about Susan and her things.

Ajit is getting better, but still stays withdrawn. His improvement is evident only in that he appears to be more connected with his daughters. He will let each girl stand on one of his feet, and then he walks across the apartment, lifting them as they cling to him and squeal with laughter.

Jasmine loves to see the girls engage him, but is becoming anxious for him to acknowledge her existence. Jasmine deliberately speaks broken English or Punjabi to make him angry, to see him react, but he does not; he simply ignores her mistakes. He plays with the girls and dines with them, but does not say anything to Jasmine. Jasmine sleeps with the girls and he sleeps on the sofa until they manage to buy twin beds. The only consolation Jasmine has is that he is there to watch the girls when she cooks, bathes, or goes to the grocery store. To her, the most important part of married life is to build a secure and loving nest for the children. Jasmine is consoled that Sohil and Komil love to play with their father.

These days Purnima and Jasmine meet quite often, mostly in the park. The more they meet, the more they like each other, and the children play together very well. One day, Purnima asks if Jasmine could watch her son three mornings a week, because she has gotten admission to a master of library science program which starts in January.

"They have evening classes, too, that you might be interested in," suggests Purnima. "We could take turns babysitting."

"Yes, I do need to stand on my own feet sooner or later since my husband is not well enough to find a job."

"I know you said he stays home a lot since being in the hospital. What is wrong with him?"

"Ah, it's a long story…I will tell you some day," Jasmine sighs. "In short, he is under treatment for anxiety. Will you help me in getting admission? I think it's a good idea to get my mind off my worries. I can take one course at a time."

Although they go to the laundromat, grocery store, and the park together, they never talk about their married life. As a matter of fact, they have not yet met each other's husband. Purnima's husband comes home very late, and leaves for work early in the morning. And Purnima has never come in to see Ajit because Jasmine has never encouraged her to do so.

At the dinner table, Jasmine is pleasantly surprised to hear Ajit asking her about Purnima. So far he has been apathetic about her daily activities, though she still likes to give him an account of her day like happily married people do. Another thing she notices is that he now collects the mail each day from their mailbox. Jasmine is happy to see this change in his behavior. Before going to bed, she opens and starts to read letters from Bibijee and Dilbeer.

> *My dear child,*
>
> *This is a short letter to give you good news that Dilbeer is engaged to an engineer. Your bhabi is a good matchmaker and Dilbeer likes the young man a lot. He and his parents live in Canada. They came to India for only one month and demand the marriage take place within three weeks. The only problem is that Dilbeer insists on getting married when you are here. I hope you can write a letter to her to make her understand to go ahead without your presence.*
>
> *Simran has not visited us for several months. I will go to her house to find out if everything is okay with them. I hope Simran can persuade Dilbeer to agree. I will write to you a lengthy letter after Dilbeer's marriage.*
>
> *With lots of love,*
>
> *Your Ma*

Jasmine sits motionless, holding the letter, not knowing how to feel. The thought of herself not present at her sister's marriage robs her happy feeling. And she feels very uneasy about Simran. The last letter she received from Simran was in September, and now Bibijee informs her that Simran has not visited them for quite some time. She must send a telegram to her dearest friend tomorrow morning, she thinks, before she tries to sleep.

The silent nights of crisp, cold, December, and the mild whisper of the remaining leaves on the nearly bare trees haunt Jasmine at night. Some nights she wants to scream—scream loud enough to rupture the unbearable stillness. Glancing through her mind's eye, the memories of her childhood scroll like the cinema talkie that she had watched once or twice a year in her village. It was shown on a big screen in the open ground.

Thinking about the painted birds on their kitchen wall, she remembers how her little sister cried that her drawing of a parrot came out crooked, and how Bibijee helped her correct it. Jasmine painted a blue peacock and her cousin drew the mango tree. Bibijee assured them that the wall paintings would remain there forever. She pictures the scene of her village park right after a thunderstorm, when insects as tiny as beetles come out in hundreds, walking softly on the wet earth. They were harmless and tiny creatures but, in their velvety coats of Chinese red, they inspired awe. She feels pity for Ajit because of his experience of such a sorrowful childhood. Sometimes she wants to hug him to fill the emptiness of his life, but then, Susan still stands in the way.

A week passes quickly and tomorrow is her sister's wedding. Tonight, the girls and Ajit are sleeping soundly. Her mind wanders to her sister's wedding—actually, it is happening right now, due to the time difference. All the relatives would have come by now. She hears them singing songs, cracking jokes, and laughing loudly; Indian weddings are so much fun. She can picture freshly homemade *laddoo, gulabjaman, jalebi* and other varieties of sweets, lying row upon row on covered tables, just as they were during her brother's wedding. At this hour, her sister and brother-in-law must be sitting for the wedding ceremony. Her sister would be looking beautiful. She sees Simran filling in during her absence, helping Dilbeer in every way. It would have been such an exciting occasion for the girls. *Why didn't we go? I had the money; I could have admitted Ajit to the hospital. What stopped me from being there for my only sister?* Jasmine questions herself before answering. *No way; it is not that easy to go abroad—the visa, the shots, and the tickets—the whole preparation needed too much time.*

Walking together to the playground the next afternoon, Purnima notices the sadness on Jasmine's face. "What is wrong? You look sad."

"My sister got married yesterday and I…" Jasmine starts, but she is unable to finish.

"You know, this is the price we all pay for living abroad. I was unable to attend my brother's wedding last year. My sister was unable to attend my wedding."

"You like living in America?" Jasmine asks.

"You know, I really love it," says Purnima. "The biggest advantage for us women is staying away from in-laws and not having constantly to deal with a joint family. My mother-in-law is such a dictator, oh my God! I am so relieved; you are lucky for not having in-laws." Jasmine does not respond, wondering what is luck, and who is lucky in this world.

Jasmine is holding Simran's letter that she collected from her mailbox earlier, but is reluctant to read it in the park due to Purnima's company. As soon as she returns home, she opens and reads the long letter, written in October, but completed and posted in late December.

*My dearest Jasmine,*

*It is one-thirty in the night, and I am sitting in my verandah pretending to be burning the midnight oil for my economics exam tomorrow. My folks are snoring inside their rooms. The October nights are humid, as you know. A soft drizzle is haunting me with memories. Do you remember our Punjabi class under the pipal tree? A bird's dropping landed on the teacher's sleeve and we could not stop laughing. The teacher made us stand in the sun for two hours and even then we were unable to control our laughter. Oh, how much we used to laugh! Now, it seems as if the laughter has flown away along with you. Yesterday, a moving cloud burst open drenching the whole class, and how much I wished you were here studying with me for the postgraduate degree.*

*I am relieved to learn from your letter that everything worked out for you. Ajit loves the girls as I predicted, and life is beginning to take a positive turn. May God bless you with a very happy married life and help you soon forget what you had to endure in the past.*

*Dilbeer is terribly sad that you will not be present at her wedding. She does understand that it is not possible for you to come, but it is her heart which refuses to accept. I will try my best to proxy your presence and help her in the shopping and preparations.*

*I did not want to burden you with my miserable life, but you are the only one who understands me. I have to tell you what is going on these days in the world of my love. A few months ago, I told my mother about my desire to marry Veer. Since then I haven't been allowed to go out except to college until I am engaged to him. I wrote a letter to Veer conveying my mother's wish that he should talk to his parents and send them or a matchmaker to our house with a marriage proposal. I wait every day until late at night and soak my pillow with tears. I have not met with him for two full months. Just as the flowing river rushes with intense desire to meet its beloved ocean, I run to the door just to have a glimpse of Veer passing through my alley.*

*Tonight as I am writing this letter to you, I cry to see a moth burning into ashes in the candle's flickering flame. The moth is so much attracted to the flame and his desire so intense that he could care less about destroying himself. All of a sudden, I see a light at the end of the tunnel. Perhaps this is how a true love's body and soul attain salvation. The kind of love I have for Veer is pure, divine, and I would feel so fortunate if I could attain salvation just like the moth. If you think about Heer & Ranjha, Sohni & Mahiwal, Romeo & Juliet, Sassi & Punnu, and so many more true lovers, they died in the end, which in some sense immortalized their true love.*

*I don't think Veer's parents have agreed; otherwise, he would have replied to my letter by now. If his love were true, he would have taken a stand against his parents. Every passing day brings my heart closer to suspicion and despair. But I do not blame him; I know*

*he loves me. It is our society that is so cruel, so ignorant,
putting horrendous restrictions on innocent young
people. The other day I scribbled some lines:*

*Walls! Walls! Walls!
High walls, low walls
Mud walls, brick walls
Whichever path she selects
Standing there walls.
One wall is her father
Standing like a scarecrow,
One wall is her mother
One is her brother
Lecturing on the mores.
One wall is her society
Tallest of them all
Helpless, woebegone
Eats a poisonous herb
And never wakes again.*

*My sister advises me to forget about Veer and go
on with my life. She does not realize— actually no one
here has a clue about the kind of love I have for him.
One glimpse of him works as a balm on my lacerated
heart. The Sufi poet, Baba Bullah Shah, describes my
condition so eloquently in one of his poems:*

*"Ranjha, Ranjha Kardi ve main ape Ranjha hoi,*

*Akho ne meinu dhido Ranjha Heer na Akho koi"*

*In essence, Heer's love for Ranjha becomes divine,
crossing the bonds of body, a merging of two souls
where all distinctions between the lover and the beloved
vanish. In his poem, Heer and Ranjha become one and*

*no one should call her by her name, Heer, because she
has merged into Ranjha...."*

Jasmine, shaken by this letter, stops reading any further
and she quickly writes a brief note to her friend.

> *My dearest Simran,*
>
> *I presume from your letter that you are depressed
> and wish to die for your love. Please, please do not think
> such thoughts. Your sacrifice (as you call it) would crush
> my heart and serve no purpose. You would defame
> your parents' name. And within our cruel cultural
> measures, your death would be seen on a scale of physical
> love—their filthy minds would never think beyond the
> condemnation of an unwed mother who was afraid to
> live in shame. I know that you have never crossed your
> limits; you have not met Veer for two months, but people
> do not know this. Our society does not understand that
> there is love that lies beyond the worldly reality, that
> such love is ecstasy of the soul, not merely the body. You
> must persuade Veer to marry you. You must wait for
> him. I will write you a lengthy letter soon.*
>
> *Yours forever,*
>
> *Jasmine*

Jasmine quickly posts the letter, and hopes it will reach
her soon. She tries to put her mind at ease, but feels helpless.
*God forbid if anything should happen to Simran...I would never
forgive myself.* Sitting in a far-away foreign land, she is unable
to communicate instantly with her, or her folks who have no
phone. Letters are so slow; she can only hope and pray for
Simran's safety.

The next day Ajit places a call to his brother in England. The brothers haven't spoken to each other for over a year. Jasmine, coming out of the bathroom, overhears part of the conversation.

"I want to find Mama to give her two slaps: one for you and one for me, for leaving us," Ajit tells his brother.

Of course, Jasmine can't hear his brother's response.

"You are sure that she is not in India?" asks Ajit."Then where has she gone?"

After a pause, Jasmine hears Ajit speak. "Of course, I will find the reason for her leaving us before I show my anger. Give me her family surname and her address in India—I must find her."

Jasmine thanks God at this evidence of Ajit's improvement. This morning she was delighted to hear him humming his favorite song in the bathroom. *Today is definitely a turning point!*

# 12

# The Distressed Visit

In Punjab, it hardly ever rains in January, but this evening it is pouring, accompanied by vicious thunder. Perhaps nature, too, wants to weep profusely.

Tents have been erected in Simran's courtyard to accommodate the mourners sitting on the ground. Simran's friends are preparing her body for the pyre. They dress her in pink bridal *salwar kameez:* a beautiful veil, bridal jewelry, pink lipstick, and blush. Their tears mingle with the henna they are painting on Simran's hands. They admire her beauty. They pray for her soul to find peace and unite with her bridegroom in heaven. *Her face is so peaceful,* they whisper to each other.

Simran's parents sit nearby, hanging their heads in shame and despair. Their breath catches in their throats, and tears flow relentlessly. Veer's parents are nowhere to be seen. They are hiding Veer from Simran's brothers, who are looking for him everywhere, hoping to slit his throat. They would like to see him cremated next to their sister, but only out of anger, not compassion. Jasmine's sister and mother try to calm Simran's hysterical sister. And the villagers, with their ignorant minds, make baseless assumptions. They are unable to comprehend that a pure, helpless virgin has just taken her own life due to the social strictures that they themselves are responsible for. Moreover, they will never blame the young man for doing anything wrong. A man in their culture can do no wrong; it is always a woman's fault.

Jasmine, far away, receives a letter from her mother. It tells her that Simran is in a coma due to a car accident, and needs time to recover. She is unable to write or speak, but the doctor says she will be fine in due time. On reading this, Jasmine starts to pray for her friend's speedy recovery and thanks God for keeping her alive. Back home, Jasmine's mother feels some regret over the lie, but ultimately decides she made the right choice; better to keep the tragedy a secret for now than to cause her daughter to fall ill with grief.

Purnima has started her classes, so Jasmine takes care of Gautam for a few hours every morning. Jasmine is taking a course one evening a week and leaves the girls upstairs with Purnima.

One morning they wake up to find a blizzard has dumped ten inches of snow overnight. From Jasmine's window the scene is absolutely spectacular. The bare branches of trees are laden with white fluffy snow. Sohil and Komil can see from their window some children playing in the snow. They can't wait to go out, but Jasmine is not prepared for the snowy winter. It never occurred to her that they would need more protection than just a winter jacket. They have no snowsuits, boots, gloves, or warm caps. When she has Gautam in her care also, she is almost overwhelmed by the energetic toddlers stuck inside the small apartment. They are too active to sit in front of the television; all they want is to run around.

Sometimes she wonders whether she can ask Purnima to hire a babysitter, but she refrains. *We are friends,* she thinks to herself. *We should help each other in time of need.*

One night when the girls are sound asleep, Ajit comes and sits on the edge of Jasmine's bed. "Jasmine, are you awake?" he whispers.

"*Hanjee* [yes]." Jasmine tenses up.

"Will you forgive me?"

"I never thought you were guilty."

"I love you. You are an angel."

She does not answer. Neither of them turn to face each other.

The next morning when Purnima comes to leave Gautam with Jasmine, one of her eyes is swollen with black and blue marks.

"Oh! What happened to you?" Jasmine asks.

"I fell down last night," she says. "It does not hurt, so don't worry." Purnima leaves quickly.

Today Ajit is going to Washington, D.C. for an interview at Georgetown University. He plans to spend the night with a friend. He wears a black suit and a bright necktie. Jasmine compliments him on looking very professional. He smiles.

"This weekend, let's go to see an Indian film showing at the university auditorium," Jasmine suggests.

"Yes, definitely." Ajit says, before leaving.

Jasmine is ready to meet Indians and make new friends. Now she can write a detailed letter telling her folks all that has happened. Before, she lied to them, but now she can truthfully write that all is well. She calls Mrs. Khan to tell her that Ajit is much better.

Purnima comes back from her class, and since Ajit is not at home, Jasmine invites her in. "Oh my goodness! Purnima, your hands are freezing, come inside, I will make you a hot cup of tea."

Jasmine sips her tea while Purmina only holds the cup, warming her hands. "What is wrong? You don't seem to be the bubbly girl I know," Jasmine says.

A tear drops into Purnima's cup of tea. She looks up to the ceiling, "Oh God, please give me the courage I need right now," she says. "I am leaving him."

"Leaving who?"

"Who else? This bump on my head, this black eye – can't you guess?"

"Oh, I am so sorry! I really believed you fell down."

Purnima shakes her head, sets her tea down, and looks towards the window.

"You know, we spent such a wonderful year in Bombay after our marriage. I remember telling my sister how happy I was, how I was treated like a princess. I don't know what has happened to Arvind in these two years of living in America."

"You should take him to a psychiatrist. Perhaps he can be cured."

"No, you do not know how…well, he thinks there is nothing wrong with him, that I am the one who needs a psychiatrist," Purnima says. "But I am not a helpless creature. I will not keep on suffering silently. I am an educated modern woman. It is an insult to my whole being to submit to his cruelty."

"But if he was so good in Bombay, what could have made him change?"

"Within one month of our moving here, his mantra was '*do as the Romans do in Rome.*' He wanted me to wear miniskirts, get a stylish haircut, and attend dancing classes. We started going out to bars and nightclubs quite often. Now he drinks even during the day, and at night becomes violent. He does not pay any attention to Gautam. He does not want me to study further for fear I will become too independent. But I am ready to be strong and stand up for myself."

"Your husband needs to be treated before you leave him," Jasmine cautions. "Think about Gautam, who will lose a father."

"Jasmine, you are talking like a helpless village girl," Purnima snaps. "Which father are you talking about? Arvind is gone all day to work, then watches television or starts a fight with me when he is home. My sister tells me to come back to Washington right away, but I want to complete my semester here."

Purnima and Gautam then go upstairs. While the girls are taking a nap, Jasmine sits still, thinking over the sad news and her conversation with Purnima. That one phrase – *a helpless village girl* – has stirred the strings of her heart's *sitar*.

*Should I have left Ajit to teach him a lesson, thus depriving my daughters of their father?* She ponders at length. *No, no, that step would have been so wrong. I think Purnima is making a mistake. I will tell her to give him one more chance before taking such a devastating step.* But the conversation has bewildered her, and has revived her hostility towards Ajit. *How dare he betray me! How in the world can I forgive him so easily?* Jasmine scolds herself.

Tonight she can hear the wind howling and the windows shaking. She feels a tremor moving through her spine. All of a sudden she is scared. She feels alone. She wonders why whenever she gets close to a person, that person leaves. *Why does this keep happening to me? First, Mrs. Khan leaves, and now Purnima is ready to move. At least God has saved Simran, but she lives so far away. I hope and pray, Simran will come to America after her marriage to Veer.*

Jasmine falls asleep and dreams about Simran, who is wearing a red sari. "Why are you wearing a sari?" Jasmine asks, laughing.

"Why not? I am a married woman."

"You got married? Why didn't you invite me?"

"You wouldn't have come, so why bother to invite you," Simran replies.

"Why are you annoyed with me?"

"I am not," she says. "I have fulfilled our desires, and emigrated. Now we will never live too far from each other!" Simran embraces her.

"Where is Veer?"

"He is coming soon. His passport wasn't ready."

Throughout the next day, Jasmine's dream keeps ringing in her mind. She writes a letter to Simran. She tells her about the dream and assures her that Veer will marry her, because she has heard that an early morning dream always comes true.

Before Ajit returns home she prepares a special dinner and *kheer* to celebrate his progress. Her little family sits down together at the dinner table for the first time. Sohil and Komil can sense the happy atmosphere and they smile and giggle.

Ajit is quite attentive and participates in their laughter. For the first time, they all sit on the sofa to watch television.

The next Saturday, they go to an Indian movie. There are quite a few Indians in the auditorium, to Jasmine's surprise. Mostly they are south Indians and Gujarati. There is only one other couple from Punjab. Everyone is very friendly; in a foreign land, people from any corner of India welcome each other with a feeling of *apnapan* (my own).

During the intermission, they exchange telephone numbers and personal information, and extend invitations. After the movie, many go together to a pizza restaurant. This is one American food that appeals to their palates, especially with the help of plenty of crushed red pepper. One Gujarati couple invites Ajit and Jasmine along to the pizza restaurant. Their names are Ganesh and Uma, a very personable couple about Ajit's age. They have a four-year-old son, Manik. Komil and Sohil are happy to see him. Ajit and Jasmine invite them for dinner the next weekend.

The train of their life starts to move on the right tracks. Their immigration is finally approved. Ajit has obtained a teaching position at Swarthmore College starting in September. They have made some friends, mostly students, who are a mix of singles, married couples, and some male students who have left their families back in India. Everybody is in need of *desi* friends.

Some singles crave homemade Indian food, which Jasmine loves to cook for them. To the girls, everyone is *Uncle* or *Aunty*. Some of the visitors are reminded of their own little ones or siblings left behind.

Jasmine writes all these details to Bibijee, Dilbeer, and Simran with delight and excitement. Dilbeer writes one letter on behalf of Simran, keeping her "alive" for Jasmine's sake.

Ajit has received a wedding invitation from Professor Lal in Punjab. He is finally getting married and urges Ajit to be his best man, just as he was for Ajit. Ajit decides to take a trip to India before starting his teaching position. He wants to find out about his mother, also. He tells Jasmine he will be visiting India only once to complete both the tasks. They have enough money, green cards, and the free time.

Jasmine's excitement knows no bounds. She quickly writes letters to inform her loved ones of their upcoming visit. She is able to accompany Ajit because her semester will be over by then. Purnima also plans to leave her husband and move to Washington after she completes her semester. Jasmine dreads the thought of Purnima leaving, but thinks it will be a little easier since she will be heading to India. She buys gifts for everyone. They plan to include a stop in London to visit Ajit's brother and family.

Sohil and Komil cannot contain themselves and keep talking about their *naani* so often that Jasmine feels she should not have told them about the trip until they were on their way. Finally all the bags are packed and the happy family of four takes a taxi to the airport and boards the plane to England.

Sitting next to Ajit on the plane, Jasmine remembers her previous trip. She imagines life is a merry-go-round; you keep going around and around, regardless of the choices you have made. She can never forgive Ajit for abandoning her, so why is she behaving as if all is fine? She knows she cannot live a lie, so why does she pretend? Ajit is holding her hand; why doesn't she take her hand away to indicate her hostility toward him? She admires Purnima for making a bold decision. But there is a vast difference between a city slicker and a country bumpkin. *We village girls are more traditional,* she thinks. *Suffering quietly is in our blood. Our mothers and their mothers believed the path of duty must take precedence over personal happiness.*

Jasmine looks at her daughters and pledges not to bring them up as weak as she sees herself. They must make their independent choices, be strong, and not suffer quietly.

After staying in London for a couple of days, they fly to India. When the plane lands, she begins to feel her father's absence. Her heart jumps when the taxi makes the turn to enter her village, but she is worried, thinking her brother might still hold a grudge against Ajit and insult him. But to her relief, Ajit explains that he wants to stay with Professor Lal. He is too embarrassed to face her family members yet, and prefers to meet them only on the last day of their visit. Komil and Sohil are too busy watching the cows and frolicking dogs to notice when the taxi drops their father at Professor Lal's residence. Jasmine looks forward to being with her family without Ajit.

At Jasmine's home, Sohil and Komil run around freely in the spacious courtyard. They hug everyone as if they had known them forever. Their cousins and many other children play with them. The village people are fascinated to hear Sohil and Komil speak English, but they are also still able to converse in Punjabi. All day long, Jasmine hugs relatives and villagers as they come to greet her. Her favorite dishes have been prepared and the aroma tickles her senses.

Every time she wants to go and meet Simran, someone else drops by. "Let us go to meet Simran," Jasmine finally says. "I can no longer wait."

"She has gone to the hospital for treatment," Bijibee says, telling the story she had ready to offer. "She will be back home tomorrow." Bibijee wants to see her daughter enjoy at least one happy day, as she delays the sad news for as long as she can.

The next evening they go to Simran's house, leaving the girls at home. Bibijee does not want them to witness their mother's grief when she learns the truth.

Upon their arrival, Simran's mother grabs Jasmine and clings to her, crying frantically. "She has left us! She will never come back, Jasmine, she will never come back." Hearing this, Jasmine stands like a statue, unable to hear or feel. They make her sit on the cot, holding her hands. They are crying but Jasmine can only stare blankly. There is a song playing on a neighbor's radio: *"dil ko itne gum mila Ke ub koi be gum nahi…"* ("My heart has endured so much grief that it has become oblivious and no longer feels pain.") Jasmine sits motionless; only her shoulders are trembling.

The women describe the whole tragedy to Jasmine to help her feel the pain. "No villager noticed my daughter jumping into the pond that day," wails Simran's mother. Jasmine's dry but loud screams shake the walls of Simran's house. But the walls of the social system that Simran had described in her poem still stand unshaken. Finally the tears come; Jasmine starts to weep, her sobs reflecting the helplessness of young hearts that become victims like Simran.

"She received your letter a day before her death," Simran's mother tells her.

"Why? Oh Simran…Simran! Why you?" Jasmine's head is shaking back and forth so hard that her hair becomes loose and flies into her wet face where it sticks. The women hold Jasmine tightly for fear she might injure herself. After a while they take her home. She has lost all her appetite but is persuaded to eat a bite and stay strong for the sake of her daughters.

Jasmine is still too sad only a few days later to attend Professor Lal's wedding, but Bibijee convinces her to do so. "Life goes on," she tells her. "One can't stop living. I know it's hard, but for Ajit's sake you must try."

Bibijee goes to see Ajit at Professor Lal's house to persuade him to stay for the rest of the time in her house. She also reminds him that Komil and Sohil will be turning three years old in a few days. To Jasmine's surprise, Ajit brings birthday cakes and toys for the girls. They celebrate their birthday with just the family; no big crowd as last time.

Ajit is pleased to see how much his daughters enjoy life here. All day long they chase the chicks, play hide and seek, and pat the animals. At night, they count the stars.

Jasmine is concerned about taking them away, once again, from this expansive and affectionate environment. But what cannot be cured must be endured. She has thought of a couple of ideas to make their life better. She thinks of buying a house with a courtyard and applying for her mother's immigration.

Jasmine's brother has sold part of his land and opened a honey business in New Delhi. Now he has come to fetch his family, but Bibijee, and his grandmother and two aunts living here will stay in the village. Jasmine would love to have her mother live with them in the States, but when Jasmine suggests the idea, Bijibee weeps. "But how can I leave this house, which is part of my blood and bones?" She wipes her eyes with one end of her *dupatta*.

"Bibijee, home is where your loved ones live. When everyone leaves, these walls will eat you alive. Home is where memories reside forever; people come and go."

"But what would I do in America? I hear that they don't even have flies that I can keep busy swatting." Everyone laughs.

"Here, you miss your granddaughters, but you will play with them there and you will watch television. There is a *Gurudwara* [Sikh temple] in New York, and one in Washington, D.C." Jasmine tries to entice her.

"No way," Jasmine's grandmother interjects. "Your mother is going nowhere as long as I am alive." Jasmine can't help but smile a little when the old woman stomps her foot and crosses her arms across her chest, looking like Komil when she is being a stubborn toddler.

Just then, the postman comes by on a bike, ringing his bell constantly, and the kids follow him through every alley. Today he delivers Dilbeer's letter from Toronto, Canada. She writes:

> *Dear Bibijee, Jasmine didi,*
>
> *Today I am missing you very much because I know today all of you must be sitting under the pipal tree, having a lot of fun. Komil and Sohil must be thrilled to run around in the courtyard. I can imagine you all sitting in the shade and all the relatives and neighbors visiting you, and everyone sipping tea. Alas! If only I had a magic carpet to fly over the ocean.*

*Anyway, do not feel too sad for me, I am very happy
here. My in-laws are so nice. They treat me as if I were
their daughter. I am glad to be able to assure you that
Raj is a wonderful person. His sisters are a bit spoiled
but they are all right with me. Some days they go to
parties without permission and come home very late
at night. My father-in-law creates a big scene, scolding
them, as they are not supposed to go out at night. I feel
sorry for all of them. Indian parents, still dwelling in
their inherited culture, deplore the exposure to western
culture. And the poor children living in two cultures are
so torn and confused.*

*I will write you more in my next letter. Now it is
time for me to help my mother-in-law make dinner.
Jasmine didi, please promise to visit me in Toronto as
soon as you come back.*

*With lots of love and hugs,*

*Dilbeer*

"Thanks a million, God, for my daughter's happy
marriage." Bibijee wipes away tears of joy.

Simran's sister tells Jasmine that their family built a small
memorial on Simran's cremation ground. Before leaving for
America, Jasmine goes there and lights a *diya* (candle) filled
with *ghee* (clarified butter). She prays for a while and leaves
a bouquet of yellow roses, Simran's favorite. A song which
Simran often used to sing echoes in Jasmine's heart: *"Ye
jindagi usi Ke hai Jo kisi ka ho gaya, pyar he men kho gaya..."*
("One who merges soul and body in love, lives forever.")

The next morning, once again, Jasmine waves good-bye.
Once again she is hiding her tears behind her smile. The only

difference from the last time is that the girls are screaming to stay back and Simran is gone forever.

Sitting in the taxi, she looks at Ajit and is surprised to see tears in his eyes. A painful squint on his face remains during the car ride. Ajit is disappointed at not finding a clue about his mother's whereabouts. Jasmine prays for some miracle to happen to make his mother appear from somewhere soon. She is afraid he might slip into depression and lose his job again. She is petrified even to think of repeating the last two years of her life. Bibijee has advised her to show more care. She also suggested that Jasmine try to encourage Ajit to talk more.

When they get settled in the plane, Jasmine asks him about his stay with Professor Lal. "We took a tour of the college. I was pleasantly surprised to see lots of changes that have taken place. There are additional classrooms and they remodeled the canteen. Postgraduate degrees are now being offered, too."

"Yes, I know. Simran was the first postgraduate student in the college," Jasmine says. Hearing no response from Ajit, Jasmine feels dejected. She still hopes to hear some words of condolence from him. She has lost her best friend and Ajit hasn't shown any sympathy other than saying he was sorry to hear the sad news. Rather than coaxing him to continue talking, she shuts her eyes, suddenly hating her life with him. *I have never known such an unemotional and uncaring person.*

Ajit closes his eyes too and replays in his mind the conversation with Professor Lal, when he opened his heart and told him the complete saga with Susan. "Poor Jasmine," he had lamented. "She is willing to overlook every fault of mine. Sometimes I think she is an angel and I am taking advantage of her."

"You know," Professor Lal had said, "A classmate fell in love with her and pleaded to marry her after hearing about your divorce papers. But she rejected his proposal for the sake of her daughters."

"This solves the problem then," Ajit had told his friend. "Why not persuade Jasmine to marry him?"

"Why? You want to be free again to love someone else?"

"Oh, no, never," Ajit had said. "I have become useless. I have no desire left in me. I will make Jasmine's life miserable."

"Well, you get yourself treated," Professor Lal had suggested. "I will take you to an *Ayer Vedic Hakim* whose treatment never fails. If you really care for your wife's happiness, then get your act together and give her the life she deserves."

Returning to the present, Ajit reaches for Jasmine's hand. She opens her eyes. "One day we will definitely find your mother," she says.

# 13

# The Art of Living

A charming stone-front Cape Cod sits majestically on a cul-de-sac of Valley Road in Swarthmore, Pennsylvania. The lawn is dotted with mature cultivated shrubs, and weeping willows stand humbly near a creek that cuts through the grassy acre lot. On one side there is a magnolia tree bursting with huge white flowers. Early June creates such magic on the winter-beaten ground. Bright yellow forsythias, daffodils, fiery red tulips and, of course, the pink and white dogwoods accentuate almost every lawn in the neighborhood.

Jasmine has invited some friends to celebrate the twins' sixth birthday. She and Ajit moved to this house only two months ago, and it is still basically empty. The previous owners sold them cherry-wood Duncan Phyfe dining room furniture and the outdoor patio chairs, so they at least have enough chairs to seat the guests. On the dining room table, Jasmine has spread a tablecloth that Bibijee cross-stitched years ago, white with little red flowers. Two small cakes, red party plates, and birthday hats decorate the table, and a few balloons hang unevenly from the chandelier. A large jug full of red fruit punch rounds out the scene.

These friends are a mix of Gujarati, Punjabi, Bengali, and South Indians, and are curious to tour the new house. Their desire to become homeowners themselves is awakened as they see their friends doing well. Their ambitions to complete their education, obtain professional jobs, and own a house are reinforced. On the way back, one of their friends comments on the house. "The outside is beautiful, but inside, the rooms are so small," she says. "I would rather have a bigger house than so much land outside."

"I love their expansive lawn," the husband counters. "Look how much potential it has! They can grow their own vegetables, and have a pool and a basketball court." And they argue on and on. Another friend, sitting in the back, joins in. "This is quite an expensive area," he notes. "I wonder how they saved so much money in just a few years of his professorship?"

Every evening, Ajit and Jasmine go shopping for furniture and other household items. Almost every time they come back empty-handed. Ajit is intent on buying only what he likes; any item Jasmine suggests fails to meet his standards. Still, he includes her in the final decision, even though most of the time she concedes to his choice. Finally they end up purchasing maple bunk beds, a toy chest, and a beautiful armoire for the girls' bedroom. For their room they get a double bed, a desk, and a chair from an estate sale in the neighborhood. They practically furnish their whole house from such sales.

"If Bibijee came to know that we furnished our house with second-hand items, she would have a fit," Jasmine says.

"We are living in America," he says. "Here, it does not affect one's status to use second-hand things. This is the most admirable quality of Americans! They are not so concerned with rigid traditions, and they believe in the dignity of labor and human equality."

Jasmine notices that some American neighbors are very friendly. Others are less so—she overhears hushed fears that the value of the property will go down if Indians start to move in.

Today is the first day of school. Sohil and Komil are dressed in pink frocks and their hair ponytails are tied with ribbons. Jasmine, as always, uses different-colored ribbons to help others tell them apart, and adds a beauty mark to Sohil's cheek for good measure. The kindergarten is just three blocks away from their house. Jasmine is pleased to see how gracious the teacher is. She greets them at the door and makes them feel very comfortable. Jasmine comes back home after leaving the girls at school, feeling relieved. This school indeed is much better than the one they attended in the city.

With the girls off to school, she sits down with a cup of tea and her mind drifts to thoughts of Simran. Her dear friend's passing away has etched a deep wound on her heart. She misses Simran's letters of philosophical wisdom. So many times, those letters pulled her out of a tumultuous state of mind. She wishes she could write a letter to her, a letter to post in the mail and then eagerly anticipate a reply from her friend, as she had done so many times.

Jasmine gets a piece of stationary and writes down her thoughts:

*Some say time is a great healing factor, but to me, time is a great deceiver. It hides the future so skillfully that we come to know it only after the fact. This morning, this evening, and this night – all are controlled by time. We cannot visualize time as it comes and goes; we can only sense it from the folds of our parents' wrinkles, or the toothless smiles of our toddlers. Time does help us in one sense; it allows us to build a wall to hide ourselves behind. We swim on the surface of the tides and hope to move on with our lives with stability. Simran's whispers in my heart always console and remind me that people die only for those who do not remember them. She lives in my heart forever.*

Having returned from India, Jasmine has buried herself in studies and in looking after her nest. Now, Bibijee has taken Simran's place with soothing letters of her own. She tells her daughter to fight against all odds for the sake of a good life, which is God's blessing. *"One cannot change the wind, one can only change the sails;"* she treasures this quote from one of Bibijee's letters. It helps bring her out of her whirlpool of sorrow.

Bibjee's encouraging words motivate her to such an extent that she completes her Master's degree in Library Science. Ajit has become extremely busy; his college is very demanding. He must publish work regularly in order to secure his tenure.

A few years pass by in a flicker of the eye. Purnima has returned to her husband. She tells Jasmine that he has stopped drinking and has started to behave normally. After one full year, he recovered and begged her to come back. Purnima did, and is now working in the local library as an assistant librarian. Although Purnima still lives in the city, she and Jasmine manage to meet regularly, resuming their friendship.

Jasmine is looking for a part-time job, as she does not want to work full time until her mother comes to live with them. Although she has a Master's degree, she hasn't been able to find a position in her field. Purnima advises her to get her foot in the door in any capacity. "The only way we foreigners can get a position and promote ourselves is by showing our capabilities and ingenuity," Purnima explains. "I accepted an assistant's position just to get in. Once they gauge my ability to do excellent work, they will recognize my degree and promote me."

After quite a few interviews, Jasmine accepts a part-time position in the newly opened Vocational Rehabilitation and Employment Services under the umbrella of the Department of Veterans Administration in North Philadelphia. Every morning after leaving the girls at school, Ajit drops Jasmine off at the trolley station that takes her to 69th Street. From there she takes another train to reach Front Street. Her division consists of one director, one manager, one assistant manager, a couple of research assistants, and eight records clerks.

For the first two weeks on the job, she feels out of place. She notices other employees staring at her when she walks by, and she hears their whispers and chuckles. She is sure they are making fun of her. The atmosphere makes her nervous and timid.

Their work desk arrangement is in an open area, with only three cubicles for the management. Each records clerk has a Rolodex to maintain client updates. Every Monday morning, the clerks hand their Rolodexes to Jasmine. She compiles the data into different categories, makes calculations, and submits the statistical report to the records manager and to the director.

The director is an older man with a very professorial demeanor, and he is a kind, gentle, and amiable boss. Jasmine reports directly to him. He gives her the assignments and while she explains the research report to him, most of the time he dozes off. Slowly his head goes down, down, down, and then with a sudden motion he raises his head, saying, "Now tell me what percentage of Hispanics we have." Jasmine repeats the numbers to him again and again. Every morning when he comes in, she greets him, "Good morning, Mr. Twinkle," and he always answers, "My name is John Teewinkle, not Twinkle." He never tells her to address him by his first name. It takes Jasmine several weeks to remember to pronounce his name correctly

One employee from a different division comes every morning to greet all the female clerks with a bold kiss on their cheeks. On the first day when he comes near Jasmine, she covers her face with both hands and says, "No kiss for me please, just say hello to me." And now when he comes near her, he always says, "Stay away from this Indian gal, Bob, stay away."

She tells Purnima about the odd behavior of the other employees towards her. Purnima wonders whether they sneer at the way Jasmine dresses. "Perhaps your clothes are out of style," Purnima says. "I'll come this weekend to examine your wardrobe."

Purnima is hysterical when she sees Jasmine in her western dress. "Oh my God! This dress is way too long for you. No wonder they laugh at you. And this one is almost see-through; you need to wear a slip under it. And you don't wear stockings?" They both laugh their heads off. Then they go shopping for new office clothes for Jasmine. She absolutely rejects Purnima's suggestion to purchase a mini dress, and also refuses her friend's urging to get her hair cut. After shopping, they go to a restaurant for lunch.

"Why don't you cut your hair?" Purnima asks Jasmine.

"I'm a Sikh girl, and keeping one's hair uncut is one of the five symbols of Sikhism," Jasmine explains.

"How come Ajit is clean-shaven?" Purnima asks. "Isn't he a Sikh?"

"Yes, he is. But he is not as traditional as I am. Moreover, many Sikhs living abroad feel strongly they should not look noticeably different. You know, it's already a challenge for a foreigner to find a job here; can you imagine a turbaned Sikh going in for an interview? It is hard enough to be accepted in the corporate world."

"But your haircut can enhance your personality, making it easier for you to mingle with co-workers, I think," Purnima suggests.

"Maybe it will. Ajit continues to tell me the same, too. But my grandmother will become very upset if I do."

"Anyway, you could look a bit more westernized by leaving your hair open, not braided like this," Purnima says, pointing at Jasmine's hair. "And you have to show your friendliness and be bold enough to communicate with them. Once they come to know you, they will accept you. Trust me."

Jasmine takes Purnima's advice seriously and only a month of extra effort on her part pays off. Now the office girls include her in their lunch breaks. Once a week they go to a restaurant where they eat fried chicken, candied sweet potatoes and collard greens. Jasmine loves this food, especially the collard greens. When Jasmine asks her friendliest co-worker, Diane, how to prepare collard greens, she tells her to cook the greens in water with a "fat bag." Jasmine doesn't understand what a fat bag is. The next day, Diane brings a fat bag wrapped in freezer paper for Jasmine, who is horrified to see the fatty pork bone inside. On Ajit's advice, she says nothing to Diane about it, but never again does she touch the portion of collard greens on her lunch plate.

In time, Jasmine completes her six months of temporary work. Mr. Tewinkle likes her job performance more than enough to open up a new full-time research assistant position. Jasmine accepts the full-time position only after talking to her mother, who has moved to Toronto. It had been easier for her sister to sponsor Bibijee to immigrate to Canada than for Jasmine to bring her into the States. Now Jasmine wants her mother to live with them to look after the girls. Her full time work starts in December, but they don't want to drive north during the winter. For now they will manage with a part-time babysitter. Ajit picks up the girls from their school in the afternoon, and a babysitter watches them until Jasmine comes back from her office.

The winter passes quickly, and they decide it's time to go to Toronto and bring back Bibijee. Very early on a chilly spring morning, they pick up the sleeping girls and their fluffy blankets and gently lay them down in the back seat of the car. The crescent moon still dangles in the misty sky. As they approach a lake, the fog becomes as thick as clouds, showing only the silhouettes of the faraway trees.

"We should have started our trip later in the morning," Jasmine whispers.

"Shut up, this isn't the time to lecture me," Ajit snaps. Jasmine shuts her eyes and her mouth, wondering how one sentence can hit Ajit like a lecture. Luckily, the twins aren't disturbed by his loud voice, but she is; she hates her life with Ajit. They drive the Pennsylvania Turnpike in complete silence.

After a while she opens her eyes to the breathtaking scene of the Pennsylvania Mountains. The enchanting shades of green dotted with white patches of snow, and the multi-colors of budding trees and flowers melt away all her hostility. "Look! Isn't the sunrise gorgeous?" She tries to break the ice, but Ajit says nothing. Silence prevails throughout the highways of New York. They have been on the road for almost five hours when Sohil and Komil wake up, and they make a stop at the service area for breakfast. She confronts him in the restaurant. "What's wrong with you? Why aren't you talking?"

"I may not get my tenure," Ajit reveals. "I needed to complete my article, but you kept on pushing me into making this trip."

"Why didn't you tell me?" Jasmine says. "We could have postponed the trip."

"You were so excited about it, so I decided not to dampen your mood. Anyway, let's not worry about it. I hope my previous articles will be sufficient to impress the committee."

Jasmine is weary of his mood swings. One minute he is angry and the next he is fine. The rest of the drive he is cheerful, singing and talking to the girls.

They stop for the night near Niagara Falls to stay with their friends who had recently moved there from Philadelphia. The next day, after enjoying the spectacular view of Niagara Falls from the Canadian side, they reach the beautiful city of Toronto. A fairly large community of Indians, with Indian shops, restaurants, and temples, creates a friendly Punjab-like neighborhood. Jasmine hates to break Bibijee away from her new friends, but Bibijee insists on lending her a helping hand in her time of need.

Komil and Sohil are overjoyed to have their *naani* sitting between them in the car on their way back to Swarthmore. Bibijee packed an Indian lunch, which they enjoyed on a picnic table at the end space of a gas station. The rest of the way, Komil and Sohil sleep comfortably with their heads on *Naani's* lap.

The next day their new life routine starts, enhanced by Bibijee's presence. Jasmine leaves home at seven every morning and comes back at six-thirty in the evening. Bibijee prepares dinner, feeds the girls, and assists them with their homework. At times when they do not listen to her, she scolds them in Punjabi, making an angry face, and Sohil whispers to Komil, "*Naani* is mad."

One evening, Bibijee tells Jasmine that Sohil and Komil keep on calling her "mad." "Do I look crazy to them?" she asks, confused.

"Ah, no, ma," Jasmine says, laughing. "Mad means 'angry,' not 'crazy,' in America."

Ever since Bibijee arrived, Ajit is hardly around. He spends his time working in the garden or at the library, reading Indian newspapers and working on his publications. After eating his dinner, he goes up to their bedroom to watch the news. When Jasmine finishes the kitchen cleanup, the girls' bath, and lunch preparations, she sits with Bibjee a little. Sometimes they go out for a walk or watch television before reciting religious hymns to put the twins to sleep.

When Jasmine retires, Ajit is usually still watching television or listening to Indian music. Jasmine joins him for a while and then goes to sleep. They do not communicate much, and when they do, it is always about work or their daughters. Although they sleep in one bed, they stay in their separate worlds. She doesn't want to disturb him, thinking he is tired. She thinks maybe he doesn't love her. Similarly, Ajit doesn't want to bother her, thinking she can never forgive him and does not love him; otherwise, she wouldn't be so distant and cold.

Jasmine yearns for someone to hug her so tightly that it stops her breath. But who? She can't see his face. She imagines a faceless silhouette; perhaps she feels too guilty to picture someone other than her husband. No one can see their inner turmoil, not even Bibijee, who lives under the same roof.

Life goes on revolving around their family and jobs. She puts every ounce of her energy into her long workdays. At home, Bibijee looks after the girls, and when Jasmine comes home, dinner is ready. With no stress of household chores, she can concentrate on her job and always gets outstanding job performance reports. While other employees fritter away their time reading romantic novels or gossiping, Jasmine continues to work on her statistical reports. After six months, her full-time employment becomes permanent.

By 1975, many Indians have settled in the tri-state area suburbs. Some of them are newly married and some have toddlers. In addition to their original Gujarati group of about ten families, there are now Punjabi Sikhs, Hindus, and South Indians. As they increase in numbers, they start to separate into their own communities. Ajit and Jasmine always mingle with all of them. They have dinner invitations almost every weekend and once a month they entertain friends themselves. Their life is wonderful on the surface. But like two covered pots, no one knows what is simmering inside.

Interestingly, each social group has unique traits which weren't apparent to Jasmine when she lived in India. Gujarati parties are full of pure, simple fun. They prepare wonderful, traditional dishes, adding a little sugar to almost all of them; rice and *daal* is the last item before dessert. They play *antekashri,* a game where one person sings a verse from a movie song, and the next in line has to sing a song starting with the ending letter of the previous one. On the other hand, Punjabi Sikhs and Hindus prepare elaborate meals including meat, and they serve liquor. While the men discuss politics, the women share recipes, crack jokes, and talk about their children. South Indians are expert in delectable vegetable preparations with plenty of hot pepper and coconut. Jasmine and Ajit enjoy all these variations, but Bibijee has a hard time getting used to unfamiliar tastes. She usually eats her Punjabi dinner at home before going to parties. Sohil and Komil are more interested in playing with their new friends than in eating the food.

Although Ajit enjoys himself when they are socializing, when he is home he never just relaxes with his family. Like a workaholic, he always finds something to be done either inside the house or outside. Perhaps this is his excuse to avoid confrontations with Jasmine, or maybe it is occupational therapy for his vacillating mind. One night, Ajit screams in his sleep, "Mama, Mama, don't leave me! No, please! Please don't go…"

"Ajit, wake up! You are having a nightmare." Jasmine shakes him.

He wakes up and starts crying like a little child, hugging Jasmine. Jasmine melts, kisses his forehead, and hugs him to soothe his tortured soul.

"I must find my mother," he says. And he goes back to sleep.

# 14

# Thanksgiving—Indian Style

A few days after a fierce blizzard in February, Jasmine stands waiting for the train home from her office in the evening. The wind blows the snow in all directions. The platform is slippery from the freezing temperature. The train is late, and everybody is moving around to keep from freezing. Jasmine's feet are numb, and she can hardly move them. After twenty minutes, the train finally arrives and Jasmine manages to drag herself to a vacant seat. The rhythmic clacking and warmth of the heated train lull her to sleep. In her dream, some girls come to her, giggling, and take her to a massage table. They start giving her a hot oil massage.

"Where am I?" she asks them.

"You are in Paris." And they start giggling again.

After the comforting massage, they take her to a small square pool filled with fragrant water. The warm water relaxes her mind and body. For a moment she feels as if she were sleeping on the rooftop back home, soothed by a cool breeze filled with a jasmine fragrance. The pool is layered with red and pink rose petals. After the bath, the girls prepare her for the evening ball with the prince of Versailles. Jasmine looks like a fairy princess in her evening dress. Her hair is braided and a red rose is tucked in one side. The brocade pleats of the gown shimmer as she moves; her blouse is of golden silk, embossed with red rubies. The diamond and ruby necklace augments the beauty of her long neck. The horse carriage comes and off she goes for the grand ball in the Palace of Versailles. She has never seen anything like this before. The magnificent palace gleams with chandeliers. Far away, at the other end of the ballroom, she sees someone familiar who waves and starts walking toward her.

"Simran, is it really you?" Jasmine exclaims. "What are you doing here? Oh, you are alive!" She touches her face and her arms and clings to her.

"I live here," she says. "To those who witnessed my cremation, I am dead. For you, I will never die."

Suddenly Jasmine wakes up to find herself sitting alone in the train. Apparently, the train made its last stop, dropped the passengers off, and parked in the parking tracks while she slept. Jasmine quickly gets up from her seat and panics to find the locked door. She runs in all directions to find an open door, but all doors are shut and there isn't even a conductor on the train. She looks outside and notices other parked trains and starts to scream as loudly as possible, "Help, help!" Although no one can hear her, she continues until the train starts to move. The train stops at the first station and as soon as the door opens, Jasmine jumps out, recognizing her own stop. As she walks to take the trolley, her legs are still unsteady from the awful scare.

When Ajit picks her up from the trolley stop, she decides not to tell him. But at the dinner table, she tries to make everyone laugh by telling this story. Bibijee and Ajit are not at all amused.

Bibijee swings her hands in the air and brings them back to hold her head, expressing deep concern. "What if the train were parked for the whole night? No one would have known your whereabouts."

Ajit nods sternly. "Make sure you always stay awake on the train."

"I can't guarantee that because I'm dead-tired by evening," she protests. "Maybe I should start taking the suburban train. Since Swarthmore isn't the last stop, I could never end up in the parking lot. But the train costs more than the trolley."

"It doesn't matter—we both work and we can afford it." After that day, Ajit drops her off at the Swarthmore train station.

In her office, new regulations and a new statistical reporting system have been presented to Mr. Tewinkle and the records manager. The next day, Jasmine overhears a conversation between the records manager and the assistant manager, Bill.

"I think they will fire him this time—you wouldn't believe it, but he slept eighty-percent of the presentation time," says the record manager. "This time the executive director noticed it and asked me if he snoozed in his office, too."

"Intelligent man, but he suffers from a chronic siesta problem," Bill says. "I feel sorry for him."

Jasmine knows they are talking about Mr. Tewinkle. She likes him a lot; he always admires her work and gives outstanding performance evaluations. She is praying for him to continue working.

"What if a new director doesn't like me?" She expresses her concern to Purnima.

"One thing about American employers is that their preference is based on work performance, nothing else," Purnima assures her. "As long as you meet their expectations, you have nothing to worry about, trust me."

After a few weeks, a consulting firm is engaged to analyze the staffing and job duties in all departments. As the consultants conduct their analysis, nervous tension builds up among the employees and there is daily gossip about who will be let go. Jasmine is also worried. As she feared, the team proposes the elimination of Mr. Tewinkle's position, and recommends the agency combine his position with the records manager's to create a new position—Client Records and Research Development (CRRD) Manager. Mr. Tewinkle is furloughed. The records manager is promoted to the newly created position and Bill becomes the records supervisor.

Now Jasmine sits in the cubicle vacated by Bill and reports to the CRRD Manager, Miss McConnell, who is much more demanding than Mr. Tewinkle. A heavyset woman with a headmistress-like style, she is ready to jump on anyone who doesn't meet her standards. She has increased Jasmine's work to include part of her own duties. These days, Jasmine has to write the descriptive attachment with the statistical report and a cover letter—Mr. Tewinkle used to do all of the writing on his own.

Jasmine continues to fulfill her assignments dutifully. Meanwhile, the pressure the CRRD Manager puts on Bill does not sit well with him at all. He starts to criticize his boss left and right, and constantly complains about the unfair treatment and impossible workload being piled upon him.

One day he explodes. "Don't you see she is taking advantage of us?" he says. "I'm going to look for another job. This is no less than slavery."

Miss McConnell is aware of his disenchantment and increasingly sour attitude, but there are no unsatisfactory evaluations or warnings in his personnel file; therefore, she is unable to fire him for several months. He starts to take whole days off at a time to job-hunt, and eventually she is able to fire him and start to interview applicants for his position. Unable to find anyone suitable, she offers the position to Jasmine.

Jasmine does not feel she can handle the supervisory position. "No, no, I am sorry, I am not qualified," she blurts out. "I don't know how to supervise people."

"You have a degree, three years of job experience, and you have complete knowledge of our record-keeping system. I am certain you can handle it very well."

Jasmine reluctantly accepts the client records supervisory position. Strangely enough, to fill Jasmine's position, Miss McConnell hires another Indian woman, Krishna, who has a bachelor's degree in business. She is a smart, witty woman from Bombay. She accepts the job, but does not like it because she thinks she is overqualified. She brags about her high-class living in Bombay, and freely tells everyone that she needs to earn money to support her husband's higher education. Once he gets his degree, they will go back to Bombay, and there she will never have to work in an office or in the kitchen. She does not get along with anyone because, basically, no one likes her bragging all the time. She is, however, excellent at her job, quick to grasp, and quick to complete her assignments, which pleases Miss McConnell who ignores her haughtiness. Jasmine is weary of Krishna's arrogance, but also feels intimidated by her and is relieved that she is not her supervisor.

One afternoon at home, Ajit overhears the girls' conversation about their homework assignment. They are now in fourth grade.

"I want to become a teacher when I grow up," Komil tells Sohil.

"I want to become a nurse when I grow up," Sohil replies.

"Why not become a doctor, or a lawyer, or an engineer?" asks Ajit.

"Because all our friends want to become nurses or teachers," Komil replies.

This response has Ajit very much concerned, and he discusses it with Jasmine in the evening.

"They finish their homework in ten to fifteen minutes," Jasmine says. "In fourth grade, I remember sitting for hours to do my homework."

"We should transfer them to a private school, where the teachers can pay individual attention to motivate students to aim high."

They start looking into private schools and are shocked to discover how expensive they are. In addition, transportation is not available for most of them. Having no extra income, they decide to stay put for a while.

Seasons come and go and their weekdays pass quickly, following the same routine every day. Their entertainment involves meeting people from their home country and finding similarities that create a home-like environment. The Sikh families meet for a religious congregation once a month in someone's home, taking turns. They teach Punjabi to the children, engage them in singing hymns, and hold camps to teach them religion, language, and culture.

Everyone looks forward to celebrating various Indian festivals. For their Sikh friends, the most prominent ones are the birthdays and martyrdoms of their Gurus, and *baisakhi* (the harvest season and the birth of Sikhism). *Diwali,* or *deepawali* (the display of lights), is the most significant festival common to all Indians. For Hindus, this festival commemorates Lord Rama's return to his kingdom after completing his fourteen-year exile. Sikhs celebrate *diwali* as the happy occasion when their sixth Guru, Har Gobind, was freed from prison. The Mughal emperor, Jahangir, imprisoned him along with fifty kings for resisting the coercion to convert to Islam. It falls in late October or early November on the thirteenth day of the Hindu calendar.

It is now the month of October and everyone is scheduling *Diwali* parties. Their Gujarati friends are hosting a party in the International House. Jasmine has invited some friends over for dinner. Although she lights a few candles and prepares some Indian sweets, it does not feel the same as she remembers. Something is always missing, no matter how hard she tries to be authentic. She remembers the enthusiasm of *Diwali* celebrations back home where houses were freshly painted, the sweets were distributed, and the children were charmed by rows upon rows of *diya* lights on every rooftop of the village.

For Americans, the month of October ends with the Halloween festival for children, and the month of November brings a special holiday, Thanksgiving. This year, their Indian friends invite Jasmine's family to Thanksgiving dinner.

"Guess what, girls?" Jasmine asks.

"What, what, tell me, tell me," Komil says, excited.

"Sheila-aunty has invited us to Thanksgiving dinner."

"Oh, goody!" Sohil says. "I want to bring the wishbone to school! Lisa is bringing one."

"No, I want to bring one," says Komil.

"No, I said it first," Sohil rebuts.

"Wait a minute, girls," Jasmine interjects. "If you quarrel, we will not go." They stick out their tongues at each other and keep quiet for a while.

Last year, the American parents of their classmate, Lisa, invited the girls to Thanksgiving dinner. Komil and Sohil raved about the turkey and the stuffing for days. They wanted their mother to cook an American Thanksgiving feast this year, but now they are going to Sheila Aunty's house instead. Jasmine promises them she will bake the turkey at home next year.

"Mommy, you will tell Aunty to save the wishbone for me," Sohil says.

"Yes, I will tell her."

Sheila and her husband live on the same street, just a few houses down. They are both medical doctors who migrated from Hyderabad in 1959. Their six-year-old son is enrolled at an esteemed private school.

As the guests enter the house, they begin to cough and sneeze. Sheila, the hostess, had accidentally burned a big, red dry chili in hot oil, creating acrid smoke. The stinging aroma brings tears to their eyes. Sheila, embarrassed, directs the children to the basement and assures the adults that the smoke will clear soon. After a while, Sohil comes upstairs and whispers, "Mommy, is the turkey ready?"

"No, I'll call you when they take it out of the oven."

The dinner starts with *idli samber*, a South Indian specialty. There are a few American guests whose mouths are burning from pepper-sting. Their faces are red and they have watery eyes and runny noses. The children are impatient for the turkey; they are not hungry for anything else. After a while, the turkey is served. The children run upstairs to see it, but there is no big, brown, roasted bird sitting on the table.

"Where is the turkey?" Sohil makes a face.

"Oh, this big pot is full of curried turkey—it is my mother's recipe. You will love it! Come on children, eat, eat!" the hostess tells them with excitement.

The disappointed children look at their mothers while they fill their plates with rice and turkey curry.

"Mommy, I want a wishbone. I told Lisa I would bring one," Sohil whines.

"Shush. I will look for one in the pot if you eat your dinner," Jasmine says sternly, forcing her daughter to be polite and to eat.

Neither Jasmine nor Sohil know what a wishbone looks like. Lisa has explained that a wishbone is like the letter "v." Jasmine finds a somewhat similar bone, wraps it in a napkin, and brings it home. At least for now, Sohil is calm.

The next day, Lisa comes to play with Sohil and Komil. When Sohil shows her the bone, Lisa tells her, laughing, "No, this isn't a wishbone."

Sohil bursts into tears and runs to her bedroom. Komil and Lisa follow her. Feeling bad, Lisa takes them to her house and tries to give her wishbone to Sohil, which she refuses. They eat leftovers at Lisa's house and when they come home, Sohil tells her mother how delicious the turkey was with mashed potatoes and stuffing.

"I'm never, ever going to an Indian Thanksgiving again," Komil declares.

These days Sohil and Komil come home from school at four in the afternoon. Bibijee feels useless and lonely during the day. She tells Jasmine that even going out for a walk in America is so boring, not seeing a single person on the way around the block. She reminisces about her good old days back home and feels very homesick. Jasmine, sympathetic, stays home for a couple of days to find ways to keep Bibijee occupied. She buys yarn and knitting needles for her to knit sweaters, as Bibijee used to love to do. Jasmine, showing her how to work the TV, turns on the most popular soap opera, *General Hospital.* Bibijee covers her eyes with her hands whenever she sees romantic scenes, and complains, "Oh, no, these shameless people! I don't want to see this."

"Bibijee, this is how their culture is," Jasmine says. "There is nothing to be ashamed of. Remember they are just actors playing out a story. By watching this you will learn English while entertaining yourself." Sure enough, after watching this show for a few weeks, Bibijee gets hooked.

One day, the girls tell Jasmine that they are embarrassed by their names and they wish to change them.

"Oh, *meriya Rubba* [oh, my God]," Bibijee says, stunned, holding her head in both hands. "Now they want to change their names. Tomorrow they would like to change their religion. I think we should all go back to our country."

"Why don't you like your names?' Jasmine asks. "They are so nice, with beautiful and special meanings."

"Mommy, they tease me," Komil says. "They tell me I am a 'commie' from Russia. I tell them I am not Russian, I am American, and they don't believe me. Am I not American, Mommy?"

"Mommy, our teacher calls me Sohilla, and her, Camilla," Sohil says. "We like these names. You know, Mommy, our classmate, Harbir—the teacher calls him Herbert, and now everybody calls him Herbert. He likes to be called Herbert, because then no one teases him."

Jasmine is speechless. She doesn't know what to tell them. She thought she had picked these names carefully to be easy for them.

Ajit, overhearing the conversation, comes into the room. "You should tell them that we are Indians and proud of our heritage," he says to his daughters.

"When we tell them that we are Indians, they ask us where are the feathers," Sohil says.

"My goodness, these kids are fourth-graders!" Ajit exclaims. "They don't know which Indians wear feathers?"

"Yes, they know it," Kohil explains. "They just want to make fun of us."

"I think we should talk to your school principal about this," Ajit says angrily.

"No, Papa, we don't want you to talk to the principal," the girls say. "We will take care of it ourselves." As a matter of fact, they are embarrassed to have their different-looking parents appear at the school.

"I don't want to hear any problem with your names again," Ajit declares. "We are not changing your names."

The girls go to their room quite disappointed that night.

Ajit receives a letter from his friend, Professor Lal. He writes that an old carpenter from Ajit's ancestral village has told him something interesting: Ajit's father migrated to South Africa a long time ago. Surely, Professor Lal wrote, there is a good chance his father would know where Ajit's mother is living these days.

Ajit calls his brother in London, asking him to travel along with him to South Africa in the summer.

"We broke our connection with our father years ago and he never tried to find us," Rajiv tells him flatly. "I am not interested in ever seeing his face again in my life. You can go alone if you wish to."

"How can you say that he never tried to find us? Perhaps he tried but could not succeed. If this is the only way I can find out about Mama, I don't mind meeting him," Ajit says, to no avail.

In the evening, Ajit tells Jasmine that he plans to go to South Africa.

"I want to take the girls to India this summer. Bibijee is so homesick and pesters me to ask you if we can go, but I was reluctant to leave you alone here," Jasmine says.

"Well, why don't you all go to India while I'm in Africa?" suggests Ajit.

Jasmine runs downstairs to tell the exciting news to Bibijee, Sohil and Komil. The girls, overjoyed, jump up and down and Bibijee's eyes sparkle with anticipation.

Komil and Sohil talk excitedly to each other about the plan, and work on the best way to share this news with their friends at school. Komil says they will sound "exotic" and "important" because they are going to get to fly across the ocean to another continent. Sohil says they must not sound like they are bragging, but they can get their classmates to share their enthusiasm if they ask what they would like the girls to bring back for them. The girls feel this may be their only opportunity to turn "being different" to their advantage.

Bibijee actually feels more peaceful than exuberant. She gets out her stationary to write the news to her sister. Jasmine is happier for her mother and daughters than for herself, since returning this time will not mean reuniting with her mother, or with Simran.

# 15

# Summer of 1973

After the painful ordeal of customs clearance at Indira Gandhi International Airport, Jasmine, Sohil, Komil, and Bibijee enter the airport lounge where Amar is waiting eagerly to receive them. Everyone greets and hugs each other, and then hurry out to the car. As Amar's driver starts to drive away from the airport, they take in the brutal heat of June, compounded by the suffocating smell of the slums of Delhi. Sitting in the front seat, Amar tells them, "Just close your eyes and noses and bear with me through this hellish area; it will pass quickly. The highway is closed due to an accident and the traffic is detoured to this road."

Sohil and Komil laugh quietly when they see some naked children bathing on the roadside, sharing a bucket of water. The traffic is moving as slowly as ants. The air is filled with black soot which shows on Jasmine's tissue when she wipes her nose.

"This is our beloved India," Amar says with a sarcastic tone. "The rich are getting richer and the poor are getting poorer. This disparity is widening day by day and there seems to be no cure."

Beggars surround the car quickly whenever it stops and Amar warns the girls not to roll down the window to give them money. He tells them the beggars will flock around the car and bring it to a complete halt. As soon as they leave the slum area, they can sense the difference: people are taking their evening strolls; women are dressed in colorful *saris* or *salwar kameez;* the air is filled with their scents and friendliness. Amar's passengers watch the people as they stop and talk with one another, or chat with the vendors while buying vegetables. Cars honk their horns and rickshaw bells ring constantly. Stray cows and dogs wander in the middle of the road, oblivious to the crowds and commerce. These colorful, noisy scenes fascinate Sohil and Komil.

Amar's honey export business has made him wealthy and he lives in a secluded, gated community of millionaires. After the *chaukidar* (guard) opens the gate to their home, the car drives through the two-acre garden filled with exotic plants and shrubs sculptured into animal shapes. The girls are amazed and point and call out "elephant" and other shapes they recognize. Amar tells them that his garden was a showcase last year and won the first prize given by the horticultural society.

Unlike their last visit to their village, here, nobody comes rushing to meet them. Life in big cities is very different; no one sleeps on the rooftop and no one drops in just to chat with them. But the girls are excited to be with their cousins, and after dinner they play for a while before going upstairs to sleep in the large room of their cousin, Rina. Bibijee also retires soon after her dinner. Jasmine decides to read a novel in the guest bedroom downstairs.

"Madam *jee*, you want me to massage your feet *jee*?"

Jasmine is surprised to see a girl of approximately twelve or thirteen years standing in her room. She is holding a cup of hot milk. She has the sweet smile of an angel and her eyes are shining like greenish-blue sapphires. Her face looks like a full moon peeping through dark clouds.

"No, no, I don't need a massage; you must be tired after working all day in the kitchen."

"No *jee*, I never get tired *jee*. Every night, after finishing the kitchen chores, I massage my madam *jee*. She is suffering from some illness, poor madam *jee*."

"No, there is no need to massage my feet," Jasmine tells her politely.

"Good night, madam *jee*!" And she walks out of the room.

*Oh, what a shame...a sweet young girl is a victim of poverty in this country. She is beautiful and could be educated, but only knows herself as a servant.* Jasmine keeps thinking about her.

After some time, the girl comes in again and whispers, "Madam *jee*, can I sleep in your room *jee*? I am scared being alone. Tomorrow the other servant will come back from her town. Then I won't be alone."

"Okay, bring your folding cot in here, but I'll be reading for an hour or two. Will you be able to sleep in the light?"

"*Jee*, I always sleep in the light, I am afraid of the dark *jee*." Soon after, she returns with her cot.

"How old are you?" asks Jasmine.

"*Jee*, I don't know."

"What is your name?"

"*Jee*, I like to be called Magni but my name is Mangni. *Jee*, when I was in my mother's tummy, my grandmother said if my mother gave birth to a girl again, she would call her 'Mangni' so that someone would adopt her. You know, 'mangni' means take away. She was worried about my father being buried under the weight of four stones."

"Four stones, meaning four daughters?" Jasmine asks.

"*Jee*, but when I was a baby, my grandmother loved me so much. Then she started saying, "Now I don't want anyone to take you away, I love you now as much as a grandson.""

"Where is your grandmother now?"

"*Jee*, now she is up in the sky as a star. One day I was trying and trying to wake my *daadi* up, but she kept on sleeping; then my mother told me that my grandmother had become a star."

"Where do your parents live?"

"*Jee*, I don't know. When I was a little girl, my mother used to beat me, and one day madam jee saw her beating me. Madam *jee* snatched me from her and said, 'I'm never giving you this girl back unless you stop mistreating her.' My mother told her to take me, and I came here with madam *jee*."

"Your madam *jee* was in your village?" Jasmine is curious.

"She was attending her relative's wedding in our village. And now when I ask her which village, she doesn't tell me."

"Where are your sisters?"

"*Jee*, I don't know," says Magni.

"Did you go to school—I mean, did your madam send you to school?"

"No *jee,* poor madam is always sick; she taught me how to cook and clean the house. Now everyone says no one can make food as delicious as Magni makes."

After a few minutes of silence, Jasmine notices Magni is sound asleep, but her story lingers on in Jasmine's western-influenced mind and she is unable to sleep for a long time. In the morning she wakes up, hearing her sister-in-law's loud scolding, "Who told you to sleep in the guest room? Why did you disturb our guest?"

Magni brings a cup of tea for Jasmine just a few minutes later. Her face is wet with tears and she is wiping her nose with one end of her *dupatta.* Jasmine feels as if Magni's tears are mixed in the tea. *Alas! If only a family who would have treated her like their daughter had adopted her, she would have had the opportunity to grow and study just like other children.* Jasmine stares at the cup and at Magni's innocent face, feeling helpless.

Jasmine's niece is in seventh grade and her nephew is in ninth. They study in a high-ranking English school, St. Stephen's. Every evening a private tutor comes to teach science to them. In comparison, Rina's seventh grade standard is much higher than that of Sohil and Komil. The math tables, the oceans, the continents, and the American presidents, for example, are at Rina's fingertips. You give her math problems, she answers instantly, whereas Komil and Sohil struggle. Everyone notices the difference and Bibijee suggests to Jasmine, "Why don't you put the girls in St. Stephens? I will stay here with them."

"No, Bibijee, the girls are fine in America. Cramming tables on fingertips does not make a student better educated. Anyway, we will not have our daughters away from us."

Another interesting thing Jasmine notices is that her nephew and niece are, in some ways, more westernized than her own daughters. Whereas Indian parents living in America stress instilling Indian values, language, and religion into their children, parents in India put emphasis on speaking English and wearing western-style clothes. In educated families, especially in big cities, conversing in English is considered modern and trendy. Even her sister-in-law, living in Delhi, has advanced much faster than Jasmine in terms of fashion and sophistication. But, Sohil and Komil know Punjabi, the Sikh religion, and Indian festivals better than their cousins.

The family trip to the village is not as exciting as they had expected, especially to Sohil and Komil. They complain that everything appears dirty; they aren't used to primitive bathrooms and smells of domestic animals. They don't like the taste of buffalo milk, which they loved when they were little. Luckily, they enjoy eating the fresh fruits and vegetables grown right at the farm, and they love the fresh aroma of Punjabi cooking.

Jasmine, too, is sad to notice all her friends have gone to their in-laws, and familiar faces have grown old. Their house looks depressed without the hustle and bustle of people. Bibijee can't stop crying during her stay in the village. Every little thing reminds her of a story. *What a pity,* Jasmine thinks. *We dwell in memories, but we refuse to face the change wrapped in them. We want them to stay the same forever, but time has no such sympathy or desire.* She takes pictures of the well, the *pipal* tree, the rooftop, the painted wall, and anyone who will pose for a photograph.

In this hot and humid season, lizards, moths, and other insects come out in abundance, especially at nighttime around the lamps. This makes the girls uncomfortable. One day a snake slithers into their courtyard. The girls panic and cry, "We want to go back to our cousins' house in New Delhi right now." Bibijee and Jasmine, too, have been disappointed by the nuances of today's village life. Therefore, they decide to cut short their stay there.

Back in Delhi, Sohil and Komil love being with their cousins. At this age, they aren't interested in sightseeing or shopping. All they want is to swim, play, and dance at the community club near their cousins' home. They have been to the art museum, zoo, center of New Delhi, and, at Jasmine's insistence, several historical sites.

Six weeks of vacation ends too quickly, and they all depart from loved ones with tears in their eyes. As they travel the thousands of miles back to America, they all try to pull their spirits and thoughts away from the life they are leaving and toward the life, friendships, and duties they must step back into.

Driving back from the JFK International Airport, they all notice how quiet the American highways are. Coming from noisy India, it feels as if the cars are floating quietly in a calm river with a distant purring sound. No stray cows, dogs, horns, or rickshaw bells disturb the serene atmosphere.

"Ah, it is no fun here; there is nothing to entertain us on the way." Sohil makes comparative remarks.

It takes almost a month for Jasmine and Bibijee to adjust back to the lonesome environment. Their bodies get acclimated quickly, and they love the comforts of American living; however, their hearts refuse to return to reality. Images of moonlit nights on the rooftops, the sun rising behind the *pipal* tree, and the rooster's wake-up call, all float in their minds. Of course, Bibijee never comes out of her nostalgia.

Jasmine has become an expert at shoving hurtful memories behind the wall she built years ago.

And life goes on; they notice how fast life moves forward when compared to the slow pace of life back in India. Jasmine ponders how different life is there, in some ways easier, as Indians live a simple and uncomplicated life. Once a person gets a job, it becomes permanent, regardless of his or her job performance. When they get married, they have no fear of divorce; their children live in a safe and secure environment. Yet, the rational part of her knows these benefits would not outweigh the cost of missing out on her fortunate destiny to live and raise her girls in America. She may have mixed feelings, but she is confident in her choices for her daughters. She knows this is where opportunities are as available as berries on a wild tree in the summertime.

******

At half past ten, one windy evening in June, Ajit's plane lands at Johannesburg International Airport, in South Africa. He takes the airport shuttle to a nearby Sheraton Hotel to stay for the night. Tomorrow he will visit the Department of Indian Affairs, hoping to get their help in locating an Indian named Sanjiv Kumar. While drinking coffee the next morning in the hotel restaurant, his attention is drawn to a newspaper. To his surprise, he sees a rather lengthy article about Indians in South Africa. Two pages are filled with a list of Indian restaurants and shops in the city of Durban, which is approximately 300 miles from Johannesburg. A very large number of people of Indian origin live in the city of Durban, making it the largest "Indian" city outside India. He immediately takes a domestic flight to Durban and goes to a motel owned by an Indian. Luckily, the owner knows of a person named Sanjiv Kumar living in Melville, a nearby suburb. Early the next morning, Ajit knocks on his door.

"Is this Mr. Sanjiv Kumar's residence?" Ajit asks the man at the door.

"Yes, yes, I am Sanjiv Kumar; may I know your good name?" The man standing at the door looks old enough to be Ajit's grandfather. He has skillfully covered his balding head by combing hair over from the sides. He wears well-fitting western clothes and appears to be a sophisticated Indian gentleman.

"I am Ajit." Clearing his emotion-clogged throat, he continues, "Do you remember your two sons who spent their early life in a boarding school, away from you?" Although a little bit suspicious whether the old man is his father, he assumes he is.

"I'm sorry—you must be mistaken. I've only one son, and my son's name is Adesh. Please come inside."

"Aren't you from Shahpur?" Ajit asks.

"Yes, I am, but I am not your father. Perhaps there is another person with my name who belongs to my town. I migrated from India decades ago. My younger brother left India quite recently; he might know. He is coming here for dinner tonight."

"I will come back after dinner then." Ajit does not want to impose. Mrs. Kumar joins them, curious.

"Have you moved here?" asks the old man.

"No, I live in America, and I have come here to search for my parents. I am staying in a motel in Durban."

"No, no, you are our guest, you will stay with us," insists Mr. Kumar. "Ever since our son left for London, we feel lonesome. And you know you can't leave an Indian household without eating. After lunch, you must bring your luggage from the motel."

"You remind me of our son," Mrs. Kumar chimes in.

In the evening, Sanjiv's brother, Ankur, tells them he knew Ajit"s father. As far as he knows, his father has settled in Sydney, Australia.

"I am sorry to tell you that your mother passed away years ago," Ankur mentions casually.

Ajit has no courage to ask him which mother of his had died, his stepmother or his natural mother. At this point, he has lost his desire to seek out either his father or mother. He is so bitter with disappointment that all he wants is to go home as soon as possible.

After a while, Ankur says to Ajit, "My mother and your birth mother, actually, were distantly related, and they studied in the same school. Do you know what happened to your mother?"

"No, I don't, please do tell me."

"Your mother was the most beautiful woman in her town, Peelu, in Rajasthan State. Unfortunately, she fell in love with a neighborhood Muslim boy, so your grandfather quickly married her off to your father against her wishes. The Muslim boy left his studies in despair and could not recover from his loss. Finally, he joined the army. After many years, your mother happened to see him again, when he was on leave and she was visiting her parents. Their love affair was rekindled. Your father came to know about her love for this man and threw her out of the house."

"Why are you adding more grief on this poor man by telling all this?" Sanjiv says quietly to his brother.

"It is okay, uncle, I want to hear. I need to hear. Please do tell me."

"To make a long story short, your mother lost custody of her sons. She became a Muslim in order to marry the man she loved, and...." He pauses, reluctant to tell more.

"Please go on, I want to know the whole story."

"Let us eat our dinner first, it is getting cold," Sanjiv quickly interrupts.

After dinner, Ajit anxiously asks, "Do you know where my mother lives now?"

"I will tell you. First you tell me where you live and what you do," Ankur tries to stall the hurtful news.

"Well, I am a professor, and I live in the USA with my wife and two eleven-year-old twin daughters," Ajit says.

A servant brings them tea and dessert, and they sip tea quietly. For a moment, Ajit feels as if he were sitting in his parental home and Ankur's wife is his mother. He wants to hug her and cry on her shoulder. She also feels a sympathetic pull of motherly affection toward him.

"Eat your dessert *Beta* [son]," she says as she comes near him and rubs his shoulder affectionately. "Do you have any memories of the Partition of India? I guess you were too young in 1947."

Ankur interrupts to prevent further prolonging of the truth. "Well, she is trying to tell you that your mother and her Muslim husband were travelling on that ill-fated train to Pakistan in which no life was spared."

Ajit feels as if a sword had pierced his heart and all those anguished years of longing for his mother have come to a nerve-shattering end. His head rests on Mrs. Kumar's shoulder and he weeps like a child. The next day he cuts short his visit and returns to America.

# 16

# A Fork In The Road

Ever since Ajit has come back from South Africa, he has been melancholy. Rage keeps boiling inside him. He feels a grudge against humanity and its religions. He blames religion for his mother's suffering because the partition of India took her life and a million more. It was due to the intolerance of Hindu and Muslim religions and their refusal to live together in harmony and peace as one nation. He stops accompanying his family to their religious meetings and prohibits his daughters from attending Sikh camps. In his eyes, the religions of the world have been the source of pain and destruction. He is intolerant of the slightest disturbance at home, and snaps at the girls and Jasmine for no reason. He stays out of the house most of the time. To keep himself occupied, he paints the whole exterior of the house, grows a vegetable garden, and buries himself in writing.

At night, Ajit doesn't say a word to Jasmine. She is afraid to ask him anything for fear he will flare up. Bibijee starts praying (even more than usual) for his health and peace of mind. He does pay attention to his daughters' education and makes them study hard. One day he turns off the television in the middle of their show.

"They finished their homework and have just started to watch their favorite show. Why do you punish them when they are doing so well in school?" Jasmine says, cringing with bitterness, and calls the crying girls back to watch television.

"How dare you challenge my authority?" he shouts and pushes Jasmine into the wall. She shoves him right back with all her strength. The girls run upstairs again and Ajit walks out of the house, banging the door.

In less than an hour, he comes back and declares, "I'm sending the girls to the Bishop Cotton School in India. This country is not suitable for them to grow up in. The educational standard is too low! Western culture is too permissive! They can come back after high school graduation. It is best they experience Indian culture for now."

"They're going nowhere," Jasmine says. "Which culture are you talking about? Your culture, which you didn't even follow? Or, my culture? Which keeps on reminding me to sacrifice myself for the happiness of others. Or, Simran's culture? That pushed her to commit suicide!"

"Why do you keep pouring salt on my wounds? When are you going to let me live in peace?" Ajit shouts at the top of his lungs, cursing her with fury.

Jasmine goes to the girls' room, her heart thumping wildly; she closes and locks the door. He comes upstairs, furious, and tries to open the door. Bibijee comes out of her room and tells him to calm down.

"Bibijee, I want to send the girls to convent school in India and Jasmine is not listening to me." He goes into his bedroom.

Bibijee no longer wants Jasmine to be submissive. She tells her to stand her ground for the welfare of her daughters.

"Ma, he is in need of therapy again. He was calm for ten years, but the problem is, he doesn't think he needs to see his psychiatrist. I can't drag him; he must go on his own." And she goes to her bedroom.

At midnight, Komil gets up crying and Jasmine rushes to her room.

"Mommy, are you divorcing Papa?"

"No, no honey, what makes you think that?"

"But Papa was telling you to divorce him."

"Sandy's parents used to fight and now they are divorced." Sohil is up, crying, too.

Jasmine makes them sit on her lap and reassures them, saying, "Just as you and Komil get angry at each other, we do too, but that does not mean we don't love each other. Moreover, in our culture, the children take priority and divorce is taboo. Therefore, you should never worry about this." Ajit and Bibijee wake up and come into the room. Ajit hugs both girls and assures them that he loves them.

"Listen to me *beta*," Bibijee tells Ajit. "Empty promises go nowhere; you must visit your doctor and get treated."

Ajit pays no heed and goes back to bed.

At Jasmine's office, Krishna has left the job after two years. A computer science graduate is hired to fill the vacant position. He is a strikingly handsome man about Jasmine's age with penetrating eyes and an athletic physique. Jasmine's heart starts racing whenever she sees him. She tries to avoid him as much as possible.

One day when having lunch with Purnima, Jasmine tells her about this handsome new coworker. Purnima starts to tease her by singing, "*kia karoon hi kuch kuch hota hai,*" which means, "what should I do, something is happening to me."

"No, no, nothing of that sort. I just like the way he walks by my desk, and he winks with a killing smile. Why does he wink at me? You know how winking is considered back home. Is he giving me a signal or something? He appears to be a perfect gentleman."

"No, no, I think here it means nothing more than a friendly gesture. I have also noticed people saying hello with a wink," Purnima assures her.

Sometimes Jasmine thinks Purnima is another Simran. She feels very close to her and shares her intimate feelings. But she never mentions Ajit's past because she knows it would spread in their community like wildfire.

Sohil and Komil will turn thirteen this coming Saturday and Jasmine has invited all their friends to a birthday party. With a full-time job and no source of catered Indian dishes, the dinner party preparation starts a week early. Every evening, she cooks items that can be pre-prepared such as kebabs, pakoras, and sweet dishes. Bibijee grinds spices, marinates tandoori chicken, and cuts onions, vegetables, garlic, and ginger.

The morning of the party, Jasmine gets up early and works constantly in the kitchen. By three o'clock, she is finished, and the kitchen is cleaned up. Ajit and the girls decorate the basement with balloons and colorful tablecloths.

At the last minute, Komil will prepare punch, mixing ginger ale and raspberry sherbet. Although the invitation time is six o'clock, they don't expect the guests to come on time. They know from experience that American guests are always punctual; therefore, they were given the party time as one hour later than their Indian friends. Bibijee and Jasmine have sewn long evening dresses for the twins, made of pink shimmering chenille with gold fringes. Jasmine wears *salwar kameez,* also pink.

The party is in full swing. Everyone is admiring the colorful variety of appetizers. As always, the ladies gather in the kitchen to give moral support to the hostess who is busy adding the final touches to the dishes. They laugh and talk, admiring each other's outfits and jewelry. Some of them crack jokes and share their concerns about bringing up children in the western culture. The men discuss politics, while enjoying a variety of snacks. Ajit and other music lovers sing songs, while some recite poetry and a few tell jokes.

The party is over. Jasmine, Sohil, and Komil hug each other, pleased with its success. Everyone is tired and goes to bed. But Ajit's mind is perturbed by the thought of his daughters being in the vulnerable phase of teenage years in a country with so much social freedom. He thinks he must persuade Jasmine to agree to send the girls to India for study; he still thinks it's not too late.

Jasmine's mind is also noisy, and she tosses and turns, unable to fall asleep though she is exhausted from the full day. She thinks about how Indian couples give the impression that they are happily married and have no trouble at home at all; whereas, Americans are like an open book—they tell you about their bad marriages, divorces, and money problems, without embarrassment.

Early in the morning, Ajit tells Jasmine firmly, "We must send the girls to India."

She objects vehemently to the idea. "The girls aren't going to study in India. They are good girls and they will be fine. And that is my final decision."

"Who are you to make the final decision? I'm their father; I know what is best for them."

"Oh, really? Where were you when I was screaming with labor pains? Where were you when I took care of them all alone in this country? If we send them back for study only, they will belong to no country. Either we all go back to settle there, or we should accept living here."

"In a few years they will want to date. Will you be able to tolerate that? When they turn eighteen, they will want to live on their own, and get married to whomever they like," Ajit says with frustration.

"Not necessarily. If we give them the proper guidance, teach them about our culture, values, and our expectations, they will choose the right path. The key to their success lies in our providing them with a peaceful and secure environment. Also, I think you should see your doctor. He might want to increase your antidepressant dosage. This daily bickering is not good."

It is a miracle that they could discuss this burning issue in such a sensible manner, without screaming at each other. Bibijee tells Jasmine that she should start talking to the girls about Indian customs and values sooner, than later. The girls have witnessed all this commotion and are scared to do anything wrong. They are worried that if they don't live up to their father's expectations, he will send them back to India for schooling. On their own, they behave properly, study hard, and speak Punjabi at home. Occasionally, Jasmine reminds them about their wonderful Indian culture, the success of arranged marriages, and their ambition for the girls to become doctors or lawyers.

At every get-together, the women express their concerns about bringing up children in such a permissive society. Some ladies, coming from rich families, never get accustomed to America's hard-working life style. They miss their servants doing every chore for them. Some of them declare they will go back home before long, yet no one goes back. They live for years in various degrees of torment—nostalgic for their homeland, worried about their children, yet ultimately choosing to stay in America.

# 17

# In the Company of the Affluent

These days, Sohil and Komil ride the school bus to their senior high. They tell everyone in their new school that their names are Sohilla and Camilla. At home, no one is aware of this change because the girls always use their given names on their notebooks. They have learned how to fit in at school, but also please their parents by being outstanding students, and both declaring their aim to become doctors. Jasmine soon discovers that American high school is much different from what she thought. One day the girls tell her they want to attend their senior prom. Mystified about what this means, Jasmine calls Lisa's mother, Mary.

"The prom is a very important tradition in high school," Mary says. "Boys and girls get dressed up for a big dance with live music. The girls especially love the formal attire and try to look like movie stars. The only restriction I put on Lisa is not to attend a party after the event. They can get into trouble at these parties." Mary assures Jasmine that it is okay for their daughters to attend the prom because it is well-chaperoned.

Jasmine is still reluctant and Ajit definitely does not want them to attend. The concept of dating, of the free mingling of boys and girls, is strange to them because Indian culture never allowed them to do so. Every day, the girls come home from school with more news about who is going to the prom, what band will be playing, and who already has their dress. They beg their mother to allow them to go. They both have their mother's beautiful eyes and complexion; Jasmine remembers in her college days how boys were attracted to her beauty, but in the Indian culture she could easily ignore them, as that is what was expected. Here, such popularity means trouble for Sohil and Komil, who may encourage and want to date their admirers.

Boys in their class have already asked them for prom dates. The girls cry and tell their mother that they will be embarrassed to say no, and will be social outcasts. Jasmine brings it up with Ajit, who cuts her short, saying, "No. No. We are not discussing this again." Jasmine goes to Mary's house and tells her the problem. She has known Mary to be a concerned and strict parent who never misses going with her whole family to Mass at their Catholic church, so she finds it easy to share her concerns once in a while. Mary understands the girls' dilemma. She suggests to Jasmine that she allow the girls to go, and that they can go to the prom from her home, and sleep over with her daughter.

"They are definitely coming back straight from the dance. They are not allowed to attend any wild parties afterwards," Mary promises.

Feeling safe to send them under Mary's supervision, Jasmine agrees. She has decided in favor of the girls, but she is nervous doing so behind Ajit's back. First of all, it is unethical; and moreover, what if something bad happens and

Ajit has to be told? Normally, she consults her mother, but on this issue she decides she better keep it to herself. Most of her Indian friends' children are younger than her daughters, so taking her friends' advice into account would be useless. She passes a sleepless night, struggling with her conscience. In the morning, however, the pleading look on the girls' faces gives her resolve. She suddenly realizes that she and Ajit are solely responsible for their daughters' anguish. Why did they bring their daughters to America, if not to participate in American life?

"You can go, but don't tell your father. And you cannot tell your friends from our community. Moreover, do not start dating your prom boys afterwards. It is strictly for this one time, you understand," Jasmine warns them.

The girls are too happy to pay any attention to the restrictions their mother has just mentioned. They will think about those later. Right now, they think only about how they will accept their prom dates. In the evening, Jasmine and Mary take the three girls to purchase their prom dresses. After shopping, they take the dresses directly to Mary and Lisa's house.

The evening of the prom day, Sohil and Komil go to Lisa's house for a sleepover—at least, that is what they tell their father.

At the dinner table, Ajit expresses his concern to Jasmine, "Sleeping at a friend's house is not a smart idea. It may not be as innocent as we think. What if the girls decide to go to a club or a movie? American parents aren't as strict as we are. They let them go out unsupervised at night."

A morsel of food gets stuck in Jasmine's throat which is tight from her nervousness. She feels guilty for not telling him the truth and blurts out, "Actually they are…" She coughs, and then quickly she changes the sentence, saying, "You are right—in the future they can tell Lisa to sleep over here, instead." Although Jasmine handles the situation cleverly, she doesn't like deceiving Ajit. Her stomach trembles with fear and she is unable to eat. She passes the night praying for the girls' safety.

The next morning when Sohil and Komil come back, Ajit tells them not to repeat the sleeping-over business. They are relieved to find they have gotten away with their adventure, and are eager to agree with their father. Later on, the girls tell their mother the details of the prom and show her the Polaroid photographs from Lisa's mother. Jasmine gets an idea of how beautiful her daughters looked in their dresses, and admires the formally-dressed boys standing next to them. *Thank God all went well.*

The following Monday when Jasmine goes to work, she learns that her boss, Miss McConnell, is leaving her job to accept a promotion, and will move to Washington, DC. She tells Jasmine to apply for her vacant position and that she has recommended her name to the CEO. In spite of her recommendation, the CEO offers the position to Richard. She hears this is because he has a degree in Computer Science from Drexel University, and automation of the client records is part of their five-year strategic plan. Almost every one of Jasmine's staff coaxes her to file a discrimination lawsuit because she is more qualified than this recent graduate with no managerial experience. Jasmine doesn't think it is wise to start a legal issue, and continues to work diligently, as always.

Richard is the man whose walk by her desk gives her heart a pumped-up beat; whose one smile with a wink makes the moment stand still for the whole day. Whenever he is away for a day, she misses him terribly. When he looks toward her, she tries to keep her eyes away or down. It was easy for her to avoid him when he was not her boss. Now, they come in contact with each other throughout the day. Since she is more knowledgeable than he, due to her extensive experience, he includes her in the executive meetings.

One day Richard tells her that the plan to computerize the manual records is inevitable; therefore, he suggests she take some computer courses for her job security and future promotions.

"Also, you should know that I will be leaving this job to start law school in six months. I know you are qualified, but without computer training they will hire a computer expert over you. I feel you deserve the promotion and some computer courses will do magic." Richard tells her to take a few courses at Temple University and he will get the tuition reimbursed by the department.

She comes home and discusses this with Ajit, and tells him that she wants to stop working. "Are you out of your mind?" he asks. "What are you going to do sitting at home? How are we going to send two girls to college on one salary? I think you are getting a great chance to advance your career, don't muck it up."

That night she is unable to sleep. Ajit doesn't know that the real reason for her to quit her job is to stay away from Richard. She remembers when Simran used to tell her that she stayed awake all night suffering pangs of separation. Then, she was unable to comprehend it, but now those words make sense to her. They resonate with her restless heart. The more she thinks about Richard, the more she tries to get closer to

Ajit. Her duty-bound heart does not allow her to think about a man other than her own husband.

She often dreams about a particularly scary place and wonders, why? In her dream, she is stranded in a maze of narrow paths with dark houses. The people are extremely scary and weird-looking. She gets lost and tries to get out, but every street has a dead end. Any people she sees have a crazy look in their eyes, and just stare at her when she asks for help. Finally she succeeds in coming out to an open road. She sees Richard's car parked there, and runs toward it with her heart pounding. As soon as she opens the door to get into his car, she hears a loud beep. She looks around and sees Ajit, looking at her from his car across the road.

Jasmine wakes up, quite frightened, and puts her arm over Ajit to feel secure. He immediately turns away, to the other side. Although she knows it won't make a dent on his hard head, she wants to share her scary dream with him. Her fear turns to sadness. *Why are men so cold? Or, is it only Ajit, and I am seeing all men through his mold? Perhaps he is the only man who can't realize that a woman needs an emotional connection.*

Her thoughts wander to Richard, as she believes that he would definitely listen to her with interest, whatever she needed to say. But then her conscience convinces her it is not right for a married woman to get involved. She feels like screaming aloud to pierce through the stillness of her sleepless night. *Oh, silent night! Move fast—please move fast.* Daybreak is hours away. She stares out the window at the sky, pitch black with a few stars here and there. Sometimes the stars seem like words written in golden ink on a black paper. They appear and disappear, playing hide-and-seek. Far, far away, she hears faint sounds of a farmer playing a flute, and the crescent moon appears to be moving slowly toward that sound.

Finally, she drifts to sleep and dreams again. This time she becomes a bird and flies over streets with skyscrapers. She soars higher and higher. When she gets closer to the sky, a few stars come down and dress her in a bridal gown. They tell her that the moon wants to marry her. She laughs. *How can the moon marry me? He does not have arms to embrace me, and he has no tongue to talk to me. Aren't these things vital in a marriage?* Then her alarm goes off, breaking her dream in the middle. Her daily routine starts.

Jasmine continues to adapt to the never-ending new things she must learn in her American life, but she still can't talk freely with Ajit. *For heaven's sake put your arms around me*, she wishes, but does not tell him. How conveniently he tells her to divorce him if she can't accept him the way he is. She admits to herself that he is a great father, a helpful and practical husband, a great entertainer, and a highly-accomplished person. Among their friends, they stand out as the most attractive and happily married couple. "You are so lucky," a friend tells Jasmine. "Your husband does so much around the house; my husband doesn't lift a finger to help me." Jasmine agrees with a convincing smile.

She continues to work, but doesn't enroll in the computer courses as Richard had suggested. She thinks it is beyond her physical and emotional stamina to study and work full time. Richard hires a technical consultant, Michael, to begin the installation of computer terminals for the department. Michael is a middle-aged computer specialist, very social and helpful. He helps Jasmine learn the newly-installed automated system. She gets stuck on almost every step, and sometimes wonders whether she has what it takes to be computer-savvy.

She gets frustrated, but she is determined to learn. Michael does not seem to mind her many questions.

"Michael, what would I do without you? I do not know how to thank you for all your help," one day she says, innocently.

"I know how you can thank me…by sleeping with me," he whispers, coming very close.

Jasmine literally freezes in shock for a few moments. With her eyes squeezed in anger, she tells him to get out of her cubicle and never enter it again. Her whole body is shaking with fury and her hand hangs in the air, ready to smack him.

"Hey, come on. I was just joking and you took it seriously. I'm sorry, it will never happen again, I promise," he says, and quickly walks away.

Purnima's husband has lost his father who left him a large fabric factory in Bombay. Being the only son, he has no choice but to go back home and take care of his mother as well as the inheritance. His field of engineering is in troubled times. Most of his friends were laid off recently and the constant stress of possibly losing his job has taken a toll on his health. So he decides to leave Purnima and his son behind to see if he can adjust to the corporate life in the congested city of Bombay. After living a quiet suburban life here, he anticipates the drastic change with apprehension.

To no one's surprise, within six months of his stay there he decides to come back. After realizing that running a factory is not his forte, he sells the business and brings his mother to the States. After several months of job-hunting, he lands a high-paying engineering job in Dubai. This time the whole family leaves, planning to return to America when the employment situation improves.

When Purnima leaves, Jasmine's world crumbles once again, and she vows to make no more close friends. She thinks this decision can protect her feelings, but it only makes her feel more depressed about her life: Richard's resignation is only a few weeks away; Purnima is gone; the girls are ready to leave for universities; Bibijee has gone to live with Dilbeer; and Ajit is completely self-absorbed, busy minting money. Communication between them continues to be cold. It is possible Ajit feels lonely too, but just like Jasmine, he keeps it to himself. They keep themselves occupied all the time. Although they attend parties, watch movies, and occasionally go with friends to New York to watch a Broadway show, they hardly ever communicate on an intimate level.

She often wonders why he shows no affection. She knows very well that it is the Indian way of subtle connection which gives a couple the feeling of intimacy. Their relationship is supposed to be taken for granted, and there is no need to be demonstrative. She attempts to explain her dissatisfied feelings as a consequence of having been exposed to western culture for so many years. After all, she has lived most of her life in America. She remembers a conversation with her Italian colleague, Cara. A couple of months ago, Cara was reading Cosmopolitan magazine and Jasmine borrowed it to read on the train. Cara laughed while handing it to her, saying, "Interestingly, my parents were happily married until my mother started to read my magazines. Now she expects too much from my father. They've started fighting because she has become aware of her needs. So… read this at your own risk." Jasmine wonders whether she has, indeed, developed unreasonable expectations of Ajit.

Tomorrow evening is her daughters' high school graduation, and on Sunday they have invited their friends for religious prayers and a dinner party afterwards. Dilbeer's family and Bibijee are arriving late tonight. Ajit and Jasmine are very proud of their daughters. They have distinguished themselves in high school, and Komil gained admission to Yale while Sohil was accepted into a six-year medical program at Penn State. Soon they will be gone, leaving an empty nest behind.

Ajit's career flourishes and he has published a few books on economics. His strategic consulting practice has been very successful, winning him a large government contract, and has made them wealthy. With growing prosperity, they buy an expensive house in a distinguished suburb of Philadelphia. Now they have an additional group of friends who are doctors, lawyers, and business people coming from the big cities of India. They all consider themselves elite and sophisticated. They converse in English, drink, smoke, wear western clothes, and hold dinner/dance parties quite often.

Jasmine feels uneasy in this group, but Ajit fits in very well. They all talk about the economy, stocks, and real estate investments. The ladies wear expensive jewelry, designers' clothes, and brag about their possessions. It feels so superficial to Jasmine. There is not-so-subtle competition among them, and every party is like a big show-off. In spite of this aura of western style, underneath they are typical Indians, pining to return home some day. They eat Indian food, celebrate Indian festivals, expect their children to marry Indians, and miss their folks back home.

Jasmine misses her old house in Swarthmore where memories were made. She had no desire to move from there, but Ajit wanted to invest his money in real estate. Ever since he has become rich, he constantly talks about money and investments. He buys expensive cars, antiques, and attends auctions. He takes pride in showing off his collection to anyone who visits. Similarly, he is proud to introduce his beautiful wife to new friends. Jasmine feels as if she, too, were a marble figurine, another of Ajit's proud possessions. At times, she feels as if she is kept in a touch-me-not glass case, decorated with precious jewels and silks. She plays along, making her face beautified with make-up, and her lips shaded in pink color.

Tonight is a New Year's Eve Party at Dr. Sheenu and Rahul Cheema's house. Jasmine looks stunning in her pink silk sari with gold brocade-work enhancing her big brown eyes. Her matching jewelry augments her graceful entrance into the party. Ajit walks alongside with pride in his wife's exquisite beauty. All eyes turn towards them with admiration for the couple.

Jasmine notices no one greets them with a humble *Namaste*; on the contrary, it is the American, "Hi."

"What would you like to drink?" Rahul, the host, asks Jasmine.

"I would like a soda, thank you."

"How come—no wine or whiskey? We don't serve soft drinks on New Year Eve. You have to drink what I offer you."

"Come on, take a glass of wine to be polite," Ajit nudges her a little.

Holding a glass of wine, she joins a group of ladies who are bragging in high gear.

"We were window-shopping in Hawaii and the moment I saw this topaz on display, I told my husband I must have this before we leave," Rina tells the circle of women, all in dazzling party attire.

One woman starts a conversation with Jasmine and after a few minutes she remarks, "Your necklace is beautiful, you must have spent a fortune on it."

"No, my necklace isn't real. I wear whatever goes with my outfit," Jasmine says innocently.

"I never wear faux jewelry... actually I learned that from my mother," says the woman, surprised by Jasmine's admission. Jasmine just smiles and the woman excuses herself to go to the powder room.

"My mother-in-law is such a stubborn mule," someone says so loudly that Jasmine can hear the conversation going on among a group of women far away.

"I fantasize only about my husband," after a while another one says.

"You don't have to fantasize about him—he is right there!" a woman says, and they all start laughing loudly.

Ajit loves this bunch of rich people. It resonates with his inner values. He loves to give financial advice, play cards, drink, and dance. Jasmine continues to accompany him as any devoted wife would, but she calls this group of friends the "Show and Tell" bunch. She attends almost all other social functions alone, making excuses for her husband every time. She has adjusted very well to her lonesome life, though at times when she is alone in the house, she lets out a loud scream of despair and frustration.

At the same time she feels wonderful about her life. She knows their greatest assets are their daughters who have grown into lovely, poised young women, both fine citizens with marvelous qualifications. They have absorbed the best of both cultures...except for one thing: they absolutely refuse the notion of arranged marriages. Whenever they come home from college, this is the only lecture they close their ears to.

A few weeks back, they were sitting in Dilbeer's house in Toronto when Bibijee suggested a young man from Punjab for Komil. He has become a medical doctor and is interested in marrying one of her granddaughters. His parents have sent his photograph along with his bio-data. Komil and Sohil reject the idea of marrying a stranger from India, and they make fun of his photograph.

"Listen to me Komil, don't get involved with a wrong person," Jasmine says. "After graduation we will start introducing you to highly-educated Indian boys. Right now you should only concentrate on your studies." Jasmine gives her daughters a serious and firm nod of her head.

"Mom, what is your definition of a wrong person?" Sohil asks.

"Don't you know?" Komil says, rolling her eyes. "Anyone other than a Punjabi is a wrong person."

"Why are Indian parents so prejudiced?" asks Sohil

Jasmine is surprised by the question and realizes that she has not done a good job at explaining the reasoning.

"The reason is not that we don't like others as people. We greatly admire them as friendly, straightforward, and compassionate human beings. It is a difference of culture and religion, which will require much more adjustment in marriage. And on top of that, the Americans like to date forever, which is unthinkable for us. Moreover, they get bored easily and need change after a while. They change their jobs, their spouses, and their houses. You will never feel secure in life if you marry one of them. They fall in love, they fall out of love; this kind of lifestyle does not suit us. Stability is not in their culture's dictionary."

"Well, you can introduce an Indian if you like, but I won't marry unless I fall in love," Komil says, and Sohil nods in agreement.

"You know my friend, Cara, from my department; she told me that the real bells rang with a Jewish coworker, but she knew that her Catholic parents would never agree. Therefore, she is dating an Italian Catholic." Jasmine believes she has provided a nice example.

"Oh, if my *real* bells ring with an American, I should avoid him and be miserable my whole life with an Indian husband listening to *fake* wedding bells," says Komil.

"No Komil, live happily ever after, just as mom has lived all her life," taunts Sohil.

"You girls don't know what happiness is. You could be miserable living with a person you married with real wedding bells. What if your beloved husband is alcoholic, unable to hold on to a job, and unable to help you in household maintenance?"

"Then I will leave him," Komil says.

"It is easier said than done. No matter that you Americans have this choice, it is not free from misery. Especially when children are involved. Let me give you an example of the Singapore lady five houses down the road. Whenever I met her in the park, she would complain about her husband. 'He is good for nothing; he never helps me in the kitchen or with the kids. He is so unromantic.' And then she fell in love with her American boss. She divorced her husband, abandoned her school-aged children, and married the guy. Now she is completely miserable. The man is alcoholic and useless. He has no money to buy a nice house. Now they live in a crummy little house and most probably she will have to work all her life. Had she stayed with her husband, she would have had a better life and their children's lives would have been much happier in a secure, happy environment. So what did she gain except ruining so many lives around her?"

"She is stupid, I'll say. We're educated people and make intuitive choices, Mom," Sohil says.

"Self-centeredness is a number one enemy of a married couple. One has to behave selflessly to create happiness. Although love is necessary, it is not the romance that makes a marriage successful. It is the sacrifice, which is possible only if one has the capability to adjust to meeting more than half way," says Jasmine.

"Tell me Mom, are you happily married?" asks Sohil.

"Of course I am. Happiness is very personal, whereas misery has no such distinction. Misery can strike the happiest person anytime, anywhere. One can't control misery, but to bring happiness into one's life is within one's reach. To me, happiness is to make a happy environment for others around you. Happiness to me is to fulfill the purpose of one's life."

"Wow! Mom, I never knew you were a philosopher in addition to a great mother."

"You girls have good heads on your shoulders — I am sure you will not be as naive as the Singapore lady. But I do want to reiterate, 'Love is blind and marriage is an eye-opener.' To select a life partner, do not follow your heart blindly. First you have to make sure he is well-educated, and doesn't belong to a divorced or uneducated family."

"That is why we want to know the person really well before we marry, and without dating a guy we wouldn't know about him," says Sohil.

"At least you should keep your mind open to the ones we introduce to you. We will know their backgrounds better than you do with the one you come across on your own." Jasmine says.

"I will go back to India if you don't marry Sikh boys." Bibijee gives them an ultimatum.

The girls know that contradicting their family's philosophy of marriage is like touching a beehive. Therefore, they use their strategy which they planned years ago. *"Act Desi, talk Desi, and wear Desi clothes in front of them."* And live as their western friends do to fit into the society which is theirs by birth. In other words, they are Americans in Indian frames. They think their parents are the confused ones. They have learned how to cleverly play a double role to keep their parents happy as well as to fit in nicely with their American peers.

# 18

# Matchmakers

Cara, an Italian co-worker, is Jasmine's best friend. Ever since Purnima left for Dubai, Jasmine is growing closer to Cara, despite promising herself that she would never make another close friend. Now they go out to lunch together quite frequently. They talk freely and share the vicissitudes of their lives.

When Cara confides that her boyfriend of two years broke up with her, Jasmine even tries matchmaking for her. So far Cara has had three broken relationships, and she talks with appreciation about the arranged marriage custom of India, telling Jasmine that she is looking for an Italian professional man. Jasmine introduces her to an Italian neighbor's brother, a teacher. Now Cara and her boyfriend meet regularly, and she intends to marry him if and when he proposes.

One afternoon while they are having lunch at a restaurant, Cara starts to share some office gossip, but Jasmine absentmindedly interrupts her. "It makes me sad that Richard is leaving," she sighs. "I like him a lot."

"You can like him, but don't fall in love with him," Cara says. After a pause, she leans in and whispers, "He is gay, you know."

"Yeah, I know," Jasmine says matter-of-factly. "He is such a happy-go-lucky person."

"Jasmine, he has a boyfriend. I mean he's…you know." Cara gives some hand signals to make her understand.

"Ohhooo! You mean he is homosexual."

"Hush, don't say it so loud!" Cara notices some heads turn toward them. "That's not something you talk about in public."

"Oh, this is news to me. It makes my heart ache a little," Jasmine says.

"You love him, don't you?"

"No, no, not really," Jasmine says, a bit too quickly. "But I had a dream about him last night. I'm glad you told me."

Cara nods expectantly, and Jasmine sighs deeply.

"In my dream, I was sitting with Richard on a bench in the park," Jasmine says. "The descending sun was slowly turning into an orange ball behind the tall trees. It created such patterns of beams, with colorful prismatic effects in the sky and the river. The fall leaves were glistening with its reflection too. He held my hand, gently transmitting a closeness that I had never experienced. What a gentleman he was, I thought. He could have taken advantage of my vulnerability, but he didn't. He understood my cultural limitations, and he wouldn't do anything to hurt me. 'If you were single I would've married you,' is all he told me. But when I turned my face towards him, it was Ajit, not Richard, sitting next to me. Feeling such relief, I thanked God."

"Why?" Cara asks, baffled. "There is nothing wrong if you care about Richard."

"You don't understand. Guilty feelings overpower me just thinking about someone other than my own husband."

The remainder of the lunch consists of friendly chatter as usual, albeit with a somber cloud looming in the background.

One evening, Jasmine is sitting on her patio in a reverie while waiting for Ajit. Fall seasons in America have always left her a trail of pleasant memories. The very first one, in 1957, totally swept her off her feet with its magical spell of beauty. Since then, she has experienced seventeen fall seasons in her new country. In the fall of 1966, their names and photographs were engraved on certificates when they were naturalized as American citizens. She remembers sitting in the court when the judge congratulated a crowd of about a hundred foreigners after administering them an oath and pledge of allegiance. She remembers her heart swelling with pride, and her eagerness for the future as a real American.

This year's autumn, however, is very dull, indeed. Ajit has become a hopeless workaholic and the girls have gone back to their universities. Jasmine sits alone on the patio watching a downpour. Torrents of water sweep the dry leaves and push them toward the creek. Watching the cruelty of the wind and the energy of the gushing water, she imagines the leaves as the pages from her memory book, and they are being swept away so terribly fast by the flowing water. She wants to run and catch them, but she remains seated. *To catch those precious moments of my life and hold them in my hand forever*, she thinks to herself, *is as impossible as finding a lost diamond in a heap of snow, or as taking a photograph of a lovely full moon hidden behind a cloud. Alas!*

Ever since Richard left, the office atmosphere has changed. It is as if he had taken the spirit of the department along with him. Since the computerized system has been abandoned, Jasmine has been promoted to Richard's old position and now spends her days in his former office. She can feel his presence in the desk, the file cabinets, and the walls and floor itself. Whenever her telephone rings, she eagerly picks it up before her secretary does, thinking it might be his call. Perhaps he has forgotten something and will come to pick it up. She knows he has gone to Boston to study at Harvard, but her heart hears whispers as if he were right beside her. Why does she miss him so much? She wanted nothing more than what she had. Just his presence and his smile had been more than enough for her.

Although this new job is quite challenging, Jasmine loves it. Taking part in meetings, she gets the chance to meet other managers. Her new boss, Mrs. Williams, is a kind and fair person who doesn't put unrealistic pressure on Jasmine.

Unfortunately, though, the good period lasts only one year. The agency's budget allocation is drastically reduced, pushing it into a major re-organization. Jasmine's division is merged into the Policy and Planning Department. Now she reports to the Director of Policy & Planning, who is a middle-aged macho American with Yale pride written all over his face. Mr. Tate is thin and short, and walks stiffly with his chin in the air, giving off a sense that he is indeed in charge.

His first meeting with Jasmine puts her off. He doesn't look at her directly. Stern-faced, he asks her tough questions quite unrelated to her expertise, just to intimidate her. She comes back from his office quite perturbed. She wants to quit her job right at that very moment, but her well-wishing staff members tell her not to give him the satisfaction.

Her new boss seems to go out of his way to make her life difficult. One day she overhears him telling another colleague that he can't stand foreign accents. He says loudly that he had an Indian professor who was such a jerk and he despised him. Then they talk about Vietnam, and he mentions that he was so fed up with seeing Vietnamese eyes; he was yearning to see American blue ones. When Jasmine tells Ajit about this conversation, he tells her to quit working.

"We are well off now," he says. "Our daughters are doing great, and there is no need for you to endure such despicable treatment."

However, when she tells Bijibee about the situation, her mother firmly tells her not to quit. "Is this my daughter I am talking to?" she says. "My daughter is the one who crossed over all the tricky and thorny paths in her life with courage and dignity. This stony hurdle should be nothing for her to cross."

"But Ma, Ajit is doing so well, and I no longer need to earn money. He wants me to quit."

"You can quit, but after proving your ignorant boss wrong about you," Bibijee replies.

The staff doesn't want Jasmine to resign either. "That is what he wants," they tell her. "Why should you give him the satisfaction? We want you to stay. Anyway, if he fires you, you have the basis for a discrimination lawsuit."

So she continues to work. A few months later, a couple of high-level officials from the Department of Labor pay a visit. All managers have been asked to present what their divisions are responsible for. Jasmine, seeing a chance to prove herself in front of those in charge, prepares her presentation thoroughly. She practices pronouncing certain words correctly and memorizes every word of her written paper. After the presentation, the CEO comes to speak to her personally.

"Your presentation was excellent!" he says. "This is the first time I have thoroughly understood the functions of your division."

Then Mr. Tate's face changes colors as the CEO tells him that in the future he wants Jasmine to accompany him to his staff meetings. She knows her boss is fuming and grinding his teeth quietly while giving a fake smile of approval.

Jasmine feels proud to report to her staff and the whole clan. She hopes that this will make her boss feel good about her, too. On the contrary, his attitude becomes even more hostile. Fortunately, Jasmine's exposure to the monthly executive meetings proves quite helpful in improving her English and boosting her confidence.

Just when Jasmine feels she has weathered the storm, an unpleasant surprise throws her work life into chaos. Jasmine is summoned for a discrimination lawsuit filed against her by one of her former employees, Denise, an African-American. About a year ago, Jasmine fired her. She had been taking far too many shortcuts in her data input work, causing major problems down the line, and she responded to repeated warnings with indifference, eventually forcing Jasmine's hand.

At the deposition, the agency's defense attorney represents Jasmine while Denise's lawyer questions her. Denise's lawyer begins with some general queries about her work history and ethnic background, and then probes deeper.

"I understand you have a caste system in India," he says. "Is it true that in your religion—I believe it is called 'Hindu'—a lower caste person is considered untouchable, and is not allowed to enter the kitchen or a holy place?"

Jasmine, shocked to hear such an insensitive question, requests to be excused to consult her defense attorney. The two of them are allowed to leave the room to speak privately.

"Does he have the right to ask me about religion?" Jasmine protests. "What if I refuse to answer? For one, there is no caste system in my religion, and secondly, I don't think such questions are relevant."

"Actually, it will be to your advantage to answer this question," her lawyer replies. "He is trying to make a case against you—that you mistreat the lower class in your country. Therefore, it is natural for you to discriminate against minorities here. You should answer this question as elaborately as you can to prove him wrong."

When they come back to the room, the lawyer repeats the question. Jasmine answers with confidence and determination.

"As a matter of fact, the caste system was not attached to any religion. It began with the arrival of the Aryans from Europe and Asia around 500 B.C. The Aryans formed groups based upon their professions. And I think Hindus eventually labeled these different professions 'castes.' The four castes are Brahma, Kshatriya, Vaishya, and Sudra. Below these are the outcastes, who are 'Untouchables.' There have been preachers against the caste system throughout the ages. By the way, I am not a Hindu, so I don't know that much about its practices. I am a Sikh, and my religion is Sikhism."

"Can you explain your religion? Be very brief."

"It started with the birth of our first Guru, Baba Nanak, in 1469, and evolved into a distinctive religion with our tenth Guru, Gobind Singh. Baba Nanak passionately preached against the caste system and the prevailing social vices of the time. He raised his voice loud and clear preaching that women should never be mistreated or abused. He expressed his ideas in celestial poetry. His philosophical hymns, plus the sublime writings of our Gurus and saints, make up our scripture, which is called 'Guru Granth Sahib.' It delivers a strong message that God has created the entire universe, and under his one light all humans are born equal. Therefore, they all must be treated equally. The Sikh holy book includes religious hymns from about 50 saints belonging to other faiths as well as to all castes."

Jasmine pauses to catch her breath. The dumfounded attorney shakes his head, searching for the right words to regain some momentum.

"You have more than thirty employees," he says. "Why did you hire only two African-Americans?"

"The hiring is done based on the civil service list," Jasmine calmly explains. "I have no control over who gets on the list and who doesn't. When I hired my secretary, an African-American, she was on the list. I interviewed three applicants, but I hired her because she was the most qualified. I did not pay any attention to her ethnicity."

The deposition continues. Jasmine stoically fields question after question, until finally, two grueling hours later, she is allowed to exit the room. When she comes out, she sees Richard in the hallway, and her heart skips a beat. He has also been summoned, and is waiting to be called. Jasmine talks to him briefly, much too briefly for her liking. He tells her that the case has no basis for discrimination and the court will definitely dismiss it.

Time passes, and as Richard promised, the case against Jasmine fails to develop further. Still, Jasmine is not happy at work. It is not the same as before, and it appears to her as if she is working in a foreign place. Her boss still doesn't treat her well. The friendlier personnel have moved on with their lives.

"Americans are known for change," Cara tells her one day, as she's planning her move to Baltimore with her new husband. "They get bored with routine and are always looking out for better opportunities."

After a few months, her boss creates a new position, the research and program development manager. Jasmine is certainly qualified, but instead of promoting her, Mr. Tate hires a new graduate. She comes home in tears. Her daughters advise her to file a lawsuit; Ajit tells her otherwise.

"No matter that we are American citizens; to them we are still foreigners," he says.

"It's a clear-cut discrimination case," her staff tells her. This time, though, she ignores all these opinions and resigns, thus ending a 15-year career of outstanding job performance.

Ajit's latest book, *How to Become a Millionaire*, becomes a *New York Times* bestseller. He is totally engrossed in a full schedule of interviews and book signings. To occupy herself during this time, Jasmine goes to visit her sister and mother in Toronto. A few days later, her daughters join her. Komil has one year left to complete her law degree from Yale, and Sohil has another year until she obtains her medical degree.

"You should start looking for suitable boys for them now," Bibijee suggests to Jasmine. "By the time they are done with studies, they should be married."

"You know, Mrs. Khan's son is engaged to an American girl," Jasmine says. "She told me that one day he came home and announced his intention to marry this girl, who is a physical therapist and older than he. He still has one year to complete his MBA. They were upset for days; finally, they were able to persuade him to postpone his marriage until his graduation. They are hoping by that time the girl will break up with him."

"Mom, don't worry about me," Komil says, with more than a hint of sarcasm. "I will *definitely* consult you before getting engaged."

"And I will not get married until I complete my internship, so you need not look for a match for me," Sohil says bluntly.

"Oh, no, I want to see a wedding soon!" her thirteen-year-old cousin pleads. "Komil *didi,* please do get married right after you complete your education."

"I suppose we should start introducing suitable boys to you soon," Jasmine says, her eagerness building. "You know it takes time to find the right match. It's not like you have to get married right away."

Komil, not wanting to dampen her mother's excitement, says nothing. Jasmine takes this as permission to start the matchmaking process.

"Let's all take a guided tour in India next May, after our finals, before commencement," Sohil says, hoping to change the subject.

"Great idea!" Bijibee says, and her eyes twinkle more brightly than they have in a while.

Dilbeer declines, explaining that her kids will still be in school.

"We can make it a shorter trip. There is time after your school is out and before commencement," Sohil say, after seeing her cousins' sad faces.

So, they all agree to take the trip during the first week of June. Ajit can't accompany them, he is too busy with his publications.

As soon as Jasmine returns from Toronto, she starts to purchase gifts for her extended family and friends back home. It is a long list, and she has to make sure no one's name is left out. All her aunts and uncles expect something American, even if it's a bar of Dove soap. Her brother's family and three westernized cousins send a list of expensive designer clothes, purses, and perfumes.

Dilbeer's family takes a plane from Toronto, synchronizing their flight time with Jasmine's so they arrive at nearly the same time at Heathrow airport. From London, they board the same flight to New Delhi. All the cousins are thrilled to sit together on the plane. After a twenty-two hour journey, they touch down in New Delhi. The cousins are overwhelmed and fascinated by the chaotic scene at the airport. After passing through the tormenting experience of customs clearance, they all breathe a sigh of relief. Jasmine's brother, standing in the waiting room, waves to them, and they exchange warm greetings.

Amar has arranged a private tour for the whole clan. His chauffeur has rented a spacious van, which everyone fits in comfortably. Starting in New Delhi, they make quick stops at the Red Fort, Humayun's tomb, and Qutab Minar. From there they leave for Rajasthan, a state known for its magnificent palaces, forts, and red-stone architecture. The beauty of sandstone has an enchanting effect on the group's inquisitive minds. They enjoy elephant rides up to the Amber Fort and Hawa Mahal.

The next stop is the Taj Mahal, in the city of Agra, one of the most magnificent monuments in the world. The story behind it is nearly as beautiful as the structure itself. In 1631, the Mughal emperor, Shah Jahan, was grief-stricken when his beloved wife, Mumtaz Mahal, died during the birth of their fourteenth child. He wanted to build a mausoleum in her memory, which would be a symbol of eternal love. The architectural design is a combination of Persian and Indian, and the layout is perfectly symmetrical. It took almost twenty years of continuous construction to complete. More than one thousand elephants were used to transport the white marble and other building materials. The exterior work of art, in white marble, is the most intricate design of Persian architecture. The interior decoration is inlaid with 28 types of semi-precious stones gathered from all over Asia.

The family stays in a nearby hotel for the night to experience the magical beauty of the Taj in moonlight. Just as they have read so many times, this architectural marvel shimmers in the river currents and appears as a dream. The next day, they take a tour of the opulent palace of another Mughal emperor, Akbar the Great. The most memorable segment of their trip involves renting a *shikara* (houseboat) on Dal Lake in Kashmir. Its breathtaking beauty has helped it become a tourist's paradise.

This is Jasmine's first experience of India as a land of such heavenly sights. It reminds her of her first landlady, Mrs.

Stevenson, who often told stories of her life in the foothills of Kashmir.

Surprisingly, the worst part of their journey occurs when they go to a small town in Punjab to visit Jasmine's maternal grandparents. From there they had planned to go to Jasmine's home village, but the rumor of a curfew and escalating unrest in Punjab prompted them to quickly leave for New Delhi. Jasmine cries profusely at the thought of leaving India without visiting her childhood home.

As it turned out, coming to Punjab in the 1980s was very unwise, in terms of timing. They had been warned by their many friends to postpone the visit to India, but they didn't care. They were unable to gauge the rapidly deteriorating conditions of their beloved state.

At this point in time, dissatisfied with the declining provincial power under the centralized government, the Sikh leaders have been agitating in a struggle for righteousness. Ever since the partition of India in 1947, the Sikhs have been demanding an autonomous Sikh state which has evolved into a desire for a separate country, called *Khalistan*. The movement has gained momentum under the leadership of Bhindrawale. By 1984, his attempts to get the government's attention became radical and violent. Random killings have widened the gap between Hindus and Sikhs. Everyone living in India fears a big *dhamaka* (Armageddon) very soon. With all this as background, Jasmine and company make the painful decision to leave India as soon as possible.

Bibijee has decided to stay because she wants to live the rest of her life in her native country with her son's family in Delhi. The girls are crying; they want Bibijee to go back with them, but Amar's children want their grandmother to live there. Understanding Bibijee's dilemma, Jasmine tries to control her tears and console her daughters. With heavy hearts, the three say good-bye as they leave for the airport.

They reach home just before commencement, the day Komil is graduating from law school, and Sohil from medical school. Jasmine plans a graduation party for them on June 15th in a grand banquet hall. She invites all their friends, relatives, and acquaintances from far and wide. She wants to make it a gala affair for the girls. She feels her life of sacrifice has borne the sweetest fruit; she is proud to celebrate her daughters' achievements.

In the meantime, she is eager to start the process of finding a suitable match for Komil. Realizing that Komil may be less than cooperative, Jasmine, with Ajit's help, finalizes the content of an advertisement to be submitted to *India Abroad*, a New York publication aimed at Indian-American readers. Of course, they do this without Komil's knowledge. Many modern Indian families post matrimonial offers this way, and Jasmine has heard they have been successful. The brief announcement reads:

> *Affluent Sikh parents invite alliance from doctors/lawyers raised in USA, for beautiful girl, slim, fair, 23/5'6", Yale law graduate. Reply w/ photograph–Box 123456.*

After a few weeks of waiting, the advertisement appears in the matrimonial section of *India Abroad*, and within a week, they receive responses asking for the girl's recent photograph and bio-data. Jasmine discards the ones with no photographs. She makes two separate piles of "possible" and "acceptable" offers to show Ajit, who further scrutinizes them. He throws out ones without impressive educational backgrounds. That leaves them with only three acceptable possibilities, to whom Jasmine mails a lengthy bio, Komil's recent photograph, and their telephone number.

One afternoon, Jasmine receives a phone call from a particularly inquisitive mother of a suitor. "Does your daughter speak Punjabi?" she asks, rattling questions off more quickly than Jasmine can reply. "How often does she go to *Gurudwara*? Has she learned to make *chapatti*?"

Jasmine answers what she can, but her patience eventually wears out, and she furiously hangs up.

"Why did you hang up on her?" Ajit scolds. "It is so discourteous."

"Well, you answer the next phone call!" she snaps. "Only then will you realize what foolish questions they ask. She wasn't a cultured woman! I would never let my daughter marry into such a family."

Finally, they receive a decent, thoughtful response from a qualified prospect. Jasmine invites the whole family for dinner on a weekend when Komil will be coming home. The boy's mother suggests to Jasmine that it should be a spontaneous meeting of the two potential life partners. She has told her children that Jasmine is an old friend, and Jasmine agrees to tell the same story. Unfortunately, she forgets to tell Ajit, so when Komil comes home, he tells her to dress up nicely this evening.

"Why?" Komil asks, frowning. "Who is coming to dinner? Some dignitary I have to dress up for?"

"We want you to meet a boy and his family, just in case you like him."

Komil throws a tantrum on the spot.

"I'm leaving right now!" she roars. "Why didn't you ask me before arranging this dinner? Did I ever tell you that I am ready to get married?"

Komil snatches her bag and storms out of the house. Jasmine runs out to stop her.

"If you walk out on us today, this door will be closed to you forever!" Ajit yells.

"My child, it is too late to cancel the dinner invitation," Jasmine pleads, clasping her daughter's hand tightly. "Just let them meet you. If you don't, your father will make my life miserable, reminding me that he wanted to send you to India for studies and I wouldn't agree."

For her mother's sake, Komil comes in, stone-faced.

"I will meet these people, but do not expect any more than that from me," she says.

The family arrives, and Komil, to her credit, manages to smile. They all sit down at the dinner table and have a general, friendly conversation. After dinner, Komil takes the boy, Imaan, and his sister, Shami, to the family room, where they talk and watch television for a while. The family leaves by eleven in the evening.

Jasmine asks Komil whether she liked Imaan and Shami.

"Well, they are very nice," she admits. "Imaan is in his final year of law school, but he is so quiet; I wonder how he will ever succeed as a lawyer. He told me that he is dating an American girl and they hope to get married next year, but he is afraid to tell his parents."

"Poor parents!" Jasmine later tells Ajit. "They have no idea that their son has a girlfriend."

She feels sorry for them, but her concern takes on a new depth as she starts to wonder whether her daughters might give her a similar shock one day. She starts to pray hard.

The next day, she tells Bibijee by phone about how the evening went.

"Keep up your effort," Bijibee says. "Such tasks take time. One day you will find the right match for her."

At a dinner party in their friend's home, the ladies discuss the difficulties they face with their offspring growing up in western culture. Most of their friends' children are much younger than Komil and Sohil. Even though only a few families are in the same boat as Jasmine, the conversation always ends up focusing on matchmaking.

"I don't know what my son is up to," Tamanna complains. "I have shown him the photographs of very beautiful girls and he does not think anyone is pretty enough for him!"

"My daughter has been introduced to several very handsome, highly educated boys, but she keeps on saying they don't click," Rakhi worries.

"I can't understand this *clicking* business," Jasmeet says. "I tell my daughter to just get married, clicking will happen eventually. She thinks I am nuts. I tell my daughter I am still waiting for the day when your dad and I will click, but we are happily married."

Everyone laughs; they could relate to that sentiment.

"I think we have to understand their side, too," Seema, a school psychologist, says. "Our kids appear to be Indians on the surface, but they really are Americans. We confuse them so much by pushing them too hard to stay within our cultural mold. We should tell them the pros and cons of both cultures and explain to them that the choice is theirs. If they make the right choice, they will be happy in their lives."

"How can we tell them that the choice is theirs?" one of the mothers demands. "What do they know about choices at their young age? We are sending *our* children to India to study there up through high school. That way, they will acquire the best of both cultures!"

Whenever they get together, the Indian mothers discuss such concerns. Meanwhile, their children enjoy their American lives. While Jasmine's search for a traditional match continues, Komil has been dating an American classmate. Whenever she is introduced to a suitable match, she goes on a "date" with him just to satisfy her parent's wishes. It keeps peace at home.

# 19

# The Lacerated Punjab

Punjab, named after the beauty of *Punj* (five) and *aab* (rivers), is known as the breadbasket state of India for the bounty of its fertile land. The sight of expansive farms with their abundance of produce is something thrilling that must be experienced first hand. During the summer season, the air is filled with the aroma of ripe cantaloupes, watermelons, and mangoes. Stray trees stand here and there at the edge of fields, loaded with sweet red berries, a favorite treat of the children. Walking back from school, students climb these trees to pick and eat the fruit, then play with the tiny round pits, throwing them at each other.

This was the Punjab of 1957 when Jasmine reluctantly departed from her parental home, where she had played hide-and-seek and house-house, and where she had painted colorful birds on her kitchen wall. At the time, she was not aware that these silly painted birds, and the memories they carried, would haunt her all her life.

The year 1984 turns out to be *annum horribilis* for the Sikhs of Punjab, as well as for the Sikhs living abroad. This isn't the first time Jasmine's beloved state has suffered atrocities. The 1947 partition of India stands out as the cruelest of all, when the blood of more than a million people flowed into the waters of five rivers. The borderline that cut through Punjab's belly to give birth to Pakistan produced not just labor pains; it led to bleeding hearts for centuries to come.

Now, the Indian Prime Minister decides to attack the Golden Temple to get rid of the militants hiding there. But along with them, thousands of innocent Sikh pilgrims are killed while attending their fifth Guru, Arjun Dev's, martyrdom day.

Jasmine thinks her daughters' graduation party will be the happiest day of her life. But the horrendous news from Punjab dampens the mood of their Sikh friends so much that Jasmine wants to postpone the party. Ajit and the girls do not agree with her and continue with the plans. Ajit sings a couple of lines of an Urdu song about the cycle of happiness and sorrow—how they keep on moving, and the balance continues in one's life, moment by moment.

Most of their Sikh friends attend the party, but their hearts and minds are clearly elsewhere. The Bhangra dance, the new trend of the eighties, continues until midnight. The shimmer of Indian outfits such as *lehnga, sari* and *salwar kameez* augments the psychedelic lights illuminating the dance floor. The exotic variety of food has been prepared to satisfy various palates—South Indians, Punjabi, and Guajarati, and a few American friends.

Tonight, the Sikhs are not in the mood to dance. Their hearts are heavy, their pride is injured, and they sit to discuss the tragic events in Punjab.

"Indira Gandhi's biggest blunder was to raid the Golden Temple, killing thousands of pilgrims, and burning the sacred Sikh scriptures, the *Guru Granth sahib*," says Kirat Singh.

"It must be avenged in the near future," Manveer Singh says grimly. "Why on earth did she have to choose that particular day?" He's met with nods and grunts of agreement all around.

Sikhs, both in India and abroad, feel oppressed and humiliated at this atrocious action. Many clean-shaven Sikhs have resumed the practice of wearing turbans and growing beards, the symbols of Sikhism. Several prominent Sikhs have returned their government medals in protest. While in Punjab, the government continues to arrest the young men and agitation grows, giving birth to Sikh radicalism. Friendships are jeopardized; tensions are rising between Hindu and Sikh friends. The Hindus are now banned from Sikh temples.

In the midst of all this, Sohil has been dating a tall, dark, and handsome Hindu classmate. His parents had migrated from Bangalore in the early sixties. Sohil's parents are totally in the dark about this, and now she is debating when she should tell them. She knows her boyfriend is ready to propose, and has suggested a Memorial Day wedding.

At the dinner table, she dares to start the conversation. "I have a classmate from Bangalore," she says. "He's an intelligent, handsome gentleman. He is a son of Hindu parents." She stops to wait for their reaction.

"So, you wish to marry him?" Ajit abruptly asks her.

"No, no, no, it is out of the question!" Jasmine exclaims before Sohil can reply. "I would rather see you married to an American than a Hindu."

"How many years have you been living in this country?" Ajit snaps at Jasmine. "With such a myopic vision, sometimes I think you still dwell in your village."

"What if his parents do not give their consent?" Jasmine says, ignoring Ajit.

"His parents are very open-minded people and they are both doctors."

"We have no problem, if his parents agree," Ajit says firmly, glaring at Jasmine.

"Come on, Mom, we both love each other," Sohil pleads.

"Do you realize what they have done to us?" Jasmine says. "Our Sikh friends will be outraged to hear this." Tears well up in her eyes. "Well, your father has given his blessing, so who am I to say anything? I guess I'm *nothing* when it comes to making important decisions!"

"Mom, your best friends are Hindus," Sohil says. "One Prime Minister's cruel action does not make all Hindus bad." Jasmine does not answer.

"I hope you can make your heart understand, because we hope to be married next Memorial Day," Sohil says.

Jasmine cries for the rest of the night, and much of the following afternoon. She has lost her appetite. Now she thinks Ajit's idea of schooling them in India would have been better after all. She should have agreed with him! In India, children learn how to respect the desires of their parents. Here in America, the philosophy is to respect your own person first, follow your heart, and don't go against yourself. Eventually, her bitterness dissipates as she realizes that some events in one's life cannot be controlled. She remembers a quote by James Baldwin which her wise friend Simran once shared with her: "Men who believe they are masters of their own destinies can only continue to believe this by becoming specialists in self-deception."

Jasmine wonders what kind of surprise her other daughter will bring this weekend. To her amazement and dismay, Komil comes home and tells her parents that she is engaged to David, a Jewish classmate. She shares many things about him, which she believes will meet her parent's approval: He belongs to a very wealthy, traditional family. His parents have never been divorced or remarried, and he believes in strong family values. He wants to go into politics, just as she does. She says she wants to marry David Leibner the next Labor Day weekend.

Jasmine feels her head reeling with this news on top of Sohil's shocking decision. Ajit agrees right away; the combination of wealth and politics strikes him as a dream come true. Jasmine, on the other hand, suffers quietly.

"Why are you so quiet, Mom?" Komil pleads. "Aren't you supposed to say something? Your silence is killing me."

"She is unhappy because of Sohil's decision to marry a Hindu," Ajit explains off-handedly.

Jasmine bolts from the dinner table, goes to her bedroom, and starts sobbing loudly. Komil follows her, and tries to console her.

"Ma, if you are so unhappy, I will break my engagement," she soothes. "I have learned from you to sacrifice my happiness for the sake of others. Without your blessing, I will not marry David."

"No, I am not crying because you are marrying an American," Jasmine says between sobs. "It is because of the way you all have treated me. You come home *after* your engagement; Sohil announces she is marrying a Hindu. Your dad treats me as if I have no brain, and no say. I've tried my best to instill our values in you girls. I wonder where I went wrong."

Komil hugs and assures her mother that she will like her fiancé.

After a few weeks, Komil brings David home to introduce him to her parents. A tall, good-looking young man with curly blonde hair, he steals her parents' hearts with his charming personality and good sense of humor. He relishes spicy Indian food and is interested in learning about Punjabi and Indian culture. He is able to ease Jasmine's initial reluctance at having a son-in-law from a different culture and religion. In the ensuing period, David becomes a regular welcome guest in their home and seems more and more a part of the family.

It is the start of the fall season of 1984, a cursed year for Jasmine's beloved Punjab. Two Sikh bodyguards assassinate Prime Minister Indira Gandhi on October 31st. Although the assassination might have been inevitable, the carnage that follows for four days is unthinkable. The rumor is that it happened under the permission of the administration. The organized arson, murders, rapes of innocent Sikh females, and other horrible atrocities are carried out across the country. Delhi Sikhs are hit the worst of all.

Though Jasmine is far from home, the violence finds its way into her life as well. Her brother, Amar, has been tortured and killed on the road. Totally unaware of the assassination news, he and his chauffeur, also a Sikh, had been driving to Rajasthan for a business meeting. They left Delhi the afternoon of the 31st and that evening, were pulled out of the car, killed, and their car burned. The news reached his family several days afterwards.

Jasmine's house is full of mourners. She sits on the floor wailing in anger, pain, and anguish. Their Sikh friends are stunned and humiliated as this unprecedented carnage adds to their suppressed rage. Their pain is beyond remedy. The only way to console each other and find peace is to read the spiritual wisdom of Gurus from Sri Guru Granth Sahib. They pray and sing religious hymns for the peace of the departed soul.

Komil and Sohil are perplexed, sad, and bitter. It is hard for them to rationalize the depth of animosity and hatred among people of different religions. In America they are aware of racial discrimination and other acts of bigotry, but have never witnessed people fighting violently over faiths. Sohil has a difficult question before her. What should she do about her wedding, scheduled to take place on Memorial Day weekend, just six months away? Now it will be so hard for her mother, and perhaps many others in their community, to accept her marriage to a Hindu. The cards are already printed and the down payment on the wedding hall has been paid.

After a few months, Jasmine's *bhabi* writes that Bibijee has become bedridden. Her grief-stricken heart has no will to get better, and the wound of losing a son is too deep to heal. Jasmine wants to go to Delhi to help her get better, but Ajit and her daughters do not want her to go. The news from India is still filled with fatal incidents. Reports say the police shoot anyone, anywhere, with no discernable reason. A stray bullet from a policeman has recently killed the innocent 22-

year old son of Ajit's friend, Professor Lal. The girls do not want their mother to place herself in such a chaotic political climate.

As the winter season sets in, the wailing winds sound to Jasmine as if they are bringing a message directly from Punjab. And she stays awake, pleading: *Oh winds of Punjab, do not tease me again and again by bringing news so upsetting. Come only if you can bring comfort to my soul and sooth my wounds with a message of peace. Who has cast an evil eye on my land, where I played with the stars, and the moon was my companion? How can there be darkness where the gurus and saints have lived and enlightened the land with their message of peace and compassion?*

When Sohil comes home for spring break in March, a new problem surfaces. Throughout the winter she has worried so much about her upcoming marriage to a Hindu that she has become quite ill. Her tests at the doctor's office diagnosed her as anemic. Her parents, worried sick, bombard her with questions.

"What has happened to my child? What is bothering you? Has Karan refused to marry you?"

"No, he has not, but I am in a quandary," she confesses. "After what happened to Amar *mamajee* [maternal uncle], I would be hurting you and *Naani* [Bibijee] so much if I marry a Hindu."

"No, no, you love him," Ajit says, before Jasmine can even open her mouth. "He is a worthy husband. You must go ahead with your plans."

"How about if I write a letter to Bibijee explaining this dilemma?" Jasmine suggests in hope. "You can decide based on her response."

"Sometimes I think you have no brain in your head!" Ajit barks. "That is such a naive proposition."

"Please, Papa, don't fight over this," Sohil says. "I think Mom is right. It would help to clear my mind one way or the other."

Jasmine writes to her mother describing Sohil's concern over marrying a Hindu. She writes that Sohil does not want to add more pain to the family's already woebegone hearts, and is especially worried about Bibijee's health. But, she loves this boy so much that it is very painful for her to cancel their marriage. She doesn't know what to do and needs her grandmother to help her decide.

Bibijee's response comes promptly. Its contents surprise everyone:

> *My dear child, Sohil,*
>
> *A religious stamp on one's forehead does not make a person good or bad. It is one's deeds that either bear sweet fruits or spread evil. During this mourning period I have read our Guru Granth Sahib many times. And the knowledge I have absorbed from it has given me tremendous peace. Our holy book is filled with humility, forgiveness, and righteousness. Baba Farid writes: "Bure da bhala kar gussa mun na hundaya" In essence, he is saying answer evil with goodness; do not fill your mind with anger. If one can conquer the mind by controlling*

*the hatred and revengeful thoughts, one can conquer the world. It is not religions that create havoc; it is the misguided and cruel people who act in the name of religion. Therefore, I am happy that you have found someone you love so much. Do not worry about those aunties and uncles who would not have the heart to forgive you. I am sure one day they will.*

*Love,*

*Naani*

# 20

# The Weddings

Memorial Day weekend begins with Sohil's pre-wedding ceremony, *Sangeet/Mehendi* (Music/Henna) on Friday evening in a *Shamiana* (tent) set up in the back yard. In an effort to create the authentic flavor of *sangeet* ambiance, multi-colored *dupattas* and silk saris are used to decorate the ceiling of the tent. The stage is covered with homespun-cotton red shawls as large as bed sheets, embroidered by Bibijee with shiny and colorful silk thread. They are considered auspicious for weddings, especially on account of their red color.

Jasmine's mother has written her an encouraging letter.

*"My dear child, let no sad thoughts trouble your heart on this auspicious occasion. Life is a fusion of happy and sad events and one should not be wrapped too deeply in one or the other. I consider life to be a long, happy sentence punctuated with sorrowful episodes. I may not be present in person, but my heart and soul are there with you, enjoying the wedding thoroughly."*

Tears well up in Jasmine's eyes. Sweeping them back, she admires her mother's wisdom as she gets busy welcoming the guests. She asks a friend's husband to take Amar's place in honoring the ritual of putting the red *choora* (bangles) on Sohil's arms, which is customarily done by a girl's *mamajee*. After that, all of Sohil's friends sit around her to get their hands painted with henna. About fifteen ladies sit on the stage, singing folk songs to the beat of the *dholak*. Occasionally, Jasmine's mind drifts, feeling the absence of her family members who were not granted visitor visas. Although she keeps smiling, her friends and sister can sense her hidden grief and sympathize. They say to each other, "Such are the consequences for all of us who belong to two continents, separated by a vast ocean."

The next day, there are two wedding ceremonies: one Hindu, one Sikh. Early in the morning, excited young women help Sohil dress in an Indian silk *salwar kameez* with heavily embroidered *dupatta* for the Sikh *anand-karj in Gurudwara* (Sikh Temple*)*. After lunch she changes into a beautiful red silk sari for the Hindu ceremony in the same hall, which is also where the reception will take place in the evening. Both the Hindus and the Sikhs complete several rituals before the wedding vows. The main difference between the ceremonies is that the Sikh holy book, *Guru Granth Sahib*, contains four special hymns, called *lavan*. The priest reads one hymn at a time while another priest sings the same hymn, and Sohil walks behind Karan holding his scarf from the end to encircle the holy alter. Each time, after completing a circle, they bow to the altar, and sit down to wait for the next round. Each hymn explains the principles of leading a righteous married life with God's guidance.

In their Hindu wedding, they complete seven circles, called *mangalfera*, around the ceremonial fire. During the first four, Sohil walks in front of Karan, and for the last three circles she walks behind him. The first four steps represent aspects of life such as *Dharma, Artha, Karma, Moksha,* and the last three steps are for the three deities — Brahma, Vishnu, and Shiva. After the *Mangalfera*, seven piles of rice are placed in front of the fire, signifying the seven vows that the two make to each other. They touch the piles one at a time to take a vow of prosperity, strength, wealth, happiness, progeny, life, and unity with God's guidance. Finally, Karan presents a necklace called *Mangal Sutra* to his bride. It represents his deep love and devotion.

Both the Sikh and the Hindu ceremonies end with blessings from their relatives and a ritual of the bride going to her in-laws' home, carried by her brothers/cousins in a decorated *palki* (carriage).

Three months pass quickly, and Komil is now ready for her own wedding on Labor Day. She also has two ceremonies, the Sikh *Anand Karj* in the morning, and a Jewish ceremony in the evening. David's parents have arranged the Jewish wedding and the reception in New York, their hometown. They insist on planning a big wedding and gala reception for their only child, and David's mother purchases an exquisite wedding gown and a diamond necklace for Komil. She wants her to look fabulous.

All eyes sparkle with admiration as Komil walks down the aisle of the synagogue, dressed in a shimmering white French chiffon gown. Interestingly enough, a traditional Jewish wedding has similarities to Indian weddings. A Jewish wedding ceremony also takes place under a canopy, known as *chuppah*. When the couple first enters the *chuppah*, the bride circles the groom seven times to claim that the groom is the center of her world. The marriage is called *kiddu shin,* which translates as dedication, indicating that Jewish marriage is a spiritual bonding. An honored Rabbi conducts the ceremony.

Jasmine feels blessed to welcome her two close friends, Purnima from Dubai, and Mrs. Khan from San Francisco. They stay with her for ten days for each wedding, filling the gap of her absent family.

After Komil's wedding, Jasmine once again plans to visit India, but her family dissuades her. Air India flight 182 was blown up by a bomb in June of 1985. There seems no end to the havoc.

Bibijee's health is getting better; at least, that is what she writes in her letters. Only God knows what her real condition is. Most likely, she does not want to put her daughters in distress by revealing the truth.

With a blink of an eye the fall season passes, and this year's Thanksgiving is at Jasmine's house. She was hoping that David's parents would invite the whole family, but they did not. And neither Komil nor Sohil could accommodate everyone in small apartments. So Jasmine ends up playing the host. The house is full of her new relatives from America and Jasmine is nervous. Everything has to be perfect. Never before has she cooked and served a complete American Thanksgiving dinner, but with her Italian neighbor's planning help, it turns out well.

Life goes on as lonesome as ever for Jasmine. She doesn't have a hobby to keep herself occupied, other than cooking. But now, there isn't much need to cook every day. She cooks only when her daughters visit them or when she invites friends over. Ajit is always absorbed with his investments and writing. Komil and David have both joined a law firm and moved to New York. Sohil and Karan live in Baltimore, close to the hospital where she is doing her fellowship in psychiatry and he in pediatrics.

The howling winds of the winter months amplify Jasmine's sense of isolation. Reading prayers and trying to think of her blessings do nothing to comfort her. She feels overwhelmed with despair, so she finally calls Sohil. "I can't take it anymore, please come home...help me," she cries.

The next day Sohil drives over to comfort her mother and scold her father for being so self-centered. Ajit denies that it is his fault.

"Why can't she do something, pick up a hobby, attend classes?" he protests. "Anybody with nothing to do can go haywire."

Sohil suggests a trip for her mother, first to visit Mrs. Khan in San Francisco and from there to Dubai to stay with Purnima for a while.

"But your Papa can't stay alone for so long," Jasmine says, her excitement stifled by concern.

"Heck with Papa, Mom," Sohil says. "You need to take care of your health first."

Sohil arranges Jasmine's trip and takes her back with her to Baltimore. From there, after a week or so, Jasmine takes off for San Francisco, already considerably happier.

When Jasmine returns from Dubai, the spring season of 1986 is in full swing. Sohil and Karan come to Philadelphia, and they all decide to visit Komil and David in New York. After the three couples spend the weekend together, Ajit and Jasmine feel blessed to see their daughters happily married and well-settled. Jasmine sometimes wonders what would have happened had she signed the divorce papers and stayed back in India. She knows the environment she chose for them in America provided the rich soil for them to blossom fully. She admires her mother, who instilled the power of determination in her.

The next weekend they spend with Sohil in Baltimore. From there they all go to Washington to see the cherry blossoms. A few days later, they come home very happy, only to find sad news awaiting them: Bibijee has passed away.

Jasmine wants to fly to India right away, but her family still advises against it. The situation is still precarious in Punjab; another plot to down an Air India flight was dismantled just recently. Jasmine can hardly bear to think of being there, anyway, without her father, brother, Simran, and now her mother. Her friends come to her house to share her grief. A few weeks of sitting with the mourners and completing the reading of their holy book keeps Jasmine's mind occupied. The recital of the scripture ends with prayers for the departed soul, and hymns which (in essence) translate: *May Bibijee's body and soul belong to God like a drop of water mingling in the ocean and as a ray blends with the sun.* When all the rituals are complete, everyone goes home, leaving Jasmine with Ajit, who is unable to empathize with the pain of a person who loses a dear one.

No one realizes that Jasmine's mental condition is worsening. In the stillness of the night, she screams as loud as she can. Ajit shakes her awake.

"Jasmine, wake up, you are having a nightmare!"

"No, this is not a nightmare. I am wide-awake. I have been awake for many nights."

"What's wrong with you? Why are you disturbing my sleep?"

She sits up, grabs his shoulders, and shakes him with full force, crying, "Because I have this rage boiling over! I am angry with those who killed my brother! I am angry with you, with our cruel society, and the whole world! Bibijee would be alive today if they hadn't killed Amar. The bullets not only killed Amar, they pierced through her heart, too. She had the strength of a pillar before Amar's death."

Jasmine stops and lets go of her stunned husband. She bursts into tears, sobbing loudly.

"I want to go, I want to go, I want to go, I..."

Ajit interrupts by smacking her face to break her out of her trance. She curls up on the bed, screaming, sobbing and hitting the pillow. This time she does not care; she wants him to stay awake with her. She is tired of his retreating to some other world where he feels no pain.

Ajit goes to the other bedroom but she follows and grabs his arm.

"I wanted to fly to India right away to attend my mother's funeral, just as Mrs. Khan did years ago," she shouts. "But you wouldn't allow me because you thought Armageddon was continuing in Punjab. What about the tempest brewing in my heart? Perhaps God doesn't want me to attend funerals in my life. So far I have missed funerals of my father, friend, brother, and now mother."

Jasmine continues on, no longer scared of him, but Ajit pushes her out of the room and closes the door.

Ajit somehow fails to gauge the seriousness of her behavior and, as usual, leaves for his college in the morning.

She is alone in the house. She begins hallucinating and touching every plant in the house. She breaks off the leaves and tapes them together to make a flying carpet. And when she does not succeed, she picks up pots and throws them on the floor one by one. She imagines her friend, Simran, standing in a corner.

"Oh Simran, when did you come? How much I wanted you to be at my girls' weddings. Why didn't you come?"

"I was there. You were too busy to notice me. And I deliberately didn't disturb you. The ceremonies were beautiful, and I'm so happy for them to marry for love!"

"You know, Simran, you still look eighteen years old with that same innocent smiling face. You froze in time, but I have become like a beaten-up copper vessel. I feel so worn out. The years have etched a world map on my face, but your face is still so beautifully soft and smooth."

Jasmine tries to touch Simran's face and, realizing she is not there, she screams with panic, "Simran! Don't go away, take me with you! Please take me with you...these walls are closing in on me. I am suffocating, oh, I can't breathe!"

Jasmine opens the garage door and runs out to the driveway. By chance, Ajit happens to come back from the college earlier than usual. He stops the car just in time to avoid running over her. She starts to laugh loudly and stares at him as if she doesn't recognize him. Finally, Ajit understands that something is seriously wrong.

When he leads her inside the house, she pushes him aside to get out again. He locks her in the bedroom and calls Sohil at the hospital where she works and tells her to come home at once. Sohil tells him to give her mother sleeping pills now and try to calm her down. In a couple of hours, Sohil gets there and gives Jasmine an injection.

She explains to her father that sleep deprivation causes a person's serotonin level to go down, and this deficiency is linked to mental illness if not treated promptly. She tells him Jasmine must sleep for twenty-four hours continuously now, and sleep eight hours every night thereafter.

"Papa, you must pay attention to Mom one hundred percent," Sohil says. "She needs your assurance that you love her and will always take care of her. You have always been in your own world, working day and night. This is a wake-up call for you to slow down. Can't you see how ill Mom is?"

Ajit breaks down in tears, and for the first time he communicates with his daughter on a personal level.

"I have brought her to this point," he weeps. "I have wronged her, and now she doesn't love me."

"That is nonsense, Papa, she does love you. After all, what is love to an Indian traditional wife? She is content to generate happiness around her loved ones. She will never utter these words to you, but she will always take care of you." Sohil hugs her father.

"I will come home every night the rest of this week," she says. "And we must not admit her to the hospital; I will look after her at home. I am sure she will be fine in a few days."

Komil comes home for the weekend, and then Dilbeer comes for a week to look after her sister. Slowly, Jasmine starts to get better, but she is still talking nonsense. Her brain concocts totally baseless stories.

"Nobody knows it, but I killed Susan," Jasmine tells Dilbeer one day. "I saw her in Ajit's bed and stabbed both of them to death. You know why I killed them? So that they can live in heaven, happily ever after."

"I met my mother-in-law last year," she says another day. "She was such a nice lady, and I told her to stay away from Alit, or he would kill her. You know, Richard came yesterday and asked me to marry him, saying he would make me very happy. And I told him, 'I'm already very happy.' Why does everybody think I'm not happy?"

Finally one morning, Jasmine gets up acting quite normal. She recognizes Dilbeer.

"Oh, what a pleasant surprise!" she says. "When did you come?"

After a few days, Dilbeer leaves and Sohil puts her mother on an anti-depressant drug. She warns her father, once again, to pay attention to her for she feels very lonely. But Ajit's lack of intimacy is too deeply embedded. Even when he tries to be caring and affectionate, he has no ability to sustain it.

Jasmine gets better but knows her family will still not allow her to go to India. The Punjab crisis is still lingering; shootings and arrests are continuing. Therefore, she secretly buys a ticket to fly to India. She must immerse the ashes of her mother in the Sutlej River soon. She had written to her sister-in-law to hold on to the ashes for her.

"Where are you going?" Ajit asks, overhearing Jasmine's calling a cab.

"I am going to India," she declares. "My mother's ashes must be immersed very soon."

"No. You are going nowhere without my permission," Ajit snaps, snatching the telephone from her hand with a jerk. "If something happened to you, what am I going to do alone?"

"You will do what you have always been doing."

A phrase pops into her mind from *Gone with the Wind*—*"Frankly, my dear, I don't give a damn"* —but she would never utter such a crude thing, as it is simply not in her traditional Indian makeup.

The cab comes, and she leaves while Ajit is trying to get hold of their daughters over the phone.

"Papa, don't stop her this time," Sohil says. "She needs to get her childhood place out of her system. And she will get better only after she immerses *naani's* ashes."

# 21

# The Deserted Village

Jasmine's nephew, Arjun, has come to meet her at the airport. The precocious little boy she remembers is now a handsome young man. After completing his MBA, he had wanted to take a tour of western countries, but as ill luck would have it, after his father's death he had to take over the responsibilities of the family honey business.

"Aunty, India has betrayed us," Arjun tells Jasmine. "My father's murderers should be brought to justice, but our government has turned a cold shoulder to investigating the despicable bloodshed. He was a well-respected and very successful businessman; everyone wanted to be his friend, and now no one seems to care he was killed! I must admit our family is in a very sour mood, and I hope we don't spoil your visit."

"I know," Jasmine sighs. "You were so proud of your father, and you were so proud of India that you made us feel as if we were traitors to abandon our own land for opportunities abroad."

"Exactly, but now my country suffocates me," he says. "There is no end to the continuing havoc. No matter that was a mistake to turn the Golden Temple into a fort, but Indira Gandhi's decision to raid it on Guru Arjan Dev's martyrdom day is beyond comprehension. The military attacked and killed *thousands* of innocent women, men, and children who came from all over the Punjab. The brutality in killing innocent pilgrims and the bloody aftermath of Indira Gandhi's assassination are unforgivable. I did love my country, but no longer do I have any respect or love for it. I remember how you used to encourage me to migrate to America, and I always shook my head 'no' but... now, I am pleading with you! Please get me and my family out of here!"

"Yes, yes, definitely," she says. "The problem is that it takes ten years to get approval to immigrate. Nevertheless, I will submit the application as soon as I am back in the States."

First, Jasmine and her *bhabi* go to the Kiratpur *Gurudwara* to pray and immerse her mother's ashes in the flowing water of the Sutlej River. In the *Gurudwara*, the priest prays for Bibijee's soul to rest in heavenly peace. He sings hymns from the Sikh scriptures suitable for the parted soul. One of the hymns means: *As the rays blend with the Sun and the river water flows into the ocean, becoming one, a righteous human being mingles into the Creator's light, skipping the reincarnation cycle.*

Then they go to their village cremation ground to set small memorial stones for her brother and mother next to her father's. As their car turns onto the road entering her village, tears stream down Jasmine's cheeks. Her last visit to the village was more than fifteen years ago, but she does not see an older version of her familiar neighborhood; everything looks strange. They drive on a concrete road, past a newly-built girls' high school, a poultry farm, and a dairy farm. Jasmine is pleasantly surprised to see so much revitalization, but her *bhabi* dampens her excitement by telling of the inflamed conditions that still prevail, creating devastation in every village.

*Where are the children?* Jasmine wonders, as she notices no one is running after their car in excitement, and no women with water vessels on their heads are stopping to watch them. The only persons who greet them are her old, frail aunt and uncle. She learns one of their sons has been arrested and the other, thirty years old, has left the village to escape the cruel hands of the police.

"Our Punjab was advancing so much," her uncle says, wiping his eyes with shaky hands. "But since the 80's, someone has cast an evil eye."

"Every day young innocent boys are being arrested," her aunt says, squeezing her nose with one end of her *dupatta*. "Now the young men and boys are leaving the villages out of fear. So many of them have taken asylum abroad. All those houses where you girls used to play are abandoned."

Jasmine presses her chest as if these words were darts piercing her heart. Her aunt's face shows so much pain that Jasmine clings to her, sobbing.

While they are in this melancholy mood, a couple of beggars come to the door and start singing a song on their *dhud and sarangi* (rural musical instruments). In essence, the song is a request for peace. *"Oh, dove of peace,"* they sing, *"come to my land, sit on the highest branch of my pipal tree and sing a song to teach the ignorant people to open their eyes. The darkness prevails only until a sliver of light beams through. Oh, Baba Nanak, we need you to come back and once again shower your enlightenment upon the darkness. Once again tell them that there is no big or small. In God's eyes all are equal; there is no Hindu, no Muslim, no Sikh. Oh, beautiful dove, come and sing a song of peace."*

Jasmine's aunt gives them alms and they move on to the next house to sing again. Her aunt insists that Jasmine and her *bhabi* sleep in her house, but tonight Jasmine wants to sleep on the rooftop of her own home. Just one more time, she wants to count the stars and experience the moonlit night. She wants to wake to the sunrise behind the *pipal* tree and hear the farmer's flute.

As Jasmine enters her own home, her soul shivers to see the dismantled courtyard walls and the missing rosewood door. The only thing still intact, though faded a little, is the kitchen wall with the painted birds. Even the *pipal* tree standing there appears listless and withered. She closes her eyes, feeling the pain of nostalgia. In her mind's eye, she sees her siblings, Simran, and her mother sitting under the tree. They are playing at a carom board and laughing loudly. She plugs her ears with her fingers.

Coming back to her aunt's house, Jasmine cries. Her aunt hugs her and tries to soothe her, saying, "Don't cry, my child. Why are you spoiling your eyes? What memories of childhood and youth are you looking for? The young are either in jail, or they have left, and the old folks have passed on."

"Aunty, I want to sleep with you," Jasmine cries. "I'm scared to sleep on my rooftop. I just want to close my eyes in a room where memories don't haunt me."

Seeing that Jasmine is suddenly her small, young niece again, her aunt relents, and they sleep in the same bed that night. In a lengthy dream, Jasmine starts walking to Simran's house where she finds out that Simran had drowned, a long time before. She passes by her primary school, now in ruins. The only participants there are rats and abandoned dogs. She imagines her primary school teacher, Maya Devi, writing math problems on the blackboard. She sees her classmates each holding a matchbox. Each student was told to bring a rectangular empty matchbox and a tiny bucket of clay from the pond. They made their own bricks by filling the boxes with clay and then drying them in the sun, and built an exquisite replica of a palace. To teach them geography, they tried to construct mountains, rivers, and oceans using clay, pebbles and sticks.

Still dreaming, Jasmine resumes her walk, not knowing what she has lost and why she must find it. She comes across a vast field full of storms, floods, snakes, and dangerous animals. She is frightened, but she hears her mother's encouraging voice and crosses the field without hesitation. Continuing farther, she reaches a city full of palaces and castles. She looks up to admire the architecture, but stumbles on a stone and falls down, realizing that it is not the place where her happiness lies.

As she turns to her right, she sees shops filled with expensive items and gold jewelry. A tall woman comes out of the jewelry store and laughs, showing off her necklace.

"Are you happy because you have purchased the most precious necklace?" Jasmine asks. The lady with the impossibly long neck starts to laugh loudly.

"Happiness is a condition of one's mind," she says in a booming, unearthly voice. "It cannot be bought with money or gold."

Jasmine continues her dream journey, yet is aware enough to wonder why her mind is tormented so. She takes her rickety feet a little farther and hears the voice of a street vendor.

"Buy this *fulkari* [hand-embroidered shawl]," he calls out. "It is woven with dreams and memories! Oh, come! Look at this!"

She feels a great emotional pull and holds the *fulkari* in her hands. She looks deeply into the embroidery, which depicts a village full of happy scenes. The intricate details pull her in more. She sees a pond with water so still that the reflection of the moon is crystal clear. The farmers in the fields are singing happily while pushing the bulls to plow. Children carrying books are walking home from school and women are balancing water pitchers on their heads. Young girls are swinging on trees in the park with their mouths open in song and laughter. This *fulkari* has awakened the village of her childhood and youth. This is how it used to be and this is what she has missed. She buys the *fulkari,* feeling no need to walk farther. The sun is about to set. She is standing on the bank of her village pond with the *fulkari* wrapped around her body.

Jasmine watches how the cattle chew constantly while they sit at the side of the pond, and she reminisces about her childhood. "Ma, why do they chew all the time?" she had asked her mother.

"That is how they digest their food," Bijibee had said. "They swallow their food without grinding, and then they bring one morsel at a time back into their mouths to chew all day long."

Jasmine lies there drifting in and out of her dream. *Where are all my people — the ladies at the well, the farmers with their bull carts, and the kids playing in front of their homes?* Her aunt had told her that these days every house has tap water, electric fans, and toilets. A few houses have televisions, and the villagers flock there to watch films. She also mentioned another reason that people don't come out: the police scare the young so much that they are leaving the village to save themselves from torture and jail. Jasmine misses the narrow dirt path zig-zagging through the fields where she and other students used to walk. Those memories are embedded so deeply in her heart that she longs to walk once again on that path, but realizes that the concrete road has replaced it. Instead of bull-carts, the farmers have tractors to cultivate the land. Poultry and dairy farms have taken over the cotton fields. Although she is happy to see the progress, she feels sad. Even the bricks and rosewood doors from her family home have been removed and taken to New Delhi to be used in her brother's new home. Her childhood friends have all married and moved to their in-laws.

She wonders, if she quietly slipped into the pond, whether anyone would notice and jump in to rescue her from drowning. She remembers how many boys were saved, but not girls, when she was growing up. She wants to glide into the water quietly, to disappear, only to come back up, floating lifelessly. This is the way Simran must have surrendered to the water. This is the only way to keep memories safe forever, so that no one will dare to destroy them. Then she hears her mother's voice, chiding her.

"Coward, my daughter is a coward," she wails. "She can no longer handle the grief."

Jasmine is startled awake, and sees her aunt standing near the bed with a cup of tea. Jasmine drinks it and tells her aunt that she must go back to America, that this village no longer belongs to her. Her aunt and *bhabi* tell her to wait a few weeks for the Diwali festival. She is reluctant, but when her aunt mentions that Jasmine's friends always come to join their parents in Diwali celebrations, she agrees.

Much to her disappointment, only a couple of friends come home. Their stories, too, are filled with heart-wrenching circumstances. And this Diwali is nothing like the ones Jasmine used to enjoy earlier in her life. Then the rooftops glittered with lights in row upon row of oil *diyas* (lamps). In her child's mind, it had appeared as if all the stars had come down to earth. Tonight there are only a few lights here and there, and not a single child is outside setting off firecrackers. Her aunt and uncle are not in the mood to bake and pass around sweets as they used to do.

She had planned to stay in India longer, but this listless festival magnifies her growing sense of alienation. All of a sudden, she thinks of the fall season. She must go back to her family in the States, and soon, to see the colorful leaves. Strangely, she thinks she will be more likely to hear the rustling leaves whisper messages to her from her mother there, than here in Punjab.

The next day, Jasmine hugs her aunt and uncle good-bye and leaves for New Delhi. There she finds waiting many letters from her daughters, and one from Ajit. They all are worried about her and beg her to come back soon. She is able to get a flight a week later. After five months, her trip of re-discovery ends abruptly, on a hollow note.

# 22

# The Metamorphosis

Jasmine's seat on the plane is near the galley, and the noise keeps disturbing her sleep. She starts to write a letter to her daughters asking them to forgive her for her intention to divorce their father. She is only 47, and can no longer tolerate a loveless and lonesome life. Their father, she writes, will never change, and these days the empty nest haunts her even more. She feels the nest and foundation she built with passion and courage to give them a secure and loving family environment is complete. Jasmine dozes off while writing the letter, and when she wakes up her letter is in the hands of an Indian lady sitting next to her. Shocked, she snatches her paper back.

"Pardon me *bhain* [sister] for my curiosity to read it," the lady apologizes. "I know it was wrong, I'm so sorry. Actually, the letter slipped from your hand and I picked it up from the ground. My name is Seema and I live in London."

Still annoyed, Jasmine decides to let it go. Seema appears to be a sophisticated middle-aged woman, with curly short hair, dyed black, but with a white strand left carefully untouched. She tells Jasmine that she is an author traveling on a book tour.

"My name is Jasmine, and I live in America." Jasmine says. "What is your book?"

"This is actually my third published book; all of my writing is on communication, relationships, and healing."

After a moment's hesitation, Jasmine decides to confide, giving Seema a short synopsis of her life with her husband.

"Tell me, what is the right thing to do in my case?" Jasmine asks.

"Do you love him?" Seema asks. "Have you ever expressed it in words?"

"I don't know how I feel, and Ajit doesn't show any emotion or affection either."

"I see…your main problem is a lack of candid personal communication with each other. Perhaps you both stay away from each other because you think he doesn't love you, and he probably feels your strong resistance. This hostility generates negative impulses and the negativity creates all kinds of problems in marital relationships."

"I don't know what to do," Jasmine sighs. "My westernized self compels me to leave him, but my Indian tradition stands in the way."

"It doesn't matter which culture you follow: divorce doesn't solve one's problems either. It can bring misery of its own kind into one's life. But, if you are in love with someone else and he is willing to marry you, leaving your husband may not be so painful."

"No, I'm not," Jasmine says, wiping her watery eyes. "But my husband depends upon me and he will again plunge into depression if I leave him."

"Then don't leave him. I think you love him and he loves you. The episode of his betrayal has confused your mind. You have forgiven him, but not from your innermost heart, and he senses that. He became a workaholic to avoid you, and you conveniently did not protest his lifestyle. His purpose in life was to become rich, and your path was to keep the peace at home for your daughters' sake."

"But is it too late?" Jasmine asks. "Am I too old to begin a relationship with him which I never had? A woman, I assume, is like a tree. It needs constant nourishment of love and care; once it withers of neglect over the years, it becomes impossible to bring it back to life."

"That is pure nonsense; a typical Indian philosophy," Seema says. "An Indian woman's life is over, especially in our villages, when she achieves her goal to get her children educated and married. You live in America, where life always finds a new beginning. You are still young, and it is in your hands to complete your life's journey with an enjoyable future. Especially sad to me are all the young Indian widows I have met when researching my book topics. They feel so lonely and miserable. Our culture should allow them to remarry."

Seema continues her conversation for a while after the plane lands at Heathrow airport. Before saying good-bye to Jasmine, Seema leaves her with one final question: "Have you ever truly paid attention to what your husband's needs are?"

Seema's question makes a lasting impact on Jasmine, and she starts reviewing her past. She remembers defying

Ajit's desire for her to look trendy. So many times, he had asked her to get a haircut and wear more non-Indian clothes and evening gowns. She had refused, because cutting one's hair is not allowed in her Sikh religion, and she was more comfortable in her traditional style. She also recalls the conversation with her sister-in-law that Ajit might need her help to come out of his cocoon; both brothers had had such a miserable childhood.

Rajiv had broken close ties with Ajit years ago, unable to accept his infidelity. Now, all of a sudden, Jasmine feels a strong desire to see Sandy and Rajiv. She has a six-hour layover, and thinks it may be possible at least for Sandy to come over to meet her. She gets their phone number from information and calls, but no one answers.

Memories of things that she chose not to do which could have pleased Ajit, or helped him heal from old wounds, start to surface, replaying one after another. It is as if she were watching a list scroll across her mind, but instead of feeling resistant or reluctant, she reads it eagerly. These are the clues which will solve the mystery of their miserable relationship. These are things she *does* have control over, and she feels ready to resolve all that she now realizes.

Noticing a hair salon in the airport, she decides to get her hair bobbed. She purchases a beautiful ankle-length dress from a nearby shop. Time passes and she is ready to board the plane to Philadelphia.

From the Philadelphia airport she takes a cab home. She has not informed her daughters or Ajit of her return. She reaches home quietly, just as she came years ago without Ajit's knowledge. Before Ajit comes home, she takes out her notepad and writes a few sentences: *Do not take my astian [ashes] to India. I wish you to immerse them in the Schuylkill River or any flowing water. After all, I owe my life to this country, which has nurtured my family and me so sincerely.* She is still young, and she doesn't know why she feels the urge to make this statement for herself and her family now, but she is more at peace in this moment than any time in a long time.

Ajit arrives home and hurriedly walks from the front door back to the bedroom, not noticing Jasmine sitting in the living room. He goes straight to the closet and brings out his suitcase. He has booked a flight that evening to New Delhi, planning to go and beg Jasmine to come back. Not having received any response to his letters, he has been shaken to the core. At first, he was only aware that he missed her cooking, but as weeks went by and he did not hear from her, his heart ached with concern and caring. It made him realize how deeply he had always loved her. After all, she was his first love. How he used to imagine his life with her before their marriage! Then Susan walked into his life, shattering all dreams, to begin new unjust ones. Now he understands his terrible mistakes, and their consequences. He blames himself for Jasmine's aloofness. He vows to pay attention to her needs and live his life on her terms from now on.

After packing, he comes to the living room and sees Jasmine sitting on the sofa.

"Oh!" Ajit exclaims. "When did you come? And what happened to your hair?"

"Ha, ha, you finally noticed me," Jasmine says, smiling. "I cut my hair short so that you would look at me, which you stopped doing years ago."

"What do you mean? I always notice you but I don't say anything."

"Unless something is wrong; otherwise, you keep quiet," Jasmine complains.

"Look," says Ajit, pointing to his suitcase. "I was coming to bring you home to me. I realize my mistakes and I apologize. Will you forgive me?"

She keeps quiet and smiles mysteriously.

"I have always loved you; now tell me if you love me too," Ajit confesses, embracing her. He knows that no matter how many years she has lived in the west, she still is shy to express her love in words. She can never bring herself to be explicitly romantic.

"I have missed you very much, and I promise to be a loving and caring life partner," she says.

He holds her hand and sings the lyrics of an Urdu song:

*Come, dear walk with me*
*Forget the past. Move forward in life*
*How enchanting the moonlit night!*

# About the Author

Daljit Ranajee was born and raised in India and migrated to the United States on December 24, 1965. After working more than thirty years in the Philadelphia civil service, she retired as a director of information technology.

She has written and published poems and short stories in her native language, Punjabi, including an anthology of thirty poems, *Pachhumi Leheran* (Western Waves). *Echoes from Punjab* is her first major work written in English.

Daljit Ranajee lives in Sarasota, Florida, with her husband. They are the proud parents of a son, Navdeep and his wife, Simi; daughter, Rimi, and her husband Arun; and three adorable and talented grandchildren, Mira, Surain, and Sarisa.

For Daljit Ranajee's artwork, poetry, and blog, please visit:

www.echoesfrompunjab.com